Text copyright © 2016 Adrian Ru

This is a work of fiction. Names o
and incidents are either products o
fictitiously. Any resemblance to re
coincidental.

The right of Adrian Russell to be identified as the Author of the work has been asserted by him in accordance with the Copyright, Designs and Patents Act 1988.

All rights reserved. No part of this publication may be reproduced, stored in a retrieval system, or transmitted in any form or by any means, electronically, mechanically, photocopying, recording, or otherwise, without express written permission of the publisher, nor be otherwise circulated in any form of binding or cover other that that in which it is published and without a similar condition being imposed on the subsequent purchaser.

Published by: Adrian Russell
Edited by: David Gaskill
Cover by: Bowraven Limited

ISBN-13: 978-1539188735
ISBN-10: 1539188736

Dedication

This book is dedicated to my wife. She is my rock and my sole mate and I love her to the moon and back. She understands my new found freedom to write novels. She's happy to let me sit and type away, at home, on holiday or in fact wherever we are. I would also like to thank my editor David Gaskill, who patiently went through my script to improve my writing before going to print. I would also like to send a huge thank you to all the doctors and nurses at Royal Bournemouth Hospital, for if it wasn't for them I would not be here today and able to publish my work.

CHAPTER ONE

As he drifted up through layers of sleep, David Lane began to sense that something didn't feel quite right. He reached instinctively for the comforting edge of his mattress. It wasn't there. And where was the duvet that usually kept him warm?

His pulse quickened. Reaching further, trying again to find the raised mattress edge, his fingers grasped something that felt like straw. Straw? His eyes shot open. He found that he was not in his bed at all, but lying on the floor of what appeared to be a cavern. Straw was scattered about him everywhere. He was stark naked and itching all over.

Fear struck him like a lightning bolt: He really was no longer in the safety of his own little bedroom at home!

'Where the hell am I?'

To find out, David jumped to his feet. Or, at least, he tried to. His legs, shaky from some kind of drug infusion he didn't understand, since he didn't do drugs, were not prepared for the suddenness of the move. He fell back onto the straw-covered surface, a jarring experience that didn't help ease the racing of his heart.

He lay there for an instant, breathing heavily, feeling vulnerable and lost. Soon, though, he realised he would have to fight his fear and try to get up again. As he tried to grasp what was going on, he picked up a handful of the straw. It was dry to the touch and had an odd, unfamiliar smell. This did not make him feel any less afraid.

'Am I going mad? Am I having a nightmare?'

Trying to calm himself, he began studying his surroundings more closely. He noted that the temperature in the cave-like room was warm, so, despite his nudity, he wasn't cold. What dim light there was came from a single source, what appeared to be an entrance to the cave, but as he looked into the blackness behind him he could feel the almost abysmal depth of an unfathomable, empty space.

A new shiver of fright went from the base of his spine to the nape of his neck. It was as if someone had just walked over his grave. With his thoughts turning to …*'where the fuck are my clothes?'*…he cupped sweaty palms over his face in frustration and racked his memory for what might have caused him to end up in such a place. He vaguely recalled going to the withdrawal point at his bank in Chelmsford, where he lived, after his social security had been deposited.

'I don't remember going to bed at all.'

He rubbed his eyelids, then, as if in some way that would help lessen his confusion. It didn't.

His mind, desperate for an explanation, soon began to grasp at straws. Train tracks, he thought. A train tunnel and tracks would make more sense than a cave. A quick look around determined no railway track had ever been there.

'But how did I get here?'

He kept challenging his brain for answers, trying to piece together the few facts he had to make sense of it all.

Again, he recognised that the warm air in the cave certainly was odd; he should be feeling cold by now, but he didn't. That wasn't normal. As he looked toward the light, he could make out trees and some sky. That definitely did seem normal, although he had his doubts.

'That can't be outside in England, can it?'

Heart still beating fast, David slowly got to his feet, being careful not to fall this time. He stood, wobbling a bit, and drew some confidence from realising he was not under immediate attack. But that feeling was undermined by a wave of emotional — or was it physical? — fatigue.

'Do I really want to know?'

Whether he did or he didn't, he realised he had to do something. But what?

He looked at the welcoming light at the entrance. At the moment, naked as he was, he was reluctant to venture out there. Then he turned his head and peered again into the cave's sloping depths. No way was he going in that direction! Staring into that impenetrable darkness sparked unpleasant images.

'What if there's something bad down there?'

That thought triggered a strange foreboding in his brain. He was still very unsteady on his feet, so he braced himself by stooping and resting his hands on his knees. He closed his eyes for a few seconds to temporarily shut out this disturbing, unwanted new reality.

'Think, David! Think!'

If only he could tap into the memories he knew were dancing somewhere at the edge of his consciousness. If only he could Just then, two men came into his mind's view. Were they real? A flash of fear shot up his spine once more. And he opened his eyes and screamed.

CHAPTER TWO

It was the sun streaming in through the window of her flat that awakened Carly Prow.

She was not one for setting her alarm, as this wasted sleep time, and she hated getting up anyway.

She also hated the curtains around the window to her bedroom; these were too small for the opening, which meant there was always a gap for the morning sun to come bullying through.

Turning away to avoid the bright rays, she closed her eyes to continue sleeping. Too late! Her nicotine craving had already begun.

Sitting up, she reached for the Silk Cut packet on her old pine bedside, pulled out a cigarette and put it in her mouth.

Next to the cigarettes was a Jack Daniels petrol lighter of her father's that she had gotten when he died a few years back.

The smell of petrol fumes filled the space around her as she opened the cover, which always reminded her of her dad. Pausing for a few seconds to smell the fumes before striking the flint, she thought back to how she had loved her dad so much and still missed him.

She struck the flint several times before a small, flickering flame arose, which she touched to the end of her cigarette, and took in a long, first drag, sucking down every last wisp of smoke deep into her lungs.

She loved the first smoke of the day.

Whilst she sat there enjoying it and contemplating what to do next, she studied her room, where parts of the green carpet that she could see were worn and threadbare and more of a light shade of grey.

Carly knew today she had to look for a job and comply with the Claimant Commitment she'd made with the Jobcentre. Not having a computer in her flat, she would have to make a visit to the library at The County Hall.

She hated looking for work; more still, she hated working. But her next visit to the Jobcentre for her regular interview with her work coach was coming up, so she needed to get moving.

Last week, the Jobcentre contacted her about a property company interview, which had been set for Friday.

She began to plan how best to fail at this interview. Not wanting to risk jeopardising her benefits, she knew she had to keep the appointment. However, she was adept at not getting hired; in fact, she had made it a fine art.

The last time she had worked was around two years ago as a cleaner for a large local company that manufactured rubber O-rings. She'd hated the work and it had only been a matter of time before she got the sack.

In the end, she had poured bleach over the carpet in the board room. As she was already on a warning for being late on numerous occasions, she had been fired immediately.

Carly finished off her cigarette, then got up to go to the bathroom.

After she'd relieved herself she studied her dishevelled look in the small, bathroom mirror. Her hair was matted and greasy and her skin looked pale and blotchy.

She then grinned and saw that her teeth were looking quite yellow; she was well overdue a visit to the dentist. Carly hated dentists with a passion, so hadn't been to one for several years.

Leaving the bathroom, she went back to the bedroom for her second cigarette of the day.

CHAPTER THREE

Peter Druker sat in his office in front of a computer screen checking his healthy bank balance and, on a separate screen, looking at a list of quoted shares that he owned.

His focus was suddenly interrupted by movement just outside the one large window in the room.

Turning his gaze to what had caught his attention, he could see a pair of Mouse Birds, which are plentiful in this part of Africa, playing about in the branches of the bushes.

He took a few moments to watch these birds with their trademark long tails and tufted crests. He smiled at the way they hopped from one branch to the next, constantly checking for danger with quick movements of their heads.

After a few moments, they flew away, prompting him to return to his computer screens and the daily work routine in his office, which was a large room with a dark, wooden desk placed in the middle.

In one corner was a coffee machine with a jug full of coffee, which gave the room a constant, newly brewed coffee smell.

He would always start his day with a black coffee to help him to think clearly. His first cup would normally be drunk whilst he sat on the veranda before starting his work.

He felt restless today and, having been distracted by the birds, he decided to get up to refill his mug with more black coffee tempered with two teaspoons of sugar.

As he put the freshly filled mug to his lips, he looked across to the desk and the computer screens that were all lined up. He stood there for a few moments thinking about what he should do next.

His agitation was not eased by the coffee. He didn't feel like sitting down, so he decided to go out onto the veranda to have some thinking time.

This allowed him to enjoy the morning sun, which was something he liked to do whilst contemplating his life. It was at times like these when he got many of his new business ideas.

He left the office and walked down the long corridor which led to the open front door. As he approached the door, he could see the sun beaming in from outside. The wooden floor made a hollow sound as he walked across it in his boots. The knots and blemishes in the old floorboards were highlighted by the sun's rays as they cast shadows across it.

As Druker reached the veranda, which was covered by a metal corrugated roof, he took in a long, deep breath of the African air.

A small table and chairs on the veranda were just catching the sun at this time of day. He grabbed one of the chairs and scraped it across the wooden floor so he could sit in the soothing rays.

As he sat there, he noticed the resident Vervet Monkeys frolicking in one of the trees in the courtyard immediately in front of the house. They were there most days, seemingly playing without a care in the world.

His coffee soon finished, he returned to his desk to fire up his diary and plan his next trip to the UK. He was keen to get the trip arranged, even though he had only just returned late last night from a five-day trip.

There were always plenty of arrangements to make and he always stayed in the same hotel in Chelmsford. Druker logged onto the Atlantic Hotel's website to make end-of-the-week reservations.

Rooms were available, so he booked two for five nights. One of the rooms was for himself; the other was for his colleague, Scott, who would be joining him on this trip like on others before.

After he'd booked the hotel, he went onto book a hire car for the duration of his stay.

Druker had a lot of property, mostly in the UK. Recently, he'd branched out into the United States, where he was buying properties on the back of the huge drop in real estate values after the

2008 crash. Now that the market was recovering, he was gradually selling them off to cash in on his foresight.

His most recent purchase was not an investment at all. He'd bought Mwatusanga Reserve, 25,000 hectares of game reserve in the Zambian Luangwa valley.

The house on the reserve where he lived was in colonial style and included a number of thatched-style outbuildings.

The reserve was perfect. It came with plenty of game, including elephants, rhinos, lions, buffalo and leopards, together with an abundance of herbivores.

Mwatusanga was not far from Mfuwe Airport, which had a runway length of 2,000 metres. This runway was long enough to take off and land his Learjet Global 5000, which requires around 1,700 metres to take off fully laden.

His reserve also had a runway, too, and was now long enough to accommodate his private jet, which had a range of 9,500 kilometres. This meant he could fly to the UK non-stop from his home in Africa.

His Learjet was too large to be kept in his own small hanger, and his facilities were not sufficient to maintain such an aircraft, so instead it was kept and maintained at Mfuwe Airport. He rented a hangar from a local private jet company working out from Mfuwe, as this meant that the plane would be regularly serviced, plus there were proper refuelling facilities at this airport, too.

Whenever he decided he wanted to go anywhere, the pilots would fly in a light aircraft to Mfuwe from Lusaka Airport and then switch to his Learjet and fly to his place to collect him.

When he'd first purchased his Learjet, his first flight was not to the UK, but instead to Cape Town in South Africa.

Druker had always been a keen diver and had not yet dived with Great White Sharks, so he decided to make a visit to Gansbaai, which was around a two-hour drive southeast of Cape Town. The small town is known for its great cage diving, and the short trip out on a boat to Dyer Island is something he'd always wanted to do. The flying time to Cape Town was around three hours with the Global 5000's cruising speed of just over 900Kmh, so this was a good trip to try it out and get used to what it was like, before the longer trip to the UK.

On his inaugural trip, he had arranged for a driver to take him to Gansbaai. He had booked a stay in the Crayfish Lodge, which was a short drive to where the harbour and the boats for his outing were situated. He had chosen this lodge for its panoramic suites and great uninterrupted views of the sea off Gansbaai. Whilst he stayed there, his pilots had been booked into an expensive hotel in Cape Town, all expenses paid.

He chartered the boat privately so he could be the only person on it; he hated the idea of spending time with other tourists whilst on this experience. The company he chartered seemed to have a good reputation from the reviews he read, and was on Kus Drive, which looked out over Van Dyks Bay in Gansbaai. The person who arranged the trip for him was helpful and happy to accommodate his private hire.

On the morning following his arrival, and on the day of his trip, it was drizzling with rain. The weather hadn't stopped the trip from going ahead, though, and they'd set off at just after 7:30 in the morning, heading out to what is known as Shark Alley, which is in between Dyer Island and Geyser Rock, where 60,000 Cape Fur Seals breed. Druker recalled the smell of rotting fish that had hit him as they first approached the seal-covered rock, which was caused by the huge amount of their fish-scented faeces that blanket the island.

Soon after they'd arrived in Shark Alley, the crew had begun to throw chum into the water and to drop a decoy, which looked much like a seal pup. It took a few hours before they had lured a couple of Great White Sharks near the boat, but in the end the trip turned out to be very successful. He had seen a number of Great White Sharks whilst he was in the cage, with two of them coming up very close to check him out. After he had come up from the cage, he remembered he had felt cold, as the weather hadn't improved all day. He'd asked the skipper to return to base, in order to get warm and because he had been satisfied that he'd seen enough.

After he had tipped the team in his usual generous way, his driver had returned him to Cape

Town's airport. He'd met his two pilots in the terminal, where he boarded his plane in no time at all. He loved the new-found freedom that his new toy had given him, and he loved the flexibility it afforded him. On the flight home, he sat in one of the plane's luxury seats, drinking one of his fine red wines and looking out of one of the windows, whilst smiling to himself.

After this visit to Cape Town, Druker had soon arranged his first trip to the UK, which had also involved organising the pilots, and arranging a hire car and hotel accommodations. The pilots would deal with all the flight arrangements necessary for this. But there were certain elements of paperwork that he had to get involved with, especially when it came to his departing and arriving directly from Mwatusanga without the need for him to go via an international airport and via immigration and customs.

CHAPTER FOUR

David's main feeling of horror, which right now was even scarier than finding himself where he was, was that ... '*perhaps someone saw me naked.*'

He thought about how, when he'd screamed, he'd imagined the possibility of something prowling in the shadows, but right now the thought of someone having seen him naked sent a shudder through his entire body. It was a deep-seated fear that was far beyond monster scary for him.

He re-opened his eyes and looked up. When he gradually got back to standing fully upright, he was careful not to hit his head on the ceiling of his newly found 'bedroom.' As he stood and turned his head, he became aware of a small, stabbing pain in his neck, a pain that ran up and into the base of his skull, almost as if someone had pierced his skin with a needle.

He reached around with his hand to feel the

skin just on the nape of his neck, to locate the point at which he'd felt the pain originate, and as he ran his fingers over the site, he could feel a small lump. It was the size of a small nut. As he explored the area with the tips of his fingers, as he pushed and squeezed the skin, it seemed as if there were something just under the surface that moved when he pushed it.

He also could feel a small cut, which had yet to properly heal. The area around this strange object felt inflamed and sore, and if he didn't know better, it was as if he'd undergone some kind of small, surgical procedure.

'But then, why would they leave the lump under my skin rather than remove it — unless someone has placed something there,' he thought.

With this discovery, his whole body shivered with a raw sense of the unknown. David felt totally out of control right now. He tried to clear his fuzzy mind and think back to a time before he'd awakened in this cave. He tried to bring forward the vague recollection of the two men, a memory he was sure would help him to work out why he found himself in this strange place. There was a stocky man with a tanned and almost leather-like skin. The second man, who didn't have the same distinctive features as the first, did have lot of very dark hair, he recalled.

'My memory is good enough to remember these two men, but why can't I remember any more than that?' he thought frustratingly to himself. *'Or was this a dream I had whilst asleep?'*

Turning back to the object under his skin and the small cut above it, he had no recollection of what had caused this injury, but he was becoming even more concerned over what the object might be.

Slightly unsteady on his feet and still feeling woozy, he walked slowly towards the cave entrance. As he moved off the straw 'bed,' he could feel the cool ground beneath his bare feet. On his way to the entrance of the cave, he studied the walls of his enclosure, which were made of a hard-looking grey rock, which seemed to him like rough granite. It looked like the cave had been cut out and formed over a long time; that many millennia had passed since it was first shaped by nature.

David observed the jagged edges of the stone face of the cave, which carved out areas of light and shadow. This shadowing effect made the walls look to him like a torrid sea, with each of the tips that jutted out appearing to form waves, as if there were an invisible storm wind blowing in from the cave's entrance. He tried to imagine ships sailing across this dark, rough ocean surface, as this wind appeared to move the rock's surface back towards the dark space behind him and beyond.

He continued to move slowly to the cave entrance and, as he turned his gaze to the light source beyond the jagged opening, he felt very uneasy. He sensed he was not alone. As he cautiously approached the misshapen oval, his tired eyes took some adjusting to the bright sunlight ahead, which gleamed inside, its beams glinting off the stones on the floor of the cave.

    David hesitated for a few seconds, contemplating his situation, and as he did, his attention was drawn to a sound. It was something which he'd not been aware of when he first arose. The soft noise suddenly became very apparent to him; it was coming from deep within the cave. David looked back and into the darkness beyond, listening intently.

CHAPTER FIVE

Graham Smith awoke with a start and found himself on the floor.

'No, it isn't the floor. It's hard ground I'm on and I'm outside in the open', he instantly realised.

As this knowledge came to him, he jumped up. In doing so, he also found that he was completely naked. Suddenly, he felt extremely vulnerable. He looked around to see who might see him without his clothes on and tried to make sense of the situation.

As he surveyed the area around where he had been lying, Graham found that he was not in his familiar home in Chelmsford, but instead in a forested area. And it was very warm.

'I'm not in the UK,' was what went through his disbelieving mind.

Graham's body was not designed for being in the wild, with its huge stomach and stubby legs; his was not a physique that would be best to get him out of trouble.

'Where am I?' he questioned. *'Why am I here?'*

He began to move forward to see if he could find his way out of the trees, to see if he could find help, but as he walked he quickly realised how hard the ground was on his bare feet, making him hobble a bit and wince, as the stones bore into his soles.

Looking around and wondering how he'd got here, he realised his mind was unusually fuzzy, a feeling that could have been from whatever had knocked him out.

'I must have been drugged with something,' he concluded. *'But who did this and why?'*

As he framed the question, dancing on the edge of his memory were images of three men, one of whom was familiar to him for some reason. They seemed to be intent on subduing and capturing him, but his persistent mental fuzziness made this memory vague.

'How did I get here, though?' he puzzled, but then his thoughts were suddenly interrupted by the sound of a bird sitting on a branch above his head, which brought him back to reality and where he was.

It sounded like a pigeon, and as he stopped and looked up to where the call had come from, his thinking cleared. He began to survey the trees in the wooded area where he stood. These were all unfamiliar to him; they made him feel very uneasy. He started to wonder what other animals might be lurking in them or somewhere else around him.

Soon his senses seemed to be on a higher alert than he'd ever experienced before. It was as if his hearing had been tuned in; every sound was magnified. His body tingled and quivered with anxiety, a feeling which he'd never had until now. It felt like a deep, primal fear was going right to his core and into his bones, even though he couldn't actually see any danger. Somehow, he sensed there was something out there or that he was being watched by dangerous creatures.

What didn't help was that he was unclothed. His nakedness made his heightened vulnerability seem even more surreal. But, in a strange way, without the thin protection of clothing, he somehow felt more a part of the wild environment that he found himself in.

After having a cursory glance around, there was nothing obvious that he could use to cover himself up with, so he began to walk again. Step by step, he moved slowly through the trees.

Graham kept his hands over his crotch, just in case he came across someone else in the bush. As he thought about this, even though it might be embarrassing, he actually hoped he would meet another person, as they could tell him that this was part of some huge joke, or, better still, help him.

The trees were not as tall as the ones back in the UK and their bark was a lot dryer than any tree he knew back home. They looked as if they had not seen rain in a very long time, as did the ground, which was hard and dry, with any remnants of grass now withered and brown.

Graham paused to look down at some large ants crawling across the semi-trodden path he was on, and there seemed to be an invisible trail they were all following, albeit in a haphazard way. There was a frenetic purpose about their movement. Some of the ants were carrying leaf parts or parts of dead insects, and in some cases the package each carried was nearly as large as the ant itself.

As he watched them, the ants made him feel extremely uncomfortable, because his feet were bare and, at the moment, he knew there was nothing he could do about that or his nakedness. This uneasiness, though, was nothing compared to his absolute feeling of being lost and alone, not just physically, but emotionally, with an overwhelming awareness of extreme vulnerability. He thought again about how he'd never experienced this high-alert feeling before, and that something deeper was going on inside.

He wondered then what sort of person would place him in a position like this.

'*Who would strip me naked and kidnap me, then put me somewhere unknown?*' he thought.

'A man with bright blue eyes is who!' he said out loud, which even surprised him, as he recalled vaguely that one of his captors had this very distinctive eye colour. But finding himself extremely thirsty and hungry on top of being lost and alone, Graham realised he needed to move on and look for help, food and water. He'd worry later about how he'd ended up being here.

As he walked, he continued to find the ground extremely hard on his bare feet. The smells he smelt were unfamiliar to him; the trees looked so different from what he knew at home; the shrubbery was of a sort he'd only seen on TV when watching African documentaries.

'But if that were the case, and I'm in Africa, how did I get here? And, if so, are there wild animals like lions, leopards, and hyenas around?' he thought. *'There could be one of those animals ready to leap out from behind one of the bushes!'*

Finally, he came to a small clearing where there were taller bushes and the grass was higher than it was amongst the trees. As he looked about, and as he moved cautiously out from the trees, he suddenly noticed on the other side of the clearing a group of animals partially hidden by the rain-starved shrubbery.

CHAPTER SIX

The dizziness that had bothered David since he'd awakened had almost disappeared.

He was now convinced that this reaction was due to him being drugged somehow.

He thought back to when he'd had his appendix operation around five years previous. He recalled the same woozy feeling he had had then.

He remembered feeling sick when he had first woken up from that operation, but also how it had significantly affected his memory, how at first he couldn't even remember why he was in hospital and how disorientated he felt.

He recalled his conversation with the doctor, who explained that short-term memory loss after an anaesthetic is common.

The wooziness he had now, and especially how it had been when he'd first awakened, was very similar to the feeling he'd experienced then. The difference this time was that he didn't have anyone around to help him remember or to prompt him with what had happened. This time he had to rely on his memory recovering on its own.

As he peered into the blackness of the cave, having become acutely aware of a sound coming from deep within, he could make out what seemed like the rhythmic dripping of water. It vaguely mimicked a submarine's sonar, which was so obvious now that he was mystified as to why he hadn't noticed it before.

He began to imagine a deep, dark pool of cool water that had been collecting over time after seeping through the rocks above the cave and leaking down from the walls. He also imagined that the rocks above the pool, where the water dripped through, would be stained with whatever minerals percolated from the ground above.

It was as if all of David's senses were finally coming together, almost as if before they'd been closed off, but it was the smell of the cave that acutely hit him now. He thought perhaps it was the dripping and the imagined pool that helped his sense of smell come alive, with the mustiness reminding him of a mouldy, damp cellar.

With his brain awakening because of fresh smells, sights, and sounds, he found himself half-turned toward the distant dripping and half-turned toward the welcoming light.

He found that he was torn between going to investigate this sound and continuing his way out of the cave. Ultimately, the bright sunlight outside attracted him more. He figured that going toward the light was more likely to give him better clues as to where he was, although he was also extremely wary about leaving the apparent safety of the cave. However, he was now more aware of his nakedness, too, and, like most people, he had never been out in the open without any clothes on.

Back at home and when he was at school, he even found going to a swimming pool extremely difficult, as he had a huge fear of people seeing his rotund body shape. Of course, when he went swimming he would have been wearing swimming shorts, but even so this was still embarrassing for him. So, now that he was totally naked and in an unknown place where someone might see his naked body, he was near panic.

This thought alone made him hesitate for a while longer; he stood motionless, listening to the rhythmic drip, drip, drip behind him. But he was now also aware of some unfamiliar sounds that were emanating from beyond the cave entrance, sounds which placed him outside of his home in the UK. Bizarrely enough, the only piece of this confusing jigsaw puzzle that was strangely comforting to him was the musty, cellar-like smell.

This smell took him back to his childhood, when he would visit his grandparents. They lived in the sleepy English market town of Saffron Walden in a quaint cottage that backed onto the town's common and a small brook. He would spend many a weekend at this cottage when his parents worked or went away. It had a basement, where he had always loved to play, that always smelt of damp; this is the smell that was familiar to him now.

Despite the familiarity of this smell, he decided that the darkness of the cave was forbidding and would not provide the evidence he sought, whereas the outside and its warmth offered an escape and possible clues to his whereabouts.

Within a few more steps, the floor of the cave became stonier and harder on his bare feet. With each step he took, although he placed his feet down very carefully, small stones still bore into the soles of his feet.

Finally, he reached the opening to his unusual waking place, furrowed his brow, and squinted against the bright sunlight. As he stood there naked and all alone, he became even more frustrated and annoyed with his faulty memory.

'How could I remain totally mystified as to what has happened to me?' he questioned. *'How is it possible to be transported from home to where I've awoken?'*

He now stood just outside of the cave, studying the landscape that stretched far out before him, looking for clues as to how he might have gotten there. As he moved further out and into the sun, he became much more aware of his naked skin and covered his manhood with both hands, for fear of being seen.

He looked down at his rotund belly and white flesh, which had never really seen the sun before, as he'd spent most of his time indoors. David's overweight condition came from eating an unhealthy diet of burgers, fried chicken, and kebab takeaways, and lack of exercise.

Feeling very self-aware, he kept both his hands firmly around his privates, to conceal his pride. However, as he looked around, there were no signs of people, no signs of what he knew as 'normal' civilisation, and absolutely no recognisable clues as to his whereabouts.

He could feel the sun beating down on him from what appeared to be a height that he'd never remembered before. The sun's rays felt extremely hot on his bare skin and he knew right away that if he spent any time at all out here, he'd burn very quickly.

As he surveyed the area outside the cave, all he could see was an unusual collection of unfamiliar looking trees and shrubs and an area of scrubland ahead that seemed to stretch out for many kilometres. The scrubland, in the main, was covered in grass which had grown quite high in certain parts, and was predominantly of a light brown colour, which was interspersed with green. He assumed this hay-like grass was that way due to the lack of rainfall. Greenery was provided by umbrella-like trees, which cast wide, circular shadows on the ground below. More green was added to the scene by small bushes, which protruded above the grass

As he turned and looked back at the entrance to the cave, he could see above it an area like a small hill. This rocky slope was covered in green plants of a type which he'd also never seen before in England. The rock areas that had not yet been covered by these unfamiliar looking plants had a mottled-like surface, as they were covered in grey and white liken, which looked a bit like mould.

The similarity between both these unfamiliar scenes — the one that stretched up above and behind him and the other that stretched out and away to the horizon in front of him — was the dryness of both the ground and plants; even the plants which had green leaves looked like they'd not seen rain in a very long time. All he could conclude was one thing: *'This place looks very much like Africa.'*

'But how could that be?' he doubted to himself. *'Impossible!'*

He paused to think. The last waking thing he recalled, aside from the vague dream-like memory of the two men that floated on the edge of his mind, was of being in England.

'How could I have been transported to Africa, some several thousand kilometres away, in what seems like such a short time frame?

'How did I get moved to a cave without me being aware?

'How is it that I'm now looking out over an African savannah?'

Had he gone through some kind of strange time warp, or could this be some weird, intense dream he was having? To his knowledge, the technology to move through time still didn't exist, and he was sure he'd never had a dream so vivid. Now that he was fully awake, he was convinced that indeed he was in Africa.

CHAPTER SEVEN

Konner Hurley landed at Lusaka International airport, having transited in Johannesburg for a few hours, arriving via South African Airways. As he walked off the plane, he was hit by the warmth of the Zambian sun and smiled, because it was autumn and cold back home in New York City where he lived. His trip was planned for just 10 days and he was looking forward to his African adventure.

Konner descended the stairs from the plane and crossed the tarmac, which led to a 'Welcome to Zambia' sign in big, blue letters above the terminal entrance. The people ahead of him were already queueing up at immigration, so he joined them and waited his turn.

When he was called to the immigration official, Konner stepped forward and presented an American passport along with his 90-day visa that he'd managed to get at the Mission in 52nd Street. The immigration officer was a large man with a bulging stomach, which under his official-looking white shirt made his clothes seem almost too small for him. Surprisingly for Konner, as he was used to unfriendly immigration officers in the United States, the Zambian officer smiled at him and welcomed Konner to his country.

This officer went on to ask him the usual questions. Within a few moments, he had stamped his passport and visa and Konner found his way to the baggage-claim area. It wasn't large and had just two baggage belts. It wasn't long before his large, black bag came along the second belt. He collected it and made his way to the customs area.

After he passed through customs and came out into the main terminal, he was met by a group of people, each awaiting the arrival of someone from the most recent flight and many holding up name plates. Konner walked over to the guy who had his name scribbled onto a large, white plate. He was a tall gentleman who Konner guessed was in his mid- to late-forties. He was dressed in khaki trousers and had a camouflaged t-shirt on. When he realised that Konner was his guest, he gave a big smile, revealing a set of very white teeth, and greeted him with, 'Welcome to Zambia, Mr Hurley. Did you have a good flight, sir?'

'Yes, I did, but it was a long trip and I'm now very tired.'

'My name is Jowidah, and please let me take your bag for you, Mr Hurley,' he offered. 'We need to make our way over to the Proflight check-in area, as we are taking a short flight to Mfuwe

Airport with them.'

'Call me Konner. How long is the flight?'

'It's just over an hour, sir,' Jowidah answered, as he grabbed Konner's bag and wheeled it towards where they needed to go. Konner followed behind.

Both men checked in on the flight at the check-in desk, and before long they were both heading for the aeroplane that was sitting out on the tarmac. The plane was a turbo-prop plane and had a single engine with a propeller on each wing.

At this point Konner began to feel nervous, as he had never been on such a small aircraft before, especially in a foreign country. He looked at the aeroplane with suspicion. Next to it was an old, red tractor, which had a white trailer attached to it. As he viewed the plane with distrust, he observed three men, all with fluorescent jackets on, milling around the fuselage who appeared to be readying things for departure.

'You'll be fine, Mr Hurley. Proflight have a good safety record and it's just a short trip to Mfuwe,' Jowidah tried to reassure Konner, as he could see the look on his face and his seeming reluctance to board the plane.

Konner looked at Jowidah, forced a smile, and then climbed the stairway ahead of him. As he reached the door, he had to duck his head due to its limited height, then was met by a lady all dressed in blue. She smiled at him and welcomed him aboard, whilst asking him for his boarding pass.

Konner was directed to his seat and Jowidah joined him and sat next to him towards the front of the plane. The two of them were followed by a few other passengers, which included an older lady who needed help getting up the stairs. She was accompanied by a younger man, who looked like he could be her son. By the way she was speaking to him, Konner assumed that this was the case, and although it was clear that she needed help, she kept telling the younger man to 'stop fussing, I'm okay, leave me alone.'

These two passengers were followed by a taller gentleman dressed in a suit and tie, who to Konner looked a bit out of place on this flight. He wondered what business he might be attending to in Mfuwe. As the man was shown to his seat by the same young lady dressed in blue, he smiled at Konner, as he took one of the seats directly in front of him. He was an older man and probably in his mid-fifties and what hair he had left on his head had all gone grey.

This man was the last to get on the plane before the door was closed, and whilst the steward did her safety checks to make sure that each passenger had their seat belt fastened, the pilot started the engines. Konner couldn't believe how noisy they were when they started up. As soon the plane was at the head of the take-off strip, things got even noisier, as the pilot pushed the throttle forward and the aircraft lurched down the runway.

The runway felt very bumpy, but after only a short distance the nose of the plane rose up and they soon were airborne, at which point Konner had butterflies in his stomach. Not long after they'd taken off, the plane began to bounce around in air turbulence. Just then, the pilot introduced himself with a South African accent and said, 'We will be experiencing quite a bit of turbulence on this flight, but we should have you in Mfuwe in the next 70 minutes, so please enjoy your flight with us today and thank you for choosing Proflight Zambia.'

The pilot's words didn't make Konner feel any better, and he thought, *'Seventy minutes of turbulence over the African plains. That's not too good.'* All he could do was look out the small window and down at the dry-looking grassland below.

CHAPTER EIGHT

David pinched his arm to see if he could wake himself up even further and to bring back his lost memories.

'This experience is definitely real,' he thought.

With that, he reached around again to the back of his neck to find the hidden object under his skin and rubbed his unhealed wound. He believed that this must surely have something to do with the two men he recalled, but he also linked them to where he found himself now. His instinct told him that whatever the object was under his skin, it had been placed there by someone, most likely by one of these men. With this thought a shiver went up the whole length of his spine.

He then suddenly remembered going to an interview at a property company based in Chelmsford. This was the last thing he had done before going to the bank for his money.

At the interview, he remembered handing a copy of his CV to a businessman he judged to be in his mid-forties and recalled the guy's eyes, which were a piercing blue colour. He recollected his feeling very intimidated by the man, as he had a real presence about him and a self-assurance that he had never experienced before.

As he thought about the interviewer, it suddenly hit him that one of the two men he recalled in his dream-like memory was this same person. He began to remember some of the questions the man had asked, which were a little unusual for a job interview. One question he recalled being asked was: 'Would you prefer to be at home not working, rather than working for someone like me?' He remembered being completely thrown by this question.

The other thought that came to him about this encounter was how the guy insisted he have a drink. David had refused, as he never liked to drink from random glasses at places he didn't know. The drink on the interviewer's table was only water, but the guy must have asked him at least five times, 'Are you sure you don't want to have a drink?'

But the comment about the water that spooked him the most was when he'd said, 'Water is precious and you could die if you don't have it.'

David recalled not having an answer to this statement, and whilst he was being stared at by the man, he forced himself to have a sip from the glass that sat in front of him. This peculiarity of the interview stayed with him, too, and now he wasn't quite sure whether this was relevant to his present predicament or not. Yes, this guy was a bit odd and certainly very sure of himself and he had made David very nervous, but surely this had nothing to do with him being transported to Africa. He also recalled that this man, who had introduced himself as Mr Blake Caldwell, had tanned skin, which indicated he had obviously been somewhere with a lot of sunshine.

Then another memory of the man's office, where the interview had taken place, suddenly hit him like a ton of bricks — it was the picture on the wall behind his desk of an African plain. The pieces of this bizarre jigsaw puzzle were beginning to slot into place.

'Was Caldwell something to do with this? If he was, how did he do this?' he thought.

He continued to rehash his interview with Caldwell, and he remembered how he had left his office feeling a bit agitated. The comment about the water made more sense to David now that he was in Africa: *'The guy was toying with me about what he had planned for me out here, the bastard!'*

As he thought about his meeting with Caldwell, he realised now that he had obviously picked up on some kind of body language at the time. As he reviewed his memories of the experience, he could remember walking to the nearest bus stop after his interview, and he could also remember catching the bus home. David could also recall arriving home and going up to his flat, but it was at this point that his memory was still a bit fuzzy.

As he tried to bring forward more of his memories, David looked up and could see that the sun was high in the sky, so he knew it must be late morning or early afternoon. It was extremely hot and he could already feel his skin burning under the sun's intense rays. Now that he'd abandoned the cool interior and shadows of the cave, a heat that he'd never experienced before bore down on him with unrelenting power.

'It never gets as hot as this, even in the summer in the UK,' he thought worriedly. Not that he ever went out on hot days, due to his sensitive skin, but also due to his reclusive tendencies. Both of his parents had fair skin and his mum had red hair, which was passed on through the genetic link to him.

He looked around to see if there was anything he could use as a cover-up, like a large leaf or perhaps some discarded rubbish or clothes. Certainly, within the vicinity of the cave there were no large-leafed plants.

Feeling completely helpless, David let out a huge sigh.

His sense of absolute exposure and vulnerability was intense in him now. He'd never felt such strong emotion before. A feeling of anger came over him, too, which he directed towards the people he had never met — or had he?

'*Who was it who placed me here?*' he raged inside, whilst at the same time hoping that he was wrong about where he was —wrong despite the fact that what he was staring at looked like something out of a David Attenborough documentary.

Despite the fact that he was seeing strange-looking plants and feeling the extraordinary heat from the sun's rays on his back and shoulders, he kept trying to convince himself that he must still be somewhere in the UK.

Whatever the case, he felt very alone and a long, long way away from home.

But then, as if to dispel any lasting doubts about where he was, there suddenly appeared an even more obvious clue to his location, and he was staring right at it.

David's heart jumped to his mouth and it almost missed a beat, as the truth hit him right between the eyes. Although he'd seen all the marks of Africa thus far, and they had to be wrong somehow, it was only now when he saw what was in front of him that his sense of isolation truly hit home and he suddenly felt dizzy again. It was almost as if he were having an out-of-body experience.

In shock, David's brain tried to work out what to do next with the information that had just presented itself.

CHAPTER NINE

Whilst in Zambia, Druker found it easy to get along with the local officials and government men, as they always liked brown bags stuffed with cash, and, as Druker always had plenty of cash, it meant he usually got what he wanted. After he'd purchased Mwatusanga, he spent time building these fake relationships. Keeping these officials on his side was important to him and was worth him spending time with them, even though most of them he didn't like at all. But since he'd become successful, he had surrounded himself with staff and people he needed and trusted when he wanted something.

The corruption levels in Zambia had played a big part in where he'd chosen to buy. He had originally wanted a reserve in nearby Botswana, but the Corruption Perception Index for Botswana was relatively low and the Southern African nation had again recently captured the title of Africa's least corrupt nation. So knowing his plans for flying into and out of Zambia, he needed to be able to rely on corrupt authorities, which Zambia seemed to have an abundance of, so he bought his reserve there.

The extra paperwork for his flights would be dealt with through him, and this usually involved him paying over copious amounts of cash, thus avoiding any unnecessary questions each time he either left the country or when he returned. During this process, customs officials reserved the right to meet him at his home when he arrived, but they'd told him that this would happen very rarely. Druker knew full well that if they did turn up, the meeting would likely involve yet more cash exchanging hands.

Once he began flying to the UK in his own jet, although he liked the idea of flying direct, he would normally stop on route in Nice, where he'd stay in the Hotel Hyatt Regent on the Promenade Des Anglais in the Bay of Angels.

Druker loved this hotel; it had its own casino, where he'd play his favourite game of blackjack. He always managed to pick up young women, either in the casino or at some of the local bars and clubs. As he couldn't speak any French, in most cases the women he chose would speak fluent English. But on occasion, he'd get lucky with girls who didn't speak much English. When there was plenty of Champagne involved, which with him there always was, language never seemed to matter too much, as all he was looking for was no-strings-attached fun.

He had been married before, but his now-estranged wife still lived in his mansion in Essex England with his only daughter, Nicola. It was when he was 26 that he had met his wife in a bar in Knightsbridge and they ended up moving out of London and out to Essex. They'd lived for 10 years together until the split-up, which was after he'd had an affair with the wife of a friend.

Since his split with his wife, he had avoided entering into long-term relationships, considering them to be hassles he never wanted again. It was easier for him to get his sexual fixes on his trips to France, but also when he was in London. His daughter was working in London as a recruitment consultant, and on some of his trips to the UK he would meet her for dinner. After dinner he would frequent the casinos in Park Lane, and invariably he'd end up with a woman who was looking to have a good time with a rich sugar daddy. He wasn't fussy about which type of woman he met, so long as there was no chance of any romance or hassle in the future.

He did meet one lady in a London bar after he'd been to a casino and she agreed to meet up with him each time he flew in, but with no strings attached. This relationship lasted for a while, but he soon got bored with her, especially after she started talking about coming to visit him in Zambia. This was a step too far for Druker, as she was getting too close for comfort, so he never contacted her again after that.

CHAPTER TEN

The final piece of evidence that David needed to confirm his location was right in front of him now — a small herd of placid-looking wildebeest grazing on the grass just to the right of where he stood. He was frozen to the spot, not knowing what to do with this new scene in this unfolding nightmare. Seeing these wildebeest made him realise how exposed he was to the wild, and despite the fact that they were grass-eating creatures, he was terrified.

Intermingled with this herd of 50 or more wildebeest were a number of zebra, too. The open plain where these animals grazed was several metres below his standing point and about 100 or so metres away, but there was no doubt in his mind what they were and what seeing them meant.

'Wildebeest and zebras?' he questioned. *'I'm definitely in Africa.'* But the 'how' question raised its disturbing head again. *'Time travel? Could this be possible?'*

He plucked up a bit of courage to move further away from the protection of the cave, and as he did, several of the wildebeest nearest to him looked up. On doing so they became agitated and made enough of a commotion to unsettle the rest of the herd. This movement signalled that danger loomed, and although in reality he posed no threat to these animals at all, their instinct, which is wired into their relatively tiny brains, kicked in. Their readiness to run at the slightest sound or the smallest of movements in the surrounding grassland, was set like the sensitive trigger of a gun. Their brains were hard-wired to view any movement as a potential threat. These animals had an overwhelming sense of survival, which was always stronger than their need to eat, especially when faced with apparent danger. The wildebeest's survival mechanism, which had developed over millions of years of evolution, simply kicked in automatically, and now the whole herd was getting agitated.

These large herbivores began to head off from where they were eating grass and away from where David stood. In doing so, the dry ground where they were eating was stirred up, as dust plumed up from their heavy hooves. The earth was so obviously dry that this small movement of such hefty animals was enough to dislodge the loose soil sitting just below the dry grass.

At this point, he hoped that perhaps he was in some sort of wildlife park, but why and how? But then looking out to the distant horizon he realised that this was wishful thinking, as it would have to be one very large park. Looking in all directions, he could see no signs of human activity, no fences to keep these animals enclosed, and no end to what was turning into an experience he sorely wished he had no part in.

As he scanned the horizon, something a bit closer to where he stood got his attention. Out of the corner of his eye he saw movement in the tall grass to his left. He was sure that this movement represented more animals. But what kind? This visual signal confirmed that there were yet more animals around him and the area nearby was beginning to come to life.

His heart began to race with a pulse he'd never experienced before. He stood frozen to the spot whilst his brain was taking in the unfolding scene.

CHAPTER ELEVEN

As Graham focused on the animals he'd seen, he realised that they were buffalo.

He froze to the spot and remembered that African Buffalos were classed as one of the Big Five on the dangerous animal list.

He began to recall something he'd read: *'Buffalos are responsible for a high number of human deaths, with some saying even more deaths than the other big five, including attacks by lions and elephants.'*

Two of the nearest buffalos turned to look at him, and as these creatures stared at him and began to stir, his heart rate jumped to the highest he'd ever experienced. The nearest creature to him snorted and raised its head, as its two huge horns, almost too big for its head, rose up menacingly. Not wanting to engage with these cantankerous animals and not wishing to be attacked, he backed off slowly, trying not to upset them.

Walking off in the other direction, he now

realised his worst nightmare. There were animals out there, and dangerous ones at that. Seeing these wild buffalo confirmed that he was in Africa.

Having disappeared back into the cover of the tall trees and out of sight of the herd of buffalos, he was not sure which way to turn, for fear of bumping into more ferocious animals. He felt even more lost and alone, and understood his deep feelings of fear, but despite them, a deeper primal feeling inside Graham urged him to keep moving on, at least initially in order to find some water.

His feet were already sore, despite having only walked a short distance, plus the back of his throat was parched from the lack of water and from the heat. Thoughts began rushing through his mind.

'What if I can't find any water? What would I do if I come across a pride of lions? How can I find something to eat and what could I eat out here anyway?'

He remembered that when he was watching 'I'm a Celebrity Get Me Out of Here' on TV, he recalled their eating insects, which, if he could find some, he could eat; this would also provide him with a source of fluid.

He then had a sudden flash of memory about the three men. He remembered them all staring down at him and he was in a box, like a coffin of some kind. He recalled, as the box had been opened, a sudden blaze of light shining down, and the men all leaning over him. He recalled the pain the bright sunlight had brought to his eyes, as his irises had tried to quickly adjust to the abrupt change in light.

He recalled one of the men leaning in, then a sharp stab in his left arm, then losing consciousness, and finally waking up here in this forest. Graham knew that at least one of the men he looked up at from the darkened box was familiar.

He struggled to recall more of his activities before ending up in that box. The last thing he remembered was returning home from the shops with some food and cigarettes to his very small flat, but other than that, things were hazy.

Finally, he forced himself to remember putting the key in the lock to his flat, which was on the third floor of a large, converted house near the centre of Chelmsford. He shared the house with five other people, most of whom were also on benefits.

Then, as he replayed his actions after opening the front door, the hairs on his arms suddenly stood up and he shivered. He vaguely remembered seeing someone standing in front of him. There was someone already in his flat! It came back to him how scared he'd felt and how he'd asked the person what they were doing there. He also remembered moving towards the person; then his memory went blank, but he sensed that there had been someone else in the room, possibly waiting behind the door.

He then began to think more about the man with the blue eyes, and wondered how he'd managed to get him out here. Thinking about the coffin he'd awoken in with the light streaming in, he concluded, *'He must have transported me in that box. But how?'* How could this man get him out of the UK, unnoticed, and into a totally different country, without legal repercussions? He was amazed that this was even possible, but obviously it was.

'What if I'm not the only one?' Graham suddenly wondered, and with this thought, goose bumps formed on his arms and a shiver ran through his body.

'This man seems to be playing god. How dare he do this to me?'

His mind then turned back to his predicament and the location where he'd awakened. He needed to think straight and work out how to get out of this place.

'Perhaps there may be civilisation not that far away,' he thought, although because he was in a wooded area, he was not able to see into the distance.

Thinking again about survival and the need for food and water, Graham recalled the ants he'd seen earlier.

'Perhaps I could eat those,' he thought, although this meant going back towards where he'd come across the buffalo. After careful consideration, he decided against this move; instead, he continued in the direction in which he'd started, which was well away from the buffalo.

He pushed on through the bush towards what

he hoped might be safety.

'*But out here, where is safe?*' he asked himself. In fact, he thought, it would be unlikely anywhere hereabouts was safe at all.

His heightened awareness seemed to numb the pain in his feet, which allowed him to continue walking. The internal anaesthetic was probably due to the high level of adrenalin rushing through the veins in his body.

Whilst he walked slowly through the trees and bushes, he was aware that his senses were on high alert. He was also well aware that his body wasn't athletically designed, due to his enlarged stomach and a lack of exercise, and certainly was not designed for being in the wild. This meant that if he encountered a dangerous animal, his ability to be able to out-run it was limited.

As he walked and kept looking all around, first to his left and then to his right, trying to see if there were any lurking threats, Graham suddenly heard the loud sound of an elephant trumpeting. His heart rate jumped another notch and yet more adrenalin was released into his blood. The sound of the elephant was coming from his right, and his initial instinct was to run away, but he was surprised at how quickly he became rational: He remembered that elephants would know where there was water.

'*I can follow them to a waterhole or to a river,*' he thought.

Graham's mouth was completely dry now, so he realised he was in desperate need of water, and having watched films about elephants, they tended to find water very easily, as they needed it on a regular basis. So going against his initial reaction to get away from this new threat, he now decided a better move would be to cautiously seek them out and follow them when they decided they needed to find water.

So he slowly made his way to where he'd heard the trumpeting sound. His heart was in his mouth, though, as he stepped very carefully through the bushes. He knew that elephants could be extremely dangerous animals, especially if they have young.

As he moved, his feet landed on stone after stone, and there were also sharp sticks, hurting them even more. Also, he still felt strange walking around totally naked. He was a bit of a prude and hated showing off his overweight body to anyone. Although he felt that it was unlikely there'd be people in his immediate vicinity, he still felt very much on show.

However, his nakedness was the least of his worries; he needed to find the elephants and then follow them to water without them getting angry at his presence. As he proceeded, he could hear the breaking of tree limbs and softer vocal sounds from the elephants ahead of him.

CHAPTER TWELVE

Druker's computer screens took up most of the desk in front of him, and so that he could read them more easily, the figures on each were huge. He leant back on his leather chair, with his hands cupped over his more than ample stomach, as he studied each of the screens in front of him.

His rotundity was a result of living the good life and eating and drinking to excess. He loved his luxury drinks, like the most expensive brandy and the best malt whiskey he could buy, having it shipped in by the casket. Another favourite of his was red wine, and, since money was no object, he would have the best wine shipped in from around the world. His latest red, bought whilst in France, was a Chateau Mouton Rothschild, possibly one of the finest clarets in the world from the Bordeaux region. Whenever he poured the lovely liquid, it reminded him of blood, with its slightly viscous nature and deep, red colour, which always brought a smile to his face. He knew that he probably drank too much, which did make him think about his father and how he'd drunk himself to death, but he loved it too much to give it up.

Druker had made his fortune from buying and selling property. He had also invested in a number of start-up businesses in Cambridge and had done well with ARM Holdings.

He had invested in this company when it had first floated on the London Stock Exchange in 1998. His million-pound initial investment turned into a multi-million pound mountain of cash as this investment took off.

His parents were both now dead, but when they were alive they had never had much money. His father came from London, whilst his mother was born in Cardiff.

His parent's meagre lifestyle had been hampered by his father constant need to drink. His father would drink his way through his wages on a Friday night down at the local pub.

As a kid he hated it when his father got drunk, as these would lead to him being abusive to his mum. On occasion his father's temper would be turned on him, too.

But when Druker was 16, he had stood up to his father for the very first time. He ended up punching his father in the face hard enough to knock him out cold. After this altercation, his father never touched him again. In the end, his eventual downfall was excessive booze. At the age of 54, his father suddenly died of a heart attack.

On the side of his desk, Druker had set a full

glass, which he'd poured only a few moments ago, to let the wine breathe. He glanced across to the screens to his left. The first computer screen on his desk was showing a map, whilst the second screen was the one showing the darkened room. The two screens to the right of these were the ones that held his financial information. These were attached to his laptop, which had the screen folded down and a separate keyboard and mouse connected through wireless.

Now that he had let his wine breathe, he took a sip and allowed it to linger in his mouth for a few seconds before swallowing, enjoying every drop.

Then he continued with his travel arrangements for the UK. He had already booked the hotel in Chelmsford for himself and one of his rangers, Scott, plus the car hire. But he still needed to arrange for the pilots to fly in from Lusaka and to have them sort out the flight arrangements to Cambridge Airport. This airport was further away from Chelmsford than Stansted Airport, but it was smaller and quicker to get through, especially on his way back to Africa.

He would leave it for his pilots to arrange the hotel accommodation in Cambridge for themselves, as they preferred to do this, but he would always pay for all their expenses and he was happy for them to stay wherever they liked.

He made the call to Citation Aviation, the operator that arranged for the pilots to fly his plane. The call was always a quick one, whereby Druker would give them his departure date and time with his required return date and time. He normally allowed four to five days for his trips; in this case, he allowed for five days, with the option of coming back sooner, which was one of the great benefits of having his own aircraft. He required them to fly out on Thursday, as he already had meetings set for Friday in Chelmsford, so this gave him enough time to sort everything else out, as it was now Monday.

With all the arrangements made, he sat back in his chair and drank the rest of the wine in his glass.

CHAPTER THIRTEEN

Scott had been out of a job for over a year before he met Druker and was nearly at the point of moving to a different country. He had been considering South Africa or Kenya, as there seemed to be more jobs there, but he preferred Zambia, as the wildlife in this region was some of the best in Africa.

When Scott encountered Druker in a bar in Mfuwe, he had jumped at the chance to work for him, especially for the amount of money offered, which was totally unheard of in these parts. The job had not been advertised, but instead this guy seemed to be going around chatting to people and talking about the job. It was the barman who pointed Druker in the direction of Scott, as he knew that he'd been looking for work for a long time now and that he'd come to the bar to drown his sorrows on too many occasions recently.

When Druker had told him about the position and what the job entailed, he was initially a bit apprehensive, but his money was fast running out. He was fortunate, though, that his parents still supported him and he would often call them to keep them up-to-date with how he was doing. His father, knowing that he'd been out of work for a while, would offer to fund him through tough times then transfer money to Scott's bank account.

Scott's wages were 20,000,000 Zambian Kwacha per month for what he did, whereas he had been applying for various jobs up to this point and knew that a head ranger would be paid between 7,000 to 8,000 Rand per month in places like South Africa, which is the equivalent of 3-3.500,000 Zambian Kwacha.

He had most of the relevant experience for a head ranger-type of role. Usually, top of the list was Big Five experience, followed closely by a qualification with the FGASA. He had a Level II FGASA qualification, which centres on being a guide in Africa, but also goes into depth on types of animals, conservation management, and even teaches the night sky, weather and climate.

One of Scott's favourite modules was Module 15 on Animal Behaviour. This subject really interested him; he was fascinated with interpreting the signs animals give off, especially the larger ones, like elephants. He also had a particular fondness for rhinos, and had spent a year working at a Johannesburg zoo with the white rhinos there.

His new boss, in talking about the type of animals on the estate, which included all the Big Five game animals, made it clear that Scott's role included their protection, but that he would explain the rest of his job in due course. He confirmed that poachers were a problem, which Scott already knew, and that he would be issued the necessary firearms to deal with them, as it was likely they would be encountered at some point. His boss was very clear about what the approach should be, though: Shoot first and ask questions later, as the poachers were pretty ruthless.

In previous jobs, he had come across the aftermath of poachers who had killed animals. Finding animals in this way always made him extremely angry. He recalled finding a female rhinoceros bleeding to death after poachers had left her without her horns, having sawn them off whilst she was still alive.

Although to date he'd not encountered any face to face, he vowed that he would make sure he made it count when and if he did come into direct contact. He hadn't yet decided what he would do, but he felt that shooting poachers would be too humane and not what they actually deserved.

Now, in his bed at the estate, he had awakened with all these thoughts running through his mind, as he recalled a nightmare he'd had in the night where he encountered a poacher, who had shot him at close range.

This morning he woke up later than he usually did. It was the sound of some birds fighting outside his window that had startled him awake this morning, and as he looked out it was already light. He looked at his phone, which showed 6:43

a.m.

'Have I got time to go to the gym?' he thought.

He loved the gym. He would go on most days, as his new job allowed for this and the site had its own personal gym. He preferred to use free weights rather than the machines, as he felt this worked his muscles in a much better way.

Scott got out of bed and dressed in his sports gear. He left his small room for the short walk to the gym, hoping that he would still have time to work out before his boss came looking for him. His room was small, but it was nice enough for him to take himself away if he so wished. However, if he decided he wanted to get away from everything, he would always prefer to venture out into the wild and spot animals instead, so he was rarely in his room, except for when he slept.

The food at Druker's place was amazing and Mulubwa, the cook he had hired, was really great. There was always plenty to eat, too, and as she knew he worked out, she would always make sure he had extra. She would always come and find him to give him extra treats that she'd made in the kitchen.

Scott and his boss had returned home yesterday in the early evening from the UK. He knew that even though he had awakened late, that Druker would probably already be up and preparing things for today, so he was waiting for the call and to receive his final instructions for this morning, which had been outlined the night before.

CHAPTER FOURTEEN

As Graham walked slowly, but hidden from sight, towards the sound of the herd of elephants, his heart was pounding. Soon he spotted movement to his right and could see the huge rump of an elephant through the trees. Not wanting to disturb the creature, he stopped in his tracks, but as he stood there he could feel something tickling him. Looking down, he saw a group of ants crawling up his leg. Then they began biting him. Shaking his leg, he let out a small screech, then realised what he had done. He had announced his presence to the elephants!

The elephant nearest him turned to the sound it had just heard and let out a huge trumpeting sound to warn him off. The ants continued to bite hard into the bare flesh of his leg as he moved back away from the elephant. The huge creature turned its whole body to face Graham, who slowly retreated. His focus was more on the elephant in front of him rather than the searing pain in his leg.

He managed to fade away into the bush and he was pleased to see that the elephant decided not to pursue him. He took this opportunity to kill the remaining ants that were still crawling up his leg.

He'd never felt as helpless as he did now and he had never felt fear like this before. Knowing there were wild animals all around and with the realisation that survival was the game, he knew there would be no let-up. He understood that he was now a part of the ecosystem. No longer was he 'Man,' the all-conquering animal above the other animals on the planet; instead, he now formed a part of the natural balance of nature and the survival of the fittest.

He found himself not wanting to die. He became determined to escape this wilderness, even though in the last few years he had often felt depressed and useless, with many thoughts of suicide. He had been claiming benefits for over five years now, since he had been made redundant, and had found it all too easy to not get employment. Now all he did was while away the endless idle hours playing on his computer at home.

He began to imagine eating either a kebab or a fried chicken meal, as he had never been as hungry as he was right now, and with these thoughts of food running through his head, he found a spot to sit so he could look at his feet.

Plopped on a bare area of dirt, he could now see how badly they were cut from walking on the rough ground. He looked around to see if there was anything he could use as makeshift shoes, but there was nothing that remotely resembled any form of foot protector.

Groaning as he got to his feet, he limped back in the direction of the elephants, which was not difficult to discern, what with the amount of noise they made whilst demolishing the surrounding trees and 'talking' to each other.

As he walked towards them, the herd seemed to be a bit farther away. It would appear that they were now on the move. Not wanting to lose touch with them, he walked a bit faster, even though his feet gave him a lot of pain. He knew he had no choice.

Pressing on through the bushes, his heart started pounding yet again, as he knew the herd was only meters away, and he didn't want to run into them like he'd done before.

The pain increased with every step he made. He was limping now, which made it harder to keep up, and although he couldn't see the elephants, he could hear them crashing through the small trees and bushes.

He was already out of breath, as this was the first form of exercise he'd done in years. He had to stop. He stood for a moment to regain his breath, whilst he leant over and put his hands on his knees.

After he'd had time to recover, he began to walk again and soon broke from the cover of the trees to a more open, grassy area. There in front of him was the herd of around 20 or so elephants, including some quite small calves. They were walking quickly enough for him to need to keep up a fast pace.

Fortunately for him, the elephants didn't seem to pay too much attention to their stalker and continued on their quest, which he hoped, was for water. He knew that, so long as he could get some drinking water, the reserves of fat in his body, which were plentiful, would keep him going for at least a couple of weeks, although he hoped to be rescued well before then.

Very much aware now that he was on an open savannah, he looked around to see if there were any other animals in the vicinity. In the distance, he could see a large herd of what looked like wildebeest and zebra, and he knew very well that where there were grazing animals, there would always be predators like lions around. Trying not to think about this too much, he continued to follow the elephants, keeping what he felt was a safe gap between them.

As he trudged along, Graham occasionally looked out across the savannah. In the far distance, he could see a mountain range, which looked gloomy. Looming above these mountains were some very dark rain clouds. Then he saw a couple of lightning bolts, followed by the distant rumble of thunder. The clouds were obviously giving up their life-giving water, as he could see the dark streaks that represented rain reaching to the ground below. This scene looked more like an oil painting — an ominous one at that; it almost didn't look real. The streaks of dark rain looked like an artist had splashed his paint brush violently across a canvas after having painted the black-looking clouds on a previously blue sky. Visually, the clouds and the shadowed mountains almost merged into one, as the sky met the land in this mighty storm.

He continued walking, following the elephants, whilst hoping these clouds and their accompanying rain would come his way. He was buoyed by the sight, as this meant that the dry land around him could get some rain and he would get water.

Between where he walked and this distant scene, he could see many umbrella trees sticking up out of the landscape. These individual trees were interspersed with larger clumps of trees, while in between them was grassland. As he proceeded across the savannah, he tried to walk under as many of the trees as he could to get as much shade as possible.

'It would be nice to have those rain clouds over me right now, as at least this would give me some respite from the heat of the sun,' he thought. *'I could also drink the rain, too, and be cooled down.'* But as he looked at how far away the storm was, he realised that it was unlikely to get here soon, if at all.

Still struggling to keep up with the herd, he had to break into a slow jog, which was even harder on his feet, and as he was already out of breath from his fast walking, he knew he wouldn't be able to keep this up for too long. He was surprised at how quickly these huge creatures could move, and so effortlessly, especially as they had some quite small calves in tow. He was also hoping that due to their sheer size and from the noise they were making, that they would scare off any animals in their path.

Getting more and more out of breath, he was partly jogging and partly hobbling to keep up the pace, whilst making sure he didn't lose sight of the herd. In the distance, he could also see a span of grass that was greener than the other grass and surrounded by a few trees. Soon, to Graham's relief, he could see an area of water. It was a waterhole. Well, actually he saw it wasn't so much a hole as a large, curved, boomerang-shaped body of water, which fortunately for him was nearer than he thought it might be.

He then saw that not far away from the waterhole was a river — a large, meandering river, which was full of water. He knew now that he would be able to drink very soon, but that he would also have to be very cautious, because rivers and waterholes in Africa harbour very deadly creatures, like Nile crocodiles and hippopotamuses.

The elephants marched on towards the waterhole, whilst he hobbled along slowly behind, not quite knowing what to expect when he got there.

As Graham slowly approached, he could see the elephants playing in the waterhole, stirring it up into a muddy frenzy. Suddenly, his heart froze. There was a pride of lions on the other side!

Graham felt sickeningly vulnerable again and a new surge of adrenalin was released into his blood stream once more.

CHAPTER FIFTEEN

The new creatures that David could see were now bounding at full pace towards the herd of moving wildebeest, and at this stage they were gaining on the huge mass of animals. The wildebeest, which by now had all gathered into a tight galloping herd, were surrounded by an ever-increasing, billowing cloud of dust. The distinctive mooing of the wildebeest echoed from the herd as they ran, with each and every one of them eager to avoid being made into the next savannah meal of the day. The distinctive sound of the accompanying zebra, like donkeys on speed, also resounded from the running herd, as these creatures panicked along with the wildebeest.

The animals that chased after the herd were sleek and had light brown-looking fur, which almost blended in with the grass they streaked through. Lions!

As they moved even faster, finally into a full-on run, David seemed to see every sinew of muscle that moved under their skin and fur.

His heart raced at almost an impossible rate, as he was experiencing feelings of fear that he'd never known before.

It was an almighty shock to his feeble body structure, but somehow deep within his psyche there were automatic systems kicking in over which he had no control.

The scene unfolding before him was becoming more like an extract from a wildlife program on TV, but the difference was that he was a part of it.

'Fuck lions!' he said out loud, yet mesmerised as if he were a rabbit in the headlights of an oncoming car.

He was stunned to discover that he was witnessing the full-on attack by a whole menacing pride of lions on this herd of wildebeest. But more shocking to him was there were no fences and no safety barriers between him and the predators.

'What if they see me and decide to chase me instead?' he couldn't help but ask himself.

He stood frozen to the spot as the herd moved off into the distance, marked by the dust that then trailed away behind them, slowly settling to the ground again.

The lions finally had to give up on the chase. They'd found no easy pickings this time and no lagging weakling to chase down quickly. It hadn't helped the pride that David had disturbed the herbivores in the first place, which had been slightly before the lions were ready to pounce, allowing the herd to get a head start on their attack.

The thoughts that were going through his mind now were jumbled. His adrenalin-rich blood had heightened his senses and his heart was pounding so hard that he was worried that it might explode in his chest.

But he soon began to feel exhausted, even just standing still and watching. Finally, he decided the best thing he could do was go back into the cave for protection. This would allow him thinking time to consider what he should do next. He was also mindful about getting out of the line of sight from the now frustrated and probably hungry lions.

'Who brought me here?' he suddenly raged. *'Was this some kind of a bizarre joke?'*

After what seemed like forever, he got back to the cave and slowly moved inside away from the entrance. As he did, he heard the roar of a lion outside, a sound that was too close for comfort. He simply couldn't believe what was unfolding before him.

'I'm in a cave in Africa with wildebeest and zebra outside and a pride of lions on the loose,' he said out loud, trying to accept this stark reality.

He couldn't go too far into the cave, as the light faded very fast the further he moved away from the entrance. This made it very difficult to see, but right now he was more worried about getting as far away from the danger as possible.

As he stood for a moment, he could almost

hear his heart pounding inside his chest. He'd never felt as scared as he felt right now. There was a peculiar rawness about what he was feeling, and he could almost taste the fear.

Whilst waiting for his eyes to adjust to the dim light, he once again tried to remember how he had arrived in this strange location. His mind was still fuzzy, and he was sure his heightened stress levels would not help him recall things more readily.

The sound of the dripping water returned to his ears, echoing in the distant part of the cave. It was much too dark to see how far back it was, and he had no idea what might also be down there lurking in the darkness. As there were lions stalking him outside, there could well be other animals that lived in the cave getting ready to attack.

He stood still for a while, frozen to the spot yet again and pondered about what he should do next, as he strained to see beyond and into the darkness. His eyes continued to adjust to the dim light around him, and as they did, he moved farther away from the entrance.

David was now straining to look deeper into the cave, trying to see this imagined pool of cool water, where the continuous rhythmic sound of mineral-rich drips was tantalisingly out of sight.

As he stood facing the darkness with a mixture of emotions — extreme fear laced with anger and frustration — tears began to well up in his eyes.

It was not only like being a fish out of water, but like a fish out of water sizzling in a frying pan on a hot stove.

Then all of a sudden from behind his back he heard something move. Not wanting to turn around for fear of seeing what it might be, his heartbeat returned to the near explosion point again.

But he did force himself to turn, albeit slowly and being careful not to make a sound. As his stare finally fixed on the entrance to the cave, his worst nightmare suddenly became apparent.

CHAPTER SIXTEEN

As Graham slowly approached the water, he watched the lions intently. They seemed to be relaxed and were not overly interested in the elephants, but, more importantly, they didn't seem interested in him, either. But the mere fact that he was only meters away from a pride of lions, and without a moat or a fence between him and them, was hair-raisingly scary.

The last time he'd been this close to lions was at Colchester Zoo, where they have a large male lion along with a few females. He recalled the male staring him right in the eyes, only a short distance away, and all that was between the two of them was a few millimetres of glass. He remembered his sense of vulnerability, despite the separation. He also recalled the beautiful honey colour of the lion's eyes, which had a deep, menacing look about them, as if he were ready to pounce.

Graham's overwhelming urge to get to the

water was stronger than his fear. He could now understand how animals felt, seemingly always very nervous before they did anything. His eyes were fixed on the lions, watching to see if they flinched, to see if they showed any interest in what he was doing, but they seemed to be very relaxed and were lying in the sun mostly with their eyes closed.

As he got closer to the water, he heard the distinctive sound of Zebra, which only reminded him that, along with these native African animals, he, too, fit the category of lions' prey. Distracted for a moment by the elephants' exuberance, he suddenly noticed that one of the lions had got up from its slumber and was looking straight at him. He froze to the spot, hoping that by standing still the lion would not show any real interest in him. Instead, another of the lions got up and began to walk towards the waterhole.

As he watched it approach the water, he was suddenly aware of a warm sensation running down his legs. His bladder had given way, releasing all the urine it had been storing. He looked down for a second to see the yellow-coloured fluid curl down his legs and onto his feet, pooling on the dry African ground. Without realising it, his body was dumping unnecessary waste in preparation for fight or flight. He had never been so scared as he was right now, being faced with a pride of lions, with one staring at him and another walking in his direction. It completely overloaded his senses.

There were other things going on inside his

body, which were doing so on auto-pilot. He could only feel the changes that were happening to him, which were completely outside of his control. In addition to his bladder release, he could feel his heart pounding inside his chest. There was a raw feeling to the emotions he was experiencing. Something deep within his psyche seemed to be building. Never had he felt so terrified, and he was not sure what to do next.

Looking at the elephants, they didn't seem to be too concerned about the lions, but then they were so much larger than him, and, as far as he knew, lions didn't attack adult elephants.

The first lion to stand up also started to make its way to the waterhole from its slightly higher vantage point, and, if possible, his heartbeat jumped even higher. As they made their way closer to the water, they were then closer to where he was lying. However, there was at least a reasonably large expanse of muddy water between him and these two large cats, and he wasn't too sure as to whether lions liked to swim. What also concerned him was that there was still the rest of the pride lying on the bank and basking in the sun. At any point they could join their two companions at the water's edge.

The first lion to reach the water seemed to stare across at him as it knelt down to drink from the brown pool. The large cat had an enormous tongue that lapped at the water, as it looked ahead at him, whilst he remained as still as he could. The second lion joined the first and also started to drink from the muddy water.

Graham stared at the two lions, not knowing what to do next. He found himself having a surreal moment — perhaps he was in some kind of nightmare dream and would wake up soon in his own bedroom. But no, everything was too real for that.

As he watched, motionless and waiting for what to do next feeling helpless, the lions stopped drinking and stood up. Much to his relief, they walked back to the rest of the pride. This gave him the chance he needed to get a drink, too.

As he got closer to the edge of the water, where the hard ground had turned into a dark, black-brown mud, he could feel its coolness with his feet. He then stepped closer and the mud became softer, until he could feel the squelchy sludge squeeze between his toes.

Now right at the water's edge, he slowly crouched to drink. He leaned down and cupped his hands together to gather some water to put in his mouth. He brought the brown liquid to his lips, as it was quickly escaping between his fingers, and took his first small mouthful of what was the foulest-tasting fluid he'd ever ingested. Before he reached down again, he glanced around to make sure he was not being stalked and looked up at the lions again.

The second mouthful was no better than the first, but as he put more and more of the filthy-tasting water in his mouth, it did begin to quench his huge thirst.

As he kept drinking, he found himself stopping at almost every swallow to glance around for danger. This reminded him of watching birds in his garden, as they approached any bread or seed that had been thrown out for them.

Not wanting to drink more than he had to, he swallowed a last mouthful of the foul liquid and slowly got to his feet. As he began to turn and walk away, he saw a huge rhinoceros approaching from the way he'd come. He froze to the spot, not wanting to be noticed by this enormous creature.

The rhinoceros was panting and snorting and walking with aggressiveness, as if to say to the other animals, 'I know I am big and strong. Don't mess with me.' The huge animal headed towards the waterhole and in the direction of Graham. His heart jumped to his mouth again, as he watched in terror, not knowing which way to turn or what to do. He could also still hear the elephants making lots of noise behind him, seemingly without a care in the world.

He slowly moved away from where he stood in the mud, and, with each step, the clay-like matter squeezed up between his toes. The rhinoceros continued its confident stroll towards Graham and the water behind him. The creature snorted and raised its head in defiance, as a warning to him to move away. It was clear where the rhinoceros was heading, and there was no way that it was going to change its path, so Graham knew it was his place to continue to move away instead.

Sidling to his left to leave room at the

waterhole for this armour-plated monster to drink, his heart was pounding hard. As he studied the creature, he could see towering above its head a huge horn that curved forward with a sharp, pointed end.

He knew this natural weapon could quite easily stab him through, and he was very aware that rhinos are cantankerous animals that are not to be trifled with. The only time he'd been this close to a rhino before was at the zoo, but then there were some very large steel railings protecting him from the creatures, whereas this time there was nothing at all.

'This must be a male rhino,' he concluded, as he watched the huge animal getting closer and closer and saw its enormous size.

As he continued to edge further away and out of the rhino's path, he glanced over at the mound behind him where the pride of lions was still lying. He was glad to see that they were still resting, so they didn't add any further danger to his situation right now. His glance was only very quick, because he was keen to keep his eyes firmly fixed on the approaching rhino, which was now only a few metres away.

CHAPTER SEVENTEEN

As David stared out the cave's entrance, his eyes focused on a large male lion standing right in front of the cave. The huge beast appeared to be gazing straight at him with its wide-set, amber-coloured eyes. The stare was so powerful and so intense, that it sent a shiver through his whole body. The fear this stare evoked in him was so potent and so deep that it brought trembling from unfathomable depths within.

Being careful to not make a sound, he slowly retreated farther back into the cave. Whilst doing so, he kept his eyes firmly on the huge feline, which appeared to be still looking right at him.

He was aware that lions are well-adapted to hunting at night, as their eyes are several times better than a human's for seeing in the dark, so he was worried that this lion would be able to see him despite the darkness.

He continued to walk backwards into the dark, whilst carefully groping the floor with his bare feet. He hoped that the cave roof was high enough so he wouldn't hit his head.

He studied the huge, maned animal, which had an enormous protruding mouth and a large, dry nose. Its eyes had a look of sheer menace in a head that seemed almost too large for its slender body, as it paced across the mouth of the cave, planting its huge paws carefully on the ground with each step. The lion then stepped closer and walked into the mouth of the cave. His heart pounding, David retreated still further on the uneven surface, trying not to make a sound.

Then he stopped as he saw a second lion — a lioness — appear behind the male. Taking another step back, he hit his head on the roof of the cave, a blow that caused him to let out a shriek.

He was aware of the lions' acute sense of hearing, and knew they would have heard his sound for certain. So even if they'd not yet seen him or smelt him for that matter, they would now know he was there. He regretted making the noise, and he ducked down to avoid making the same mistake again.

He rubbed his head with his right hand, whilst using his left hand to touch the ground. By now he was on his knees, crawling along the cave floor and away from the big, threatening cats.

His head throbbed; as the pain grew, he swore under his breath.

The lions seemed to hesitate now, only having entered a short way into the cave. Both creatures stood watching intently, as if uncertain what it was they could see, whilst contemplating their next move.

David was being careful not to make any more noise and was still hoping that, although they seemed to be looking straight at him, it was too dark for them to actually see into the cave.

The distance between David and the lions was only a matter of a few metres — a distance that these huge creatures could cover within seconds. Knowing this, and also knowing that the lions could probably see him and smell him, David's heart was pounding so hard that it almost shook his whole body. He was completely at a loss as to what to do.

The male lion took another step inside the cave, which brought him even closer to where David was crouched on the floor, whilst at the same time continuing to smell the air, trying to pick up the scent of its next meal.

David edged back further still, desperately trying not to make a sound.

CHAPTER EIGHTEEN

The flight to Mfuwe had been extremely bumpy, and Konner was relieved when the Jetstream aircraft touched down on the runway with a loud thud. Jowidah had filled him in on the trip and that they'd be met by his colleague at the airport, who would take them both to Lechwe lodge.

The lady in blue then spoke to the passengers, whilst the plane was taxiing to a stop: 'Welcome to Mfuwe. Please stay seated until the aircraft has come to a complete stop. Thank you for choosing Proflight Zambia. I hope we will see you again soon.'

The runway at this airport seemed to be even more uneven than the one at Lusaka, as the pilot taxied the plane to a standstill near to the terminal. As soon as the plane stopped and the seat-belt signs were extinguished, all the passengers were on their feet, gathering their belongings and queueing up to leave.

Konner stood up, grabbed his hand luggage from the overhead locker and stood in line in front of Jowidah, waiting for the doors to be opened. Before long, both he and Jowidah had got off the plane and had gone through the terminal. They both met his colleague and walked with him to his waiting Land Rover. His vehicle had seen better days, as it was dented with few panels unscathed. It turned out that his colleague was of Dutch origin and his name was Bram.

Bram was a tall gentleman, around 1.95 metres in height. He was built like a body builder with large arm muscles and a big chest. When he introduced himself to Konner, he shook his hand and nearly broke it. He took Konner's luggage from Jowidah and proceeded to load it into the back of the vehicle.

'The journey to the lodge will take nearly three hours, but once we get off the main roads and onto the bush tracks, you'll begin to see plenty of game,' Bram explained. 'We need to get going, though, as it's better to get the driving done whilst it's still light.'

'You get in the front, Mr Hurley,' Jowidah offered, 'you'll get a much better view of the animals there.'

With this instruction, Konner went to the front of the vehicle, pulled on the door, which creaked as it opened, and climbed in. Even though the windows in the Land Rover were open, it smelled of dirt. The inside of the vehicle looked like it hadn't been cleaned since it had left the showroom many years before. In the centre of the vehicle was a rack, which housed a rifle. The difference between the inside of the Land Rover and the rifle was like they were owned by two different people. The spanking-clean rifle looked like it had just been taken off the shelf in a gun shop, and Konner recognised it as a Winchester Model 70 Rifle.

Konner knew this rifle was a .458 calibre, which was etched on the side of the gun before the words '*Win. Magnum,*' and it was capable of stopping any large animal in its tracks. This included an elephant if shot in the right place.

The classic walnut stock had been kept in impeccable condition, and the red butt pad was a giveaway to him that this was the Super Grade African rifle. Konner knew the Model 70 bolt-action rifle was widely considered to be the finest bolt action rifle ever produced in the United States. He knew also that it had achieved legendary status among shooters and collectors, and had been nicknamed 'The Rifleman's Rifle.'

Within moments Bram was in the driver's seat, with Jowidah in the rear, and they were on the road heading out of Mfuwe. The roads were tarmac-covered to begin with, but this soon changed to gravel, which was in terrible condition. Before long Bram had turned off what was a bad road onto what was a single track road, which led to the entrance to the South Luangwa National Park. The entrance was marked by two large black-and-white gates and a large yellow sign saying *Welcome to South Luangwa National*

Park. To the right of the gates, and a larger but faded sign, was the park rules and fees sign.

As Bram approached the gates, the road at this point was wide enough for two vehicles, but the gate on this side of the road was closed. A man dressed in a green army-like outfit came out from a green cabin to the left of the road and approached the vehicle.

Bram and the guard on the gate exchanged words, and it was clear that they knew each other from the friendly conversation they had. The park guard then waved them on and through the gate, but Bram had to drive onto the other side of the road to get around the gate that was on his side of the road.

Immediately on the other side of the gate was the Luangwa River, and just before the bridge was a green and yellow sign. This sign emphasised one of the main park rules, which was *Animals have right of way*. As they crossed the river over the bridge, Konner looked down and could see the tell-tale backs of hippos wallowing in the river below, but there were also a couple of hippos lying on the sandy bank.

The road soon turned back into a rough track and the Land Rover came into its own over the terrain. Bram drove with purpose along the bumpy roads, but did try to avoid the larger holes in the track, although despite this Konner was bounced around in his seat.

They had been driving in the park for around an hour when they came across a huge bull elephant standing in the middle of the track. The grey creature was side-on, but with its head and tusks pointing towards the oncoming vehicle. Bram slowed down and then pulled the vehicle to a complete stop around 30 feet from the animal.

'He's huge,' Konner commented to Bram.

'Yes, and we need to be careful, as he may charge if he feels threatened by us,' Bram replied.

'So how are we going to get past him?' Konner questioned.

'He'll move, eventually; we just have to be patient,' Bram replied, and as he was in the midst of saying this, the elephant turned its head and moved away into the bush.

'It's probably good that he's on his own, as he doesn't have a family to protect,' he said. 'If he did, we would have had to keep way back to avoid a charge.'

Once the creature had disappeared, Bram put the Land Rover back into gear and proceeded along the track. Along the way, they saw many other animals, but none as impressive as the elephant. They eventually arrived at the lodge, which was right on the edge of the Luangwa River.

CHAPTER NINETEEN

Druker's office door opened and in walked Scott. 'Hey, Druk,' he said. 'Confirmation that we've sent out the first two experiments. We took Lane out first and put him in the cave in zone two, as we agreed this morning, and we also put Smith in zone two, but several miles away in a small, wooded area.'

Scott was a tall, dark-haired young man in his late twenties. He had a tanned face from being out in the African sun for the most part of each day. However, as a kid he'd obviously suffered badly from acne, as the surface of his face was severely pitted from the scars it had left. He was fit and muscular, working out most days in Druker's gym. He was wearing khaki clothes and a baseball hat, which he'd got from the Bahamas when he was out deep-sea fishing there a few years back with his parents.

'Good,' Druker replied. 'Let's see how long these little shits last out there. I'm willing to take a bet with you that they last for less than a day. Are you willing to take up a wager?'

'Nah, not a betting man, but if I were, then I think they might last a bit longer, especially Lane. So long as he stays near to the cave, he may stand a chance,' Scott replied, as he glanced at the screen showing the tracking units.

As they discussed their first two experiments, both men looked across at another computer screen with a map and two pointers on it, one with the name *Lane* attached to it and the other labelled *Smith*.

'There they are, and you can see the tracker units are working just fine, even though Lane is in the cave. So let's see how long he lasts, but there's been no movement yet,' Druker said.

'We hid that booster unit just outside the cave, just as you instructed us to do, and it's obviously working, whereas Smith is out in the open,' Scott said, 'so let's see how long they last.'

As Scott was about to leave the office, Druker instructed him, 'Don't go far, Scott, I might need you.'

'Okay, boss,' Scott replied in his usual compliant fashion as he turned and headed out the door.

CHAPTER TWENTY

Graham decided to walk more hastily away from the water and the approaching rhino, in the same direction he'd already started to move, whilst at the same time hoping the animal was more interested in getting a drink than attacking him.

When the rhino reached the spot where he'd been standing, it stopped and turned to look around. For an instant it stared at him, raising and then lowering its head again as a warning to Graham. He stopped walking for a moment and slowly crouched down, hoping that this gesture might calm the creature, which was standing only a few metres away. The rhino lowered its head to the ground and snorted, and as its nose touched the dry soil and the air escaped out of its nostrils, a small plume of dust rose up.

The rhino turned its huge bulk to face him, and as it did so, it lunged forward. At this point, Graham was still in a crouched position and, as he tried to recoil back, he lost his balance and fell backwards onto the hard ground. The dirt and stones dug into his bare back as he fell, but when he looked up, he could see to his relief that the rhino had moved away. The huge creature was heading for the water again, but he stayed on the ground, not daring to move until the rhino began to drink.

He watched the huge creature walk further into the waterhole. With each step the ground beneath its feet sank down under its weight and into the mud below.

As the rhino began to drink the murky water, Graham very carefully began to get up from where he'd fallen, turning on to his side and then using his hands to help him rise, trying not to make too many sudden movements for fear of alerting the rhino or the lions.

Finally, he got to his feet and began to walk slowly away from the waterhole and the creatures that surrounded it, not really knowing where to go or what to do next. He could feel his stomach churning, which was likely to be from drinking the brown, fowl-tasting liquid, and he was surprised that he'd not thrown it all up.

He stopped for a moment to scan the surrounding savannah. He knew that he needed to stay fairly close to the water, but he also felt he needed to be able to hide away from the animals within some bushes and trees. Unfortunately, where he stood there was little immediate cover on this side of the waterhole, whilst on the other side and behind the lions there were plenty of trees between them and the river beyond. He stood still, looked around and surveyed the land again, looking for the best direction to head in. Over to his right were the closest trees, which he felt was his best option, rather than being in the open savannah.

His feet were hurting badly from all the walking he'd done already and from chasing after the elephants earlier. He had nothing to put around his cuts, so he had to bear the pain and move on. Heading towards the area of trees in the direction of the sun, he could now feel the full heat of it on his face and chest. He knew that later he would be in much pain from severe sunburn, but by getting to the cover of the trees, this would help his problem.

'If that rhino hadn't turned up, I could have rolled in the mud and covered my skin to protect it,' he thought with annoyance.

He then heard the sound of zebra again in the distance, with their distinctive call, like someone with a strange type of laugh, which only helped to remind him of exactly where he was.

Continuing to hobble along, he looked at the ground for things he might be able to eat, but there was only dry grass that was yet to benefit from the distant rainfall he'd seen earlier. There were also the seemingly hundreds of small stones that all dug into the soles of his very sore feet, which brought tears to his eyes.

He suddenly stopped, frozen in his tracks, as

he heard the unmistakable roar of a lion, the resonant, belching-type of sound that comes from deep inside the lungs of a male. It's a sound that can be heard from many kilometres away by other lions and, of course, other animals in the area.

The roaring was coming from the pride at the waterhole. One of the male lions was obviously making himself heard and letting every other lion in the area know that he was present and that he was boss. This sound sent shivers through his body and, as the voice of the zebra earlier had reminded him of where he was, the lion's roar only served to accentuate his predicament and how vulnerable he felt.

Feeling totally lost and alone, he continued to stumble across the African ground. He was constantly on alert and checking all around for danger. He didn't know where that danger was, but he knew full well there was yet more to come. The group of trees seemed to be so far away and his progress was very slow.

The sun seemed to be getting hotter by the minute and he could feel the skin on his body being burnt. The height of the orb indicated to him that it must be close to midday, which was the time of day to avoid it most. But he had no choice in the matter, so he battled on, walking towards what he hoped would be some kind of refuge for the rest of the day. As he walked, he could see that the zebra he'd heard a few minutes earlier were interspersed with a number of wildebeest. It would appear that they were all heading towards the

Nothing Left But Fear

waterhole that he'd left behind, which would be interesting with the pride of lions waiting there.

The herd of mixed animals seemed to make light work of the hard African plain, as they meandered down towards the life-giving water. He continued trudging towards the cover of the trees, whilst at the same time keeping an eye on the herd and for other animals that might be lurking nearby.

As Graham watched the herd approach the waterhole, he could see them get very agitated, which was of course because of the lions, but their urge to drink water outweighed their fear, as, like him, they had an overwhelming need to drink and the ever more overriding instinct to survive.

He realised even more now that his body was not in a fit state to be in the situation he was in. If he were to run from a predator, he didn't stand a chance — not that many other humans would, anyway.

Having no clothes to hide behind made him feel truly exposed and as vulnerable as he could ever imagine, although this vulnerability was not so much the worry of being seen by people - it ran much deeper than that - the nakedness exposed him to his core - it made him a part of nature on the one hand, whilst on the other highlighted how his body was no longer designed to be a part of it.

Looking back to see where the herd was, he could see that it had reached the waterhole. Huddled together, each animal was restless, due to the presence of the lions on the opposite bank. The herd moved as one and almost had a combined life of its own, as it gradually shifted and nudged ever closer to the water. Then, as he looked up to where the lions had been, he noticed they had moved; they were no longer lying on the mound overlooking the waterhole. He began to panic, as with his first scan of the area, he couldn't see any lions at all. But then he suddenly noticed a couple of them crawling through the grass in a way that made them look like commandos.

One of these lions was not too far from him; in fact, it was probably only 200 metres away. He then saw something move ahead of him in the taller grass. It was another of the lions. He was shocked at how they'd somehow got ahead of him. Without him even noticing, they had worked their way around the boomerang-shaped waterhole and on to this side where he, the zebra and wildebeest were.

'Where are the rest of the lions now?' he wondered. *'Are they after me or are they more interested in the herd behind me?'*

His heart rate jumped a notch in response to this newly discovered threat.

The adrenalin level in his blood rose still higher, as he realised what was happening around him. The lions were creating an ambush style attack and he was right in the middle of it. In different circumstances, this would have been exciting to watch, but given his present situation it was spine-tinglingly terrifying.

His heart was pounding, and then his bowels and bladder let go. He felt the warmness of his urine run down the inside of his legs again and he could smell that he had just opened his bowels, too. His whole body was getting him ready for fight or flight. He was dumping excess weight in preparation for running, yet he knew full well that he'd never be able to out-run these vicious cats.

CHAPTER TWENTY-ONE

The cave floor was at a slight incline, rising up as it went deeper into the rock face. David continued to slowly back up, as the male lion continued to sniff the air, trying to pick up his scent. It opened its mouth in a grimace, showing off huge canine teeth, as it appeared to be smelling the air with its mouth as well.

His heart was still pounding, and if it was possible, it was beating even faster now and almost increased in stages with each step the lions took closer to his position.

As David edged yet further back, the two big cats seemed to be slightly confused. He was not sure whether they were unsure about going further into the cave, or whether they were confused about what prey they had found. Either way, he hoped that they would decide against attacking him and move away, as he was certain that his heart was about to explode.

The lioness wasn't quite so far into the cave as

the male, and made a small, gruff sound, which made the male turn around.

With the male lion slightly distracted, he moved still further back into the darkness, as his heart continued to pound. He had never been so scared in all his life.

Fortunately for him, the sound made by the lioness seemed to be a signal to the male, which now turned and walked away from the cave and towards the lioness. Then they both disappeared from view.

With his heart still pounding, he knelt frozen to the spot, not knowing what to do next. Should he go even further into the cave? Or should he stay where he was and wait until he thought it would be safe enough to come out?

'But when will it ever be safe?' he thought, not even certain he was safe in the cave. *'What if the lions have set up camp just outside the entrance, and how can I find this out without going outside to see?'*

The nightmare that was unfolding before him seemed to be getting worse by the minute. His predicament was now totally overwhelming. In all his life so far, he'd never felt so outside of his comfort zone and never known fear on this scale. The taste he'd noticed before came back to him; it was a kind of metallic, bitter taste, and he noticed his mouth was extremely dry, making it difficult to swallow.

The sound of the dripping water suddenly brought his mind back into focus again and it seemed even closer than before. His eyes had adjusted a bit more to the dim light that barely reached where he crouched in the cave, but as he turned to face where the sound of dripping was coming from, it was too dark to see a thing.

'Perhaps if I could get to the water, I would at least be able to have a drink,' he reasoned, *'which might help with my parched mouth.'*

He sensed his situation was getting critical, and he knew that he needed to drink some water soon just to survive.

Realising that the lions seemed to have gone for now, he turned to face the darkness of the cave behind him. He contemplated going towards the entrance, but decided that the safest option at the moment was to continue crawling on his hands and knees towards the rhythmic dripping sound, which appeared now to be resonating around the cave.

He moved very slowly, not only because he couldn't see a thing, but also because the rock surface was hard on his knees. Also, as he moved, he was careful to put out his right hand in front of him to test the way.

Many scary thoughts were racing through his mind: *'What if I touch something?'* or worse still, *'What if something touches me?'*

Suddenly, his urge to get to the source of the water was not strong enough for him to push further into the cave. He paused where he was, scared to move forward and terrified to move back.

For what seemed like an eternity, he was frozen to the spot. He imagined all kinds of animals in the dark closing in on him and devouring his body with huge teeth. He forced back tears, feeling totally helpless and vulnerable.

In the end, he turned back to face the cave entrance once again. As he sat there looking towards what appeared to be a quite small aperture, he began to wonder again how he'd ended up here. He then thought about the two men and the strange interview he'd had back in Chelmsford, and one of the men was the same in both these memories.

He then remembered another detail: He had awakened in a cage in a darkened room. How his brain had failed to recall such a significant incident until now was a puzzle. But because of the bizarre nature of events, he was still uncertain that these weren't dreams that he'd had.

As he stood there facing the cave's entrance, David now recalled a part of this new memory where two other men came to his cage. He recalled one of them telling him to *'shut the fuck up'* when he'd simply asked for something eat. This is where his memory became fuzzy again, so he brought his thoughts back to where he was now, as it seemed more important to decide what he should do next.

The small source of light coming in through the cave entrance would, in normal circumstances, be welcoming in such a dark environment. But he knew what animals lurked out in that light-filled space, animals with teeth and animals that eat meat. So, instead, this sight was of no comfort whatsoever for him, other than providing a light source within his new-found prison.

He felt exhausted, even though he'd not really moved much since waking up from his drug-induced coma. His body was on a constant level of high alert, something that it was not used to, but certainly something that no human was used to in this modern age. However, he knew what he was experiencing right now was what all wild animals experience every day of their lives.

'People constantly talk about stress and being stressed, but in the modern world the stress that people experience bears no resemblance to this,' he thought. *'The stress of meeting that deadline or the stress of catching a train on time are really nothing compared to where I am now.'*

But David knew that staying where he sat was not an option. He had to do something. In the end, he decided to make for the single light source where he'd been before. At least there was a chance of finding help, despite the obvious dangers he knew existed. If he stayed in this cave, the only people who would find him were the people who had put him here in the first place, and that might be never.

Keeping close to the floor to prevent himself from hitting the roof of the cave again, he crawled away from the dripping sound. However, the thought of those lions sent another shiver down the length of his spine. He recalled the male lion's intimidating stare, an image that began to evoke in him the same primal feelings as before. Despite this, he continued his slow crawl towards the entrance, watching intently for any movement outside, whilst at the same time thinking about how he might find something to eat. It was a strange feeling for David — despite the huge levels of fear and stress he felt, he was beginning to feel hungry. He had no idea how he would manage to find food. He had no training in survival, and he had no idea about what was edible or not out there.

With the likelihood of lions still roaming around outside, he felt trapped. Tears welled up in his eyes again, only this time he was not able to hold them back. They flooded down his face and he sobbed uncontrollably as he began to fully comprehend just how serious his predicament was.

He thought of the safety of home and how he wished that he would suddenly wake up from this nightmare and be free of the hell hole in which he found himself.

Wiping the tears from his face at last, and being careful not to hit his head, he decided to get up and walk towards the light again. Very slowly, he approached the cave's entrance. As he stepped cautiously outside and peered around, he couldn't see any of the lions. Nor could he see any of the wildebeest, which were obviously long gone.

The sun seemed even higher in the sky now and it was starting to get even hotter, as he felt its insidious rays hitting his face and body.

Looking around, he wondered which way to head and where he might find some help.

'There must be other people around; there must be a park keeper or someone, surely,' he thought, trying to take a more positive stance.

All he could see ahead of him was an expanse of scrubland and the trees beyond. Maybe if he could get to the trees and take cover there, as he walked for help, he would be a bit more protected.

But as he surveyed the ground ahead, David heard something behind him. As he spun around he caught something in the corner of his eye, moving on the hill above the cave. His heart began pounding yet again, although he knew it hadn't yet properly recovered from the earlier lion episode.

He hadn't realised how fast his heart could beat until the episode with the lions, and now, finding himself in the proximity of something else, made it all come back once more.

CHAPTER TWENTY-TWO

On Konner's arrival at Lechwe Lodge, Bram parked the Land Rover near to what looked like the main building and said, 'We're here! Come on into the lodge where we'll sort you out with a drink.'

Jowidah got out and quickly came around to meet Konner, as he was getting out, too, and said, 'Follow me, sir. What can I get you after such a long journey?'

'Give me cold beer if you have one, Jowidah.'

'Yes, we do, we have Castle Beer, which is brewed in South Africa. There's also Mosi beer, which is brewed in Zambia, and a beer called Dr. Livingstone's Lager, or you can have a Budweiser.'

'What's the Dr. Livingstone's Lager like, as that sounds interesting?'

'That's brewed in Lusaka with fruit from the baobab tree. It's good; I recommend you try it, and they've been kept nice and cold.'

'OK, give me one of those.'

'Dinner will be served at 6 p.m., sir, so would you like a small snack with your beer?'

'Yes, I'm really hungry. I don't get on well with airplane food.'

'Coming up, sir.'

Jowidah disappeared into the building and left Konner standing by the Land Rover, as Bram attended to the luggage. 'I'll take these to your room, if you would like to follow me,' Bram said.

Konner followed the largely built man as he picked up his luggage like they were toy bags and walked up the two steps onto the veranda and through the open front door. The floors were all made of wood and had been varnished in a dark, redwood colour, and the walls were painted white with numerous paintings dotted about which looked like local scenes.

About halfway down the entrance hall was the skin of a zebra splayed out, which still had its tail attached to it, and on the way to his bedroom, Konner glanced into what looked like the lounge, where he could see on the wall the head of a huge, maned lion.

'Wow, that's amazing. I'm hoping to get one of those on my stay,' Konner commented to Bram.

'We should be able to, sir; it just depends on where the male lions are when we go out tomorrow,' Bram replied. 'We may have to drive quite far, though, and it's an early start.'

'That's OK with me. I just want to get a trophy.'

'What shooting have you done to date?' Bram asked.

'I've done plenty of bear shooting and shot many deer so far, but this is something I've been wanting to do for a long time.'

'What type of bears can you shoot in the US?'

'In Alaska, with the right permit, you can still shoot grizzly bears, which is what I've done. I got one that was nearly 1,500 pounds.' Konner paused for effect. 'He was one hell of a bear.'

'Yes, that's one large animal. You know, male lions are only between 400 to 500 pounds, so nothing on that scale, so I hope you're not going to be disappointed.'

'I want to get the biggest I can, though. Is that possible? I know they can grow to around 550 pounds.'

'Well, on our territory there are none that big, which is where we can shoot uninhibited. There's a pride of lions with two males. These are probably only around 400 pounds each, maybe a little bit more.'

'For me, I always like to get the biggest, and when I booked and spoke with Dravin he thought it would be possible,' Konner fished.

'Well, I know we've seen a group of male lions roaming the plains over on our neighbouring territory. They sometimes stray onto our land. Animals don't recognise our man-imposed borders, and wander where they like,' Bram said. 'They are all pretty large males, and one of them could well be around 500 pounds.'

'Great! Then that's where we should go.'

'I'll need to check with Dravin, as we're not supposed to shoot on that land, and it's owned by an English guy. It may be that he's spoken to him.'

'Isn't it so vast out here that they'll not know what we are doing?' Konner probed.

'Yes, it is, but we have to be careful or we'll end up getting shot ourselves for poaching.'

'That wouldn't happen, would it?' Konner said with concern in his voice.

'Yes, it could. Certain landowners, and in particular the ones that get regular tourists looking to go on safari, don't like hunters. But the English guy, whose name is Druker, isn't set up for tourists, so I don't really know his views,' Bram said.

'However, I do know that a couple of the guys that work for him are not in favour of animal shooting, as we came up against them before when we were just on their borders shooting elephant.'

'But shooting a fellow human — surely that wouldn't happen?'

'You're in Africa now, sir. We are out in the middle of nowhere, and it'd be pretty easy to shoot someone and no one would be any the wiser. Feed the carcase to the vultures and there'd be no evidence,' Bram said as they arrived at Konner's room.

'Here we are. You have an en-suite bathroom and your towels are on your bed; breakfast will be eaten on our way tomorrow, as we'll be leaving at

5 a.m.,' Bram said, placing Konner's bags on the floor next to the bed.

The room was bright and airy, with a large window open to the air, and as Konner looked around he could hear the chatter of some birds in a tree just outside.

'I'll leave you to it, and I'm sure by now that Jowidah has managed to rustle up a beer and a small snack for you.'

'I'll follow you back right now.'

'I'm not going back that way right now, sir; you'll have to find your own way for now,' Bram said abruptly, which shocked Konner, who was not expecting a reaction like that.

'But I'll make that call to Dravin for you, to see if we can go looking for those three large male lions tomorrow, whether they are on our territory or not.' Then he disappeared down the hallway.

Konner made his way along the corridor away from his room and back to where he'd come from. On the way he couldn't resist going into the lounge to take a closer look at the lion's head. As he walked into the room, the enormous head stared at him with feelingless, amber eyes. The mane was dark in colour. It looked like a very mature male, from his understanding of what male lions looked like.

'Sir, your beer,' Jowidah announced, which made Konner jump, as he was completely engrossed in his examination of the creature. 'Beautiful head, isn't it.'

'Er, yes, it is,' Konner said, as he was a bit

shocked at being found snooping around the house.

'That was shot by Dravin about three years ago. He was a magnificent creature and I think around 540 pounds.'

'I'm looking forward to tomorrow and shooting my first lion,' Konner replied, as he took a swig of the Dr. Livingstone Lager. 'That tastes good, and it's cold, too. Nothing worse than a warm beer.'

'Would you like a pretzel snack, sir?' Jowidah offered, as he held the bowl up to Konner.

'Yes, thank you. And call me Konner.'

'Dinner is in about 45 minutes, and it will be held outside on the veranda,' Jowidah said. 'You'll be dining on your own, as you are our only guest this week, and Dravin is away on business.'

With this Jowidah left the lounge and Konner was alone once more. He decided to walk back to the front of the building and out onto the veranda. He looked around the small holding and took in the warmth, as it had been cold when he left New York. He was careful to keep out of the sun, as he had sensitive skin, and although he had put on some sun cream, he preferred to keep out of the glare as much as possible.

There were some chairs to the left of the front door, set facing out into the open area in front of the lodge. So he decided sit in one of these to drink his beer and eat the pretzels.

As he surveyed the area around the building,

he saw that the ground was hard and dry. It looked like it hadn't rained in a while, although he'd been told it was the beginning of the rainy season.

As he sat there, he thought about the next morning. He could hardly wait for his adventure to begin.

CHAPTER TWENTY-THREE

There was something moving amongst the greenery in the rocky area above the cave. David squinted, trying to see what it was before deciding on whether or not to retreat to the protection of the cave.

'How big is this animal? Is it dangerous?' he thought.

And then he saw what had made the noise: It was a large baboon moving around in the small trees above the cave. In fact, as he looked closer, there were a few baboons in the branches looking down at him from the safety of the trees.

Not sure whether these creatures were dangerous or not, he backed away slowly, eyeing the cave entrance. Then he shrugged and decided his only option was to go looking for help.

As far as he saw it, the only place that help might exist was somewhere other than here, so he needed to make it across the plain, which stretched out behind him. He turned around again slowly, not wanting to alert the baboons any more than he had to, and looked out over the foreign landscape that seemed to go on for ever into the distance.

He began to work his way down the slightly rocky slope towards the flat land where the grass grew and where the wildebeest had been grazing before. However, as he walked, he was looking around and still on high alert, as it was only a short while ago that he had watched a pride of lions in action.

His heart was in his mouth as he edged his way down very slowly. The dry ground, which had loose gravel over the surface, made him slip and slide, as he gingerly descended. The gravel he found hard on his bare feet.

As he progressed slowly step by step, David kept treading on sharp stones, which made him recoil with pain. He found that even the tiniest of stones bore into the undersides of his feet and hurt.

Above him something caught his eye, which made him freeze to the spot, worried about whether or not it represented another form of danger. He quickly realised, though, that it was a large, eagle-like bird circling in the sky high above the tree tops.

The bird floated effortlessly on the ascending thermals that were generated by the heat rising from the sun-baked land below. The bird's enormous wing span was spread out and he could see the individual feathers at the wing extremities fanned out like huge hands. The wings were perfectly designed to catch every wave of thermal heat, allowing the creature to waste no energy as it glided above the savannah searching for its next meal.

As he observed this soaring creature, he decided that it didn't present any danger to him.

He soon began making his way across the open plain, feeling absolutely defenceless. For the first time in his life he was truly alone, and although he had lived on his own for quite some time now, this was different; it wasn't just loneliness, it was complete isolation. He was also feeling totally exposed, not only because he was naked, but also because he knew there were dangerous animals around.

He knew that predators could recognise vulnerability, and that they were always ready to take advantage of any opportunity that presented itself. He knew there were no rules in the wild; it was a place where only the strong survive.

By now he was walking a bit faster, even though his feet were hurting from the stones, and soon he had reached the trees. However, instead of feeling better for having done so, he felt just as insecure and vulnerable, as the trees could be hiding his next animal nightmare.

As he moved between the trees he found that the grass got thinner, but also there were more broken branches and yet more stones that made it harder on his feet. As he moved even further into the cover of the trees, he saw something move in amongst them. What he'd seen was grey in colour and appeared to be huge. His heart was already pounding, and it felt like it was about to jump out of his chest. He tried to swallow, but his parched mouth was now so dry, it was almost impossible to do so.

Keen to keep distance between himself and whatever this creature was, he trod carefully around a tree. But then he stepped on a twig, which made his presence known.

In response to hearing the sound of the breaking twig, the creature moved and turned to face David. As it moved out from its cover, David stood frozen, not wanting to move a muscle in the face of this new threat.

CHAPTER TWENTY-FOUR

Whilst Scott had been at the gym that morning, Druker had come to find him, as he suspected he would. He'd managed just half an hour of training before the interruption, but had to stop as soon as his boss arrived, as he knew that today was very important to him.

Scott was well aware of his own anger issues, which were something he had grown up with. This meant that he was always wary of it kicking in with any new boss. He had ended up in arguments before with previous bosses; this was why his last job had come to an end, when he had got into a fight and was sacked as a result.

He had spent a few years in the UK at a boarding school from the age of eleven, which is where he'd acquired the English part of his accent. But because he'd spent the beginning of his life in South Africa, his accent was tinted with a South African twang.

At school he was always getting into fights,

and, because he was always bigger than most, he usually won. As a result of him mostly winning, the teachers would come down harder on him, since his assailants would usually end up extremely bloody and there would not normally be a mark on him.

His anger issues followed him into his later life. He would find that in bars, especially if he'd had a drink or two, he would end up in fights on a regular basis. He would make sure that he could handle himself and would go to the gym religiously to work out, but he also attended boxing classes.

He had a boxing bag in Druker's gym, so he would keep up his boxing as far as he could. This was good for him to let out any steam and to help him keep his anger issues in check.

He had returned home last night with his boss in his jet, with their first two marks. Druker explained to Scott that the individuals they captured in England were to be referred to as marks. He insisted on this because he didn't want them to be seen as people. Druker would explain that when anyone referred to other animals on a game reserve, they were referred to as a collective, like lions or elephants, and not by individual names. Druker was adamant that these captives were not people anymore, but merely animals back in the wild, and they were there to see how long they could survive. He allowed only brief references to their names in order to identify the individual mark they were referring to.

His boss had decided to get two people on this last trip to the UK, which was to begin the project, and Scott was there to help with their capture. Before the trip, they had been briefed by the vet, who had given them all the necessary medication, anaesthetics, and syringes for the capture to go smoothly.

During the capture, Druker had explained that it was vital that they inject the people as soon as possible. This ensured they were neither able raise an alarm nor put up any serious resistance, but Druker was also keen that the person had little chance to think about what was going on.

Once they had sedated there first captive, who in this case was a man called Lane, they got him to their car. They then had to get the next person and sedate him, too. Their next plan was to get the pair of them to Cambridge Airport as soon as possible, and, as they were flying in a private jet and because the airport was very small, there were not the usual customs and immigration procedures to follow. This made things very easy for them to get their captives to the aircraft without much fuss. They'd both been very nervous, though, as they approached the airport, as this was the very first time they were taking two people out of the UK in this way.

In order to get Lane and Smith from the car to the aeroplane, they put both men into wheel chairs and thus were able to wheel them to the plane. It didn't matter that they were sedated, as there weren't the usual checks that happened on scheduled airlines. However, as they were approaching the plane, one of the refuelling men commented on the two sleeping men in wheel chairs. Druker simply passed them off with a quick comment about it being a long day.

Once they were on board, their two captives were placed into separate boxes that Druker had someone make especially for this purpose. The inside of the boxes were retrofitted like coffins, as they were lined with a similar material and were of similar size and shape in order to accommodate a person.

The vet had explained the dosage they needed to give to their captives and the intervals over which they should be injected. This was in order to keep them sedated throughout the flight and hopefully up to the point they were deposited in the wild. This way the captives would not remember anything about their journey. It was Druker's idea to completely confuse his captives, so when they awoke for the first time in the wild, they'd be completely lost and wonder what had happened.

Scott was tasked with this job, to keep an eye on the intervals and to administer the injections, but between each injection, he would put the lid back on the boxes, which were locked down so that the captives could not be disturbed during the flight. Each box had its own supply of air, which was fed directly through the aeroplane's air-conditioning system, so that each captive was able to breathe.

The vet was going to be meeting them when they arrived back to base, in order to put a tracker unit into each of them and to check over the 'patients.'

As they had finally landed at just past 5:30 in the evening, it was already going dark. As they taxied to a stop, they could see the vet's plane already sitting on the side of the runway.

They had been met that evening by Joshua in one of the Land Rovers. Accompanied by the vet, he came roaring up and stopped in a cloud of dust right next to the plane.

CHAPTER TWENTY-FIVE

Graham could still feel the urine and faeces on his bare legs, as he stared at the huge lioness ahead of him. Then all of a sudden, as he could not take his eyes off the big cat except to glance across at the second lion to his right, he heard the sound of hooves. The herd of zebra and wildebeest behind him had erupted into a frenzy of fear and were stampeding to escape! Looking around at what was happening, he could see the herd heading his way — right into the waiting teeth and claws of the lions in front of him.

As the whole panicked herd reached where he stood, he froze to the spot with his heart pounding. There were more wildebeest than zebra, and the animals dodged and ran around him on both sides. Luckily, he wasn't trampled. The sound was almost deafening and he could feel the thunder of the hooves beneath his feet. Not knowing which way to look or what to do next, he glanced towards where the lions were crouched in waiting and could see the lion ahead of him leap into action.

The herd also saw the huge lioness, as she leaped forward, but for one poor wildebeest it was too late; she was on the animal and too close for it to avoid the inevitable. The lion jumped with her front legs and claws outstretched onto the back of the wildebeest, as the muscles and sinews in her lean body showed through her skin and fur. Her leap ended with her reaching around with her mouth, which latched onto the animal's throat, as her whole body almost somersaulted over the wildebeest. She wrestled the animal to the ground not much more than 30-40 metres away from where he stood.

When the other lions joined her to finish the kill, the first lioness had already begun to sink her teeth into the neck of the wildebeest, crushing the windpipe beneath. The animal was letting out bleating sounds; it sounded like a young cow, as its legs flailed around.

The beast never stood a chance. Graham could only watch the poor creature kick and jerk almost in defiance at its inevitable doom. The last few flickers of life came from its hind legs, as they twitched a few final times and then stopped moving. The lion kept her grip on the animal's neck, as if to squeeze out every last drop of life from this magnificent creature, as the rest of the pride joined in and started to bite into the animal's skin. He knew the animal was already dead, but it appeared to him the other lions were beginning to eat the beast whilst it was still breathing.

As he stared at the scene, he saw that it stood between him and possible safety in the trees ahead. He hoped that the lions were now preoccupied with their kill, so this might give him the chance to get to the trees unnoticed. Not wanting to move right away, he was mesmerised as the lions ripped into the flesh of the now motionless wildebeest.

It then dawned on him that this was food that the lions were eating, and what he could quite easily eat, too, but he also recognised there was one huge problem: There were now six hungry lions tucking into this large lump of fresh meat.

There was no way he could even think of budging these animals away from their food, so instead he began walking towards the shelter of the trees. Since he now had to circle around the feast ahead of him, that increased the distance he had to walk. He really wanted to wash himself first, since he had faeces on his legs, but he didn't want to go back to the waterhole, as this was further away now than the trees. He was also not happy going over to the river, which ran to his left and at this point seemed to have a rather large drop to the water's edge, for fear of encountering other sinister creatures.

Graham hobbled on towards what he hoped was safety. But before he'd taken too many steps, he saw movement in the grass ahead of him and around the edge of the trees. Something was coming towards him. Then he saw what it was, and quickly realised there were several of these creatures emerging from behind the trees.

CHAPTER TWENTY-SIX

Druker sat at his desk surveying his computer screens. He lit up a cigarette, taking a slow drag as he studied the tracker map screen intently, then letting out the smoke in a long, drawn-out breath.

He noted that the marker that signified Lane had finally moved and was still moving.

As it progressed, Druker got agitated and stood up, whilst staring at the screen and seemingly not knowing quite what to do next. Lane had obviously left the cave and begun to move around, and he was heading in a northerly direction.

He started to pace the room, whilst maintaining his stare at the screen, with his face moving almost owl-like, as he moved around. He took another long drag on his cigarette and scowled. *'The fucker's moving and the tracker's working,'* he thought, surprised at how he was reacting to what was going on.

His experiment was actually in progress and this person, who he'd brought all the way from the

UK, was finding out the hard way what it was like to go back to nature. He was wondering what might be going through Lane's mind right now and he also wondered how long it would be before he encountered a dangerous animal, and what would happen when he did.

'I bet he doesn't last long; he can't. He's not a real wild animal,' he thought, almost challenging his notion that he might not last the day.

Finding it very difficult to relax, he left the room to find his colleague again. He walked out onto the veranda and shouted, 'Scott!' at the top of his voice.

'Scott!' he repeated again, more impatiently this time.

Within seconds, Scott came running across the other side of the yard from behind a small out building.

'What is it, Druk?' he asked.

'The little fucker is up and moving!' Druker exclaimed, as he turned to walk back into the wide doorway. Scott followed his boss back to the office.

'Which one?' Scott asked.

'Lane.'

Scott and Druker entered the office. They were both almost bursting with excitement. Druker pointed to the screen monitoring Lane and Smith and said in a challenging manner, 'Look, he's moving, so how long do you think he'll last, Scott?'

'Hey, Druk, as I've already said, I'm not going

to bet on this; we will just have to see how it goes,' Scott replied, 'but if those hungry lions have anything to do with it, then not very long.'

'We'll see,' Druker replied triumphantly. 'I bet the fucker is shitting himself right now and I'll bet you he's as confused as fuck.'

Then he added, 'He's decided to walk north and away from the cave and it's nice to see our trackers are working just fine. I'd love to see the look on Lane's face right now, as judging by the dot, he's now well away from the cave.'

Scott looked at Druker and realised how much this project meant to him and how it obviously satisfied some very deep-seated torment that Druker was holding onto.

Whilst they were talking, both men were still staring at the computer screen, fascinated by this moving dot. They both seemed mesmerised by the whole thing and neither of them looked away from it each time they spoke to one another.

'We must keep a close eye on his movements and make sure we monitor the park for any other human activity, especially if any safaris come our way,' Druker instructed.

'We don't want my project ruined before we even properly start by someone stumbling onto it by accident, now do we?'

'No, sir, we will keep monitoring the radios for any clues to rangers coming into our area,' Scott replied agreeably, as he knew full well that if Druker got mad about something he could go completely berserk.

'Who is monitoring the radios now?' Druker asked.

'Joshua is, sir; when you called me I left him in the radio room and he was on it,' Scott said.

When Druker had purchased the reserve, it had come with existing rights for the nearby reserves to use, in conjunction with their own acreage. This did add a bit of risk to his project, but with the site so large, the chances of someone stumbling upon his individual experiments were remote.

Of course, this was important for the free movement of animals across one site to the other. No one wanted the animals to be fenced in, as it provided for a better environment for the wildlife to be able to roam free.

He decided that where there were two marks out at once, he would restrict them to one area, whilst keeping them far enough apart so as not to find each other. Also, with their radio monitoring system, this gave them an advantage and a head start when anyone was coming onto their land. It might not always work, as the other rangers didn't always use the radio, but they had the risk covered as far as they could.

'He's gone quite far from the cave, actually, considering it's the heat of the day and he has bare feet,' Scott remarked.

'Yes, he has, and I bet his back is hot and burning from the sun,' Druker replied with the slightest of grins on his face.

'There were lions in the area when we dropped

him, as we saw the pride not far from the cave,' Scott explained. 'They may leave him alone, as it is very hot, but then again they may see him as an easy meal and be tempted to attack.'

'You didn't tell me that before. And you're still not willing to take a wager on this one?' Druker challenged him again.

'No, sorry boss, it's not my thing. Besides, you have already claimed he'll not last the day, so what would I bet here?' Scott remarked, smiling at his boss before noting, 'Hey, look, Druk, the other mark is now moving.'

'So he is. So he is,' said Druker. 'Smith didn't sleep for very long, then, after you left him.'

'No, I guess the drugs were close to wearing off when we dropped him off,' Scott confirmed.

The two men stood staring at the screen, watching intently as the two markers moved slowly along. It was several minutes before either spoke again, as they seemed to be transfixed by watching the moving dots.

'I wonder which one will last the longest,' Druker finally said to break the silence.

CHAPTER TWENTY-SEVEN

David now found himself face to face with a huge rhinoceros, and, despite the rhino's bad eyesight, because he was so close to the animal, it had also seen him.

He also saw that there was a smaller creature standing next to the rhino. He realised that this was a mother and her baby - now he appeared to present a threat to her offspring.

The beast with its massive bulk and curving horn started to grunt, then made a move towards him, as he tried to hide behind the nearest tree. However, very soon the two-ton rhinoceros was coming at him fast, and he found that he needed to run.

He dodged through the trees, running for his life, as he heard the huge beast not far behind. As he ran, he was now not aware of the hard ground digging into his feet. The adrenalin suddenly pumping freely through his veins numbed any pain his feet might feel.

He knew almost instinctively to dodge left and right while running to make it harder for the animal to catch him, as the creature's huge bulk made it more difficult for it to change direction in the way that he could.

Soon the grunting he could hear was not far behind him as the enraged animal hurtled through the grass.

With each stride he made and as each of his feet hit the surface, he could feel the ground vibrating with the immense weight of the creature that thundered along behind him.

And then he felt it — a huge blow to his back as the rhino made contact, sending agonising pain down his spine despite the high levels of adrenalin coursing through his body. The huge animal's horn had hit him square in the back. Flung like a rag doll, he instantly found his face in the dirt.

It was as if he'd been hit by a freight train, with his own momentum combined with the rhino's blow sending him sliding along the rough ground. He knew this meant that his skin was being torn away, leaving deep gouges on his face and chest. As he came to a stop, more searing pain shot all the way up his back and into his neck and head.

Knowing that the psychotic animal was not going to leave it at one hit, all David could do now was to instinctively pull himself into a tight ball.

He curled up, waiting for the next blow for what must have been just seconds, but which seemed like an eternity. Then he began to scream, hoping in some way that this might scare the ferocious beast away.

CHAPTER TWENTY-EIGHT

Hyenas! Graham recognised instantly that these were the creatures emerging from the trees and heading towards the lions and their kill. He knew all too well that hyenas were opportunists and would scavenge when they could, taking every opportunity to steal the hard-earned meals of others, seemingly most of the time those of lions.

He was quick to realise that although the hyenas were probably focused on the bloody carcase of the wildebeest, that the lions were still chomping on, he was still very much out in the open and vulnerable to an attack by them too. He knew he would be such easy prey for them.

The hyenas continued to emerge from the cover of the trees and he could see the lions now getting visibly agitated. One of the lions broke away, making an aggressive surge towards the approaching pack of hyenas, letting out a loud roar.

The hyena nearest to the lion backed off rapidly, making sure not to get caught by it, but at the same time baring its teeth in a minacious grin. A second lion then turned and snarled at the pack of hyenas, which were now circling the pride and their wildebeest meal.

Graham stopped where he was to survey his options, but all the time knowing that he was out in the open and completely defenceless. The hyenas blocked the most direct route to the safety of the trees and the lions were ever more agitated and restless with the closing net of harassing beasts.

The hyenas continued to make their unmistakable cackling and snarling sounds at the lions. There seemed to be more and more of them arriving from the cover of the trees and grass and Graham counted probably 30 or 40 in total. The lions were snarling back at the hyenas and gesturing to leave their kill alone, but the hyenas were intimidating and they outnumbered the lions by around five to one.

The lions were not going to give up without a fight, though, and ran at the aggressive leaders of the clan. The commotion was very loud now, as each lion tried to grab a bit of flesh from the dead wildebeest in between snarling and biting at the hyenas. Although the hyenas outnumbered the lions, they had to be careful, as lions individually are larger and stronger and could quite easily kill a single hyena, but there were so many of them that the lions were fighting a losing battle.

He was not sure what to do. The two sets of predators were so intent on each other and on the dead wildebeest, that they ignored him, but for how long? He began to work his way to the cover of the trees, at the same time giving an even wider birth to where all the action was taking place in front of him…his heart was pounding!

The trees seemed like such a long, long way away, and yet in reality were only probably about 100 meters from where he was. Would it be better to run? But this might attract more attention than his slow walk; besides, his feet hurt so much, running was not really an option.

The fight between the hyenas and lions raged on, with the hyenas getting bolder and louder, as the clan closed in on the kill. The male lion made it his role to fight the hyenas off, but as there were so many and coming from all directions, he was never going to win. The fighting got more and more intense and the stress levels got higher by the second.

The hyenas would take it in turns running at the lions to take a nip at their legs when they were not looking and then the lions would turn and fight back. Each of the lions would turn and lurch at the hyenas whilst bearing their teeth, but each time the hyena being targeted would be too fast and get away, only for another one to come at each of the lions from a different direction.

Neither the lions nor the hyenas could afford to get injured from this fight, so the battle of cat and mouse continued. The lions were reluctant to give up their prey, whilst the hyenas were hungry and equally as persistent to take it over. The persistence of the hyenas eventually paid off, as the outnumbered lions were forced to run away from their food. The hyenas jumped in and were soon ripping apart what remained of the carcass.

The cackling and arguing continued, but now this was between the hyenas, as each wanted to get a piece of the meat and carcase. Graham watched mesmerised by what he was witnessing, as he saw a whole leg being ripped away from the wildebeest's body. As the hyena that had won this prize ran off with the leg dangling from its mouth, its hope of eating the leg in peace was dashed, as it was chased by a few of the others in the clan, each as desperate and hungry to eat.

Although he continued to walk in the direction of the trees and couldn't tear his eyes away from the feeding frenzy, Graham suddenly realised that the dispossessed lions were now heading in his direction.

He froze to the spot as the pride of lions headed towards him. If only he had made more ground whilst the animals were fighting, he'd be nearer to the trees and close to relative safety. Seeing the eyes of the lions ahead of him and the size of the huge male lion, his heart was in his mouth. He realised very quickly that the lions had spotted him and that he was in their hunting sights, as two of the lionesses lowered onto their haunches and were now in attack mode.

As they continued to advance, he instinctively

turned to run.

He was no athlete, and with his injured bare feet on the hard ground, he made slow progress. He knew that the lions were probably hot on his tail. He couldn't see any lions as he glanced back, but he was sure they continued the chase and it wouldn't be long before he was being pulled down and suffering the same fate as the wildebeest.

Within seconds one of the lions would have its huge mouth and teeth around his neck, crushing every last ounce of life out of him. He imagined the other lions joining in to tear at his flesh as the life in his body drained away. He could only imagine the pain that would sear through him until he welcomed the solace of death, when all his agonies would disappear.

As he ran, the seconds seemed like minutes and time seemed to slow to a snail's pace, as if everything were in slow motion. He could sense everything around him in absolute detail, as his sight seemed to be enhanced. The lions must be close now, as the seconds of his running went by, and he was surprised at how long it had seemed, as he glanced back again and spotted one of the lionesses almost on him.

Even though he knew these were to be the last few seconds of his life, Graham seemed to be thinking extremely clearly and braced himself for the inevitable.

CHAPTER TWENTY-NINE

Druker was sipping his usual red wine when he began to watch the tracker screen a bit more intently. It appeared from the tracking dot that Lane was moving faster than he had been previously.

'He's running. I wonder what from?' Druker thought, taking another slurp.

He got up and began to pace around the room impatiently, as he saw the dot representing Lane had now suddenly come to a stop. Druker was wishing that he had cameras mounted out in the field so he could witness what was happening. He had considered investing in cameras before he began his project, but this would have been impractical, what with the size of area he owned and needed to cover.

He was staring at the screen, almost willing the dot to move, which would indicate that it wasn't all over. Although in reality he didn't care too much if his marks died, he wanted them to last a while too, so that he could enjoy his little experiment with people he considered to be lowlife types.

'It was a good job I have booked my next trip to the UK, as I have a feeling it might already be all over for one of my first marks,' he thought.

He continued to pace around his office, not quite knowing what to do next, which was unusual for him, as he'd always been sure of himself and nothing ever really flustered him. This clearly did.

'Perhaps I'll go and get Scott again and then get him and Joshua to go out and take a look,' he thought.

'No, I must be patient. This is the first one, and I don't want to mess it up by going out there too soon. He could well be having a rest.'

As he looked at the screen, the dot representing Lane was still stationary, but the one representing Smith was still moving slowly in the same direction as before. Despite the excitement of what was happening, he put his glass down and left his office to go to the kitchen, as he was beginning to feel hungry.

He had a lady that did all his cooking for him, as he never really enjoyed cooking himself. He'd had a late breakfast this morning and had told Mulubwa he would have his lunch a bit later than usual, but now he was already feeling hungry, so he went to find her, to see if she could get the meal done sooner.

'Perhaps it was all the excitement,' he thought as he walked towards the kitchen.

'Mulubwa,' he called, as he entered the room.

'Yes, dear, what can I do for you?' she replied in her usual calm and polite manner.

Mulubwa was a large lady and had spent most of her life in Kakumbi. She had been the cook for the previous owners, and when he took the place over, he was keen to keep her on. She lived on site in one of the small houses, so really it was a good life for her, as she got paid for her work and had no accommodation costs. Thomas, her husband, lived on site, too, working as the gardener, but he also doubled up as a handyman, so any small jobs that needed attending to he did.

He was also keen for them to keep quiet about what was going on, as they were sure to find out, so he upped their salaries, which they were more than happy with. Neither of them asked any questions and he said nothing to them, but they soon understood why their wages had more than doubled when their new boss took over, once the marks arrived. However, he explained to the men in charge of the experiment they must keep things away from Mulubwa and her husband as much as possible so they didn't really get to know what was going on.

Mulubwa always dressed in very bright-coloured clothes and today was no exception. The dress she was wearing was predominantly a very lively yellow, with black streaks running across the width of it. She would also always wear a Kente style hat, which again had brilliant colours, which usually matched her dresses.

Druker loved her cooking, and especially liked it when she made authentic African-style dishes.

Mulubwa smiled at him as he came into the kitchen, and stopped what she was doing.

'I'm feeling a bit hungry, despite my late breakfast, so any chance of getting my lunch sometime soon, please?' he asked.

'Of course, my dear, I've done all the prep work anyway, so how does 20 minutes sound to you?' she replied.

'Perfect. I'll eat it on the veranda, please.'

'No problem. I will have the table set for you in a short while, dear.'

With that answer he left the kitchen and went back to his office, whilst he waited for her to finish his lunch for him.

He immediately went to the tracking screen to see if Lane had moved, but it appeared he hadn't changed position at all; the dot seemed to be in the same place. He went to his computer to check when the last movement was and confirmed Lane hadn't moved now for about half-an-hour. However, it did show that he had moved a couple of metres prior to his current stationary location.

'Perhaps he is crawling along the ground injured,' he thought, trying to explain the small progress his computer was showing.

CHAPTER THIRTY

David was still curled up for what was just a few seconds when the rhino struck again. It was using its elongated horn to toss him up into the air.

With each blow, his body was being mangled more and more. The massive impacts were crushing his internal organs, which bore little protection from his skin and his small layer of sagging muscle.

As the rhinoceros proceeded to gore at him, his screams got louder and louder. He was being pushed around like a toy, as the animal snorted and grunted and the ground around him erupted into a huge cloud of dust.

Then the rhinoceros suddenly stopped its punishing onslaught and retreated from the scene with its head held high, letting out a few last grunts as it departed. David lay motionless. He was in shock and almost unconscious at this point. He was aware the animal wasn't there now, but he hadn't seen it disappear into the trees to find its calf.

As he came around, he realised that he must have passed out or had been knocked out from the beating he'd taken from the protective mother. He was unable to move, although he slowly opened his eyes. The adrenalin in his blood was now at much reduced levels, which meant that he could feel intense pain all over his body. But as his senses started to awaken again, he began to smell blood and quickly realised that the blood had to be his own.

He tried to move and un-curl his shattered body, and as he did he looked down and realised that he'd got a huge gash across his stomach. The slash was deep and went right through to his abdominal cavity, and as he tried to sit up he could see that his intestines showed through the rip.

It was now that he realised the seriousness of his situation and that if he were to survive he would need help very soon. As David sat there and watched blood ooze from his near mortal injury, he began to feel sick, but he also struggled to keep his eyes open. He was now going in and out of consciousness, and when he was awake, images of his family were all he could think about — his parents that he'd not seen for quite some time were at the forefront of his mind.

'They will never know what happened to me,' he thought, as tears rolled down his face.

He then began to wonder what he had done to deserve this and whether his behaviour at home was connected in some way. Lying there in the dust feeling sorry for himself, he began to reflect on his life. He knew now that it had been completely wasted. Realising that it was too late to do anything about it, tears flowed more freely from his already blood-shot eyes. Muttering to himself, he found himself asking for someone to come and help him, but he knew that this was never likely to happen.

As David lay there, he could feel the sun beating down on his exposed body and that his mouth had become parched even more. He began to resign himself to the idea of dying and never seeing his family or England ever again, but then he was suddenly aware of the sound of laughter, or what sounded like laughter, nearby. It was a sound that was familiar to him, but he was not quite sure why.

'Maybe someone has come to help — but why would they be laughing at me?' he thought. *'Perhaps they are laughing at my nakedness.'*

Only he couldn't really care about that right now.

CHAPTER THIRTY-ONE

Scott was having a break for a while and sat out in the sun on a small, wooden chair that was positioned just outside his room. He idly watched a pair of Vervet Monkeys that were playing in the trees next to the main house. These monkeys seemed to be resident to the area, as they would often be in this tree. On many occasions, Mulubwa would bring food out for them, which of course encouraged them to stay around.

He was reflecting on his job, which had only been explained to him after he'd accepted the role. He knew full well that each of Druker's employees would have been told the same thing as he was.

Once he'd begun his new role, his boss explained to him that he was keen to look after the marks on their way out to Africa, as he wanted to make sure they were fit enough for the ordeal they were about to embark upon. After that, they were to be treated like animals.

Druker had also explained on a few occasions that if during their work they came across poachers, that they would not be tolerated and were to be shot on sight. Scott wasn't quite sure whether Druker was only concerned about poachers killing animals because of them playing a key part in his experiment, or whether he did in fact care about these creatures, like he did.

Each of them carried a small hand gun on their person at all times, together with keeping rifles in their Land Rovers, just in case they came across any poachers. Poachers were always heavily armed and were usually after rhinos or elephants for their horns and tusks, to export them to China.

He also began to reflect on how much he was being paid for his role. He recalled his interview and his second meeting with Druker, which was held in the office in his home, only at that time the room didn't have quite the number of computers and monitors as it did now.

The job that he had originally applied for, or what he thought he was applying for when he met Druker in the bar, was the job of an animal tracker. However, now that he had the job, this initial description wasn't too far from the truth — only the animals he was tracking were a bit different from what he'd expected.

Druker had asked Scott a number of questions, some that were relevant to the job he was looking to fill, and some that were quite strange questions at the time. These questions did seem odd back then, but now they made complete sense. Druker was testing people to see whether they would mind working on his weird project. Druker was also, and more importantly, trying to find out whether he could trust anyone he hired, as he was obviously concerned that they might turn him in to the authorities.

He recalled thinking, despite the fact that Druker had a more than generous stomach and was clearly not in very good physical shape, he was obviously not a man to be trifled with. There was something about his body language that he instantly knew there's no messing with this guy.

What he was surprised at was how he managed to select the right men; it was as though he had a sixth sense about the way they would react to his experiment. Either that, or all men in this part of Africa were so desperate for money they simply didn't care about what work they did.

Scott reflected for a moment more on what he was doing here and how he felt, knowing that he was responsible for putting people in direct danger. He also considered how he'd feel when one of the marks was killed out in the bush - the result of all this thinking was one, clear thought: *'Fuck it! Let it happen!'*

CHAPTER THIRTY-TWO

The laughing sound that David could hear was more of a cackle, and he realised instantly that it wasn't human at all; there wasn't anyone laughing at him.

It was a menacing sound, not a pleasant one. It sent his fear to primeval levels, as he sensed the company around him was a hostile one, a presence that told him he was being stalked.

Eyes closed, he was slumped in the dirt, not moving and barely conscious, when yet more pain hit him. He felt something grab at his leg and a new intense pain seared through his body. The adrenalin that was already flowing through his veins from the rhino attack had long since subsided to a level that didn't anaesthetise this new pain. And then something grabbed at his stomach and he could feel his intestine being drawn out, at which point he opened his eyes to come face to face with his worst nightmare.

He realised that he was being eaten alive. He

was staring into the eyes of a wild animal, with a menacing snarl and large, yellow teeth coated in saliva, which was almost dripping from the tips of its teeth. The laughing made sense now, as he recalled from his trip to Colchester Zoo where they had laughing hyenas.

He then felt and heard the crunch of his leg bone being crushed in the huge, powerful mouth of another hyena. He screamed in vain for help and tried to lash out at his aggressors with his now very weak arms, but it was futile; his fate had been sealed after the rhino attack. The hyenas had been drawn to the smell of his blood and were never animals to pass up an easy meal.

The last thought that went through David's mind, as the scavengers gorged themselves on his bloodied flesh, was, *'How did I end up in this place?'*

He saw the picture of Africa in the office of a tanned man with blue eyes…then he drifted away.

CHAPTER THIRTY-THREE

Druker was still staring at the tracking screen and the stationary dot that represented Lane, which had not now moved for over an hour. He got up to fill his mug with more coffee, as he'd finished his wine, and when he returned to the screen again, he realised that there was something different — the spot marking Lane on the map had completely disappeared, which left the one dot representing Smith.

Not quite realising what this meant and thinking there must be a problem with the system, he went to his computer to check the settings and to refresh the page, but this simply confirmed that Lane's tracking spot was gone.

'Looks like he's been got,' Druker thought to himself. *'Unless the device has got a fault or run out of power.'*

He then grabbed his radio, instead of going out to get Scott to call him in, and within a few seconds Scott was back in his office staring at the same screen, which lacked the dot representing Lane.

'What does that mean, Druk?' Scott asked.

'Well, it could mean the tracker unit has failed or that the battery has run out.'

'Is that possible?'

'I guess it is, but these units cost a lot each, so it's unlikely. But to make sure, will you and Joshua or Ken go and take a look right away?'

Before Scott left his office, Druker was able to go into the system and give him details of the location at which the unit had stopped transmitting. Druker gave him the hand-held tracking device to take with them, just in case Lane's tracker appeared whilst they were out looking for him.

He left Druker's office right away to find one of his colleagues. Joshua was still manning the radios, listening in for local tour guides, whilst Ken was standing out in the yard cleaning his guns. Scott shouted to Ken to join him, and started to explain to him what had happened as they walked to the nearest Land Rover.

'We need to go over to Area Two and see what has happened to one of the marks. Get in with me and let's get going,' Scott said, as he jumped into the driver's seat of the Land Rover.

CHAPTER THIRTY-FOUR

As they set off in the direction of Area Two and the cave where Lane had been left earlier that day, Scott told Ken about what had happened in Druker's office.

He explained to Ken that they had an idea of where the mark was and the possibility that the tracking unit had failed, but said he was sure that something more sinister had happened to the guy.

'I suggest we go to the base of the cave where we dropped him off this morning and then track his movements from there,' Scott said.

'So, what do you think has happened to him then, Scott?' Ken asked.

'Well, my guess is that he's been attacked by the lion pride which is in that area.'

'What a way to go — although it would probably be quick, I guess,' Ken replied.

The journey to the area they had designated as Area Two would take them around 40 minutes to drive. The beginning of the drive was on tracks leading out from the homestead, but then these soon disappeared into rough bush, at which point they would have to go off-track and work their way across country, which is where the Land Rover came into its own.

Scott was still getting to know the area, whereas Ken had been there a bit longer and guided him when he was not sure of the way to go. Just as the track disappeared, they came face to face with a pair of giraffes, which were startled by the vehicle's speed, and they began to run.

Not wishing to scare these animals, Scott slowed the Land Rover down, and veered away from where they were heading and watched as the pair slowed to a walk. When Scott had got away from the giraffes, he changed his direction and sped up again, as he was aiming to get to where Lane was and back to base again before night set in.

The two men didn't speak much on the way there, as Ken wasn't one for conversation, and the drive was very noisy anyway, due to the rough ground they were traversing.

When they eventually arrived at the area near the cave, Scott said, 'Is it worth taking a quick look in there?'

'Not if that tracking device was working up to the point it disappeared. He's not likely to be here,' Ken replied.

Scott thought about it for a second.

'Yes, I think you're right, and we haven't got time to waste. But it might help to go up to the entrance to pick up his tracks,' Scott said.

They both got out of the vehicle, and as Scott began to walk up the small incline and up to the cave's entrance, Ken stayed with the Land Rover. Within a few seconds, Scott had found signs of Lane's movements.

'Ken, if you get in the Land Rover and drive alongside me, I'll track him from here.'

Scott had been taught how to track animals when he worked at a game reserve in South Africa's Kruger National Park. He was taught by a colleague there named Emmanuel, who had been tracking animals since he was a young lad. Emmanuel had been happy to show Scott the little signs that were left behind by animals as they moved through the bush. He'd also told him that it was just as easy to track humans, which is something he was tasked to do on many occasions in order to track down poachers, so he taught Scott this skill, too.

Scott had soon picked up the impressions that Lane had made with the balls of his feet in the softer areas of the ground around by the cave.

'I spotted some fresh lion spoor up there near the cave as well as Lane's footprints. There was a male and at least one female lion walking around outside the cave,' Scott explained to Ken.

'So, you could be right. Maybe it was those lions that got him,' Ken said.

'It certainly looks that way right now, but looking at the signs, Lane left the cave after the lions moved away. His footprints have gone over theirs in many places.'

Scott continued tracking away from the cave as Ken drove the Land Rover slowly next to him. The signs that Scott was looking for were very clear and fairly easy for him to see, so he was able to move quite quickly. It also helped that he knew from the details Druker had given him that Lane had walked in this general direction.

They approached the tree covering, which had taken them around 20 minutes to get to and now it was more difficult for Ken to stay near Scott, as the trees were, at points, quite close together. This didn't slow Scott down, though, as he continued to pick up the signs that Lane had left behind on his terrifying trek.

Scott then picked up on something new and began to get excited, as in addition to Lane's trail, there were rhinoceros spoor, too, that was also fresh. After he walked on for a few more metres, he picked up on the fact that a rhino had charged. This was apparent because the imprints were slightly deeper and wider apart than they had been when the creature was simply walking. The charging rhino spoor seemed to be following the spoor of Lane, which also showed that he, too, had been running. The evidence of action was beginning to tell Scott a story, so he picked up his pace, with Ken looking on and following as closely as he could.

Scott turned and shouted to Ken, 'We're getting closer; there are some rhino tracks here, too!'

The look Ken gave indicated that he couldn't hear what Scott had said, but the tracker pressed on in any case while his colleague followed in the Land Rover.

Scott saw that the chase had come to an abrupt end, and he could see indents in the ground that looked like Lane had been pushed to the ground. The rhino spoor was also very concentrated in the same area. Then Scott spotted something in the dirt near to where there seemed to have been a battle.

As he stood there looking at the blood-stained ground, Scott could also see the spoor of hyenas that had over-printed the rhino tracks. The hyena markings made sense, as they'd seen a few of them scurrying off into the bushes as they had arrived

As he stood there studying the evidence, his walky-talky sprang to life. It was Druker, speaking in code.

'You'd better get over to Mark Two, as callers have arrived and you need to go over and help,' Scott heard Druker say.

'Callers' was code for tourists and Scott knew immediately what Druker meant. They had to get over to Smith right away to prevent these tourists and their guide from spotting him.

Scott ran to the Land Rover whilst shouting to its driver. 'Hey, Ken, we need to get over to Smith. I've just had the boss on the radio saying that there are tourists in the area and we need to get Smith out of there right away.'

Scott jumped into the passenger seat and picked up the portable tracker unit as Ken put the vehicle into gear and headed in the direction Scott was pointing.

'He's about half-an-hour away, I'd estimate,' Scott shouted to Ken. They bounced about on their seats as the Land Rover sped over the rough terrain.

CHAPTER THIRTY-FIVE

Graham was running for his life. It was as if his legs had taken on a new strength. As he ran, he kept bracing himself for the inevitable, surprised at how long it was taking for the lions to reach him.

His lungs were at the bursting point now; he couldn't take in enough air to provide the amount of oxygen they needed to continue his flight, and his legs were now beginning to turn to jelly. However, desperate to avoid the lion's attack, he managed to keep up a decent pace.

Everything was happening in slow motion around him, whilst his vision became like a tunnel and shut out everything to his peripheries. The ground in front of him was clearer than it had been all day; it was as if it had been sharpened with a magnifying glass. The details on the trail were so clear that he managed to place each of his feet down without stumbling.

Despite his weakening legs, he succeeded in

dodging all the larger stones or branches that were in his way. His brain seemed to have mapped out this route and it was like he had managed to put it into slow-motion play, to help it to assimilate his escape.

Just as he was beginning to slow down, and just as his body was giving up, it happened. He felt the full force of the lion's claws and paws on his back, and fell to the ground with a hard thud.

But as he waited for the final blow to his neck, he heard the loud crack of what sounded like a gun. The sound was unmistakable to him, and as the lion fell back from him, he looked up from where he lay. He saw the lion running away, with the rest of the pride in quick pursuit. *'At last I've been saved,'* he thought.

He could now hear the sound of a vehicle coming from behind where he lay and as he turned his head, he saw a Land Rover pitch up right next to him. A big cloud of dust erupted from the tyres as it approached and stopped. The cloud of dust engulfed him where he lay on the ground, making him choke, at which point he began to get up.

Graham looked at the vehicle, which was an open-topped Land Rover with a roll bar. There were two men in the front. The driver was a grey-haired man with a chiselled face, tanned skin and dark shades. His passenger was a large character, young and probably in his late twenties. He had a singlet style t-shirt on to show off his very muscular and sculpted body. This guy clearly worked out a lot and, like the driver, also had tanned skin. But he had a pitted face, which looked like it was from teenage acne.

As he got to his feet, Graham was suddenly aware of his nakedness and realised he was very exposed. He covered his modesty, as he smiled to the driver.

'Thank you for saving my life. I really thought that was it for me,' he said to the two men.

The driver looked at Graham and then turned to his passenger, as they both got out of the Land Rover, and said, "You get him quickly, before those bloody tourists get here." The larger of the two men approached Graham, whose smile soon vanished, his expression changing to one of confusion.

'Who are you?' Graham asked the huge man, as he came up to him and grabbed him by the arm. The musclebound man didn't reply.

'What are you doing and why are you being like this with me?' Graham demanded, but the two men ignored his questions and began dragging him to the back of the Land Rover. Graham tried to resist, but he was already very weak from his time in the bush and exhausted from his adrenalin-rushed lion experience, plus this guy was very much stronger than him.

As he was forced to the back of the Land Rover, he noticed that in the back of the vehicle was an animal cage, which was fixed to the floor. The driver opened the gate of the cage and Graham soon realised what was about to happen.

'Stop! What are you doing to me? This is

insane! I'm not an animal!' Graham shouted at the two men.

Suddenly, the pain he felt in his back was excruciating, as the huge man had punched him in the kidneys, causing him to fall the ground.

'Get the fuck up, you ponce!' the man shouted, grabbing his arm once more and pushing him towards the back of the vehicle.

As he was getting to his feet, this man pushed him again, which made him stumble forward and hit his head on the edge of the Land Rover. The pain was immediate and immense, but the man, who had a South African accent, didn't let go and forced him to his feet. Despite the weight and size of Graham, the man moved him about almost like he was a puppet.

The other man now joined in the struggle, as they both pushed and shoved him towards the open gate of the cage. His head was forced through the opening, and then he felt both men grab his legs and lift him up and into the empty cage.

'He's got crap on him and now I've got it on my hands. You dirty little shit!' the larger of the two men barked.

The disappointing realisation was now coming over Graham that these men were a part of the reason he was here in the first place, and they were obviously linked to the blue-eyed man.

'Why are they now rescuing me? Why have they saved me from the lions?' he thought, but remembered that he'd heard one of them say, 'Get

him quickly, before those bloody tourists get here.'

'What's going on and where are they taking me?'

Graham heard the gate of the cage close behind him and, as he turned around, he saw them lock the bolt and the driver of the vehicle put a padlock on the lock to stop him from escaping. Then they threw a cover over the cage to conceal their cargo, which plunged him into semi-darkness.

'My god, I'm part of some crazy sort of kidnapping,' he thought. *'Where are they taking me now?'*

The Land Rover was shunted into gear and lurched backwards, jolting him against the bars of the cage. The vehicle then lurched in the other direction, as it was driven hard towards — where? He tried to steady himself inside his prison, but the ground was very bumpy and the driver didn't care about avoiding rough areas. Graham bounced and lurched from side to side, hitting the metal bars of the cage, adding pain to his cuts and bruises.

His head was also pounding from the blow he'd suffered when he hit the back of the Land Rover. His body had never suffered so much punishment in all its life.

He decided to shout for help, as he realised that his two 'rescuers' were clearly trying to hide him from someone, and he hoped that they might be around. Just as he started to shout 'Help!' over and over as loud as he could, so that his lungs could not shout any louder, he found himself flying forward and hitting the front of the cage with a hard bang.

The driver had slammed on the brakes so hard that he was thrown forward within his small prison, and he hit the cage bars with such force that it winded him. He heard one of the men get out of the vehicle, then the cover over the cage flew back. He squinted, trying to re-adjust to the bright sunlight.

Soon Graham could see the barrel of a gun pointing straight at his head, and the driver holding the gun. 'Shut the fuck up, you god-dammed slug!' he snarled. 'If I hear another sound from you, I'll shoot your fucking brains out and all over the back of this truck.'

Graham was stunned as he stared at the man and then down the barrel of the gun. He said not a word because he knew that this guy meant what he said. The cover was replaced over the cage, to conceal him from whoever was around outside, and with a hard jolt the vehicle started on its journey again. He continued to struggle to avoid hitting the sides of the cage as the vehicle lurched from side to side, hitting the lumps and bumps of the African plain. But this time he remained silent, not wanting to rile the man any more than he already had done.

The journey for Graham went on for what seemed like an eternity. He was hot and hurting badly, not just from his bare feet and the lion attack, but also from the continual battering of the cage and the throbbing in his head where he'd hit the side of the Land Rover. Just as he was beginning to wonder if the journey would ever end, all of a sudden the vehicle came to a quick stop. For a second time he was flung against the front of the cage, aggravating the pain to his bruised body.

He heard the two men get out of the vehicle and start speaking, but couldn't quite make out what they were saying, as they seemed to walk away from where he was. He sat still in his cramped prison, daring not to make a sound for fear of being shot.

'Perhaps it would be better to be dead, if this is all the life I have left to live,' Graham thought.

As he lay in the cage, neither daring to move nor make a sound, he heard voices again and footsteps approaching his darkened prison.

CHAPTER THIRTY-SIX

Konner's alarm went off and, as he looked at his phone, it showed it was 4:45 a.m. Bram had said they needed to be on the road by 5 a.m. He dared not snooze the alarm and got up right away, as he didn't want to be late. He was excited to get his first lion kill.

'Dinner was good last night,' Konner thought, and wondered what breakfast might include.

On getting up he went to the bathroom to have a quick shower before getting dressed. Afterwards, he put plenty of factor 50 sun cream on his face and arms, which were the only exposed parts of his body. He had decided to wear long trousers to avoid having any more flesh showing than he needed to.

Once he'd got dressed, he left his room to look for Bram and went down the corridor to the front of the building, which is where he'd been told to meet him in the morning.

As Konner reached the front door, he was

greeted by Jowidah with his customary smile followed by, 'Good morning, Konner.'

'Good morning, Jowidah. It's a good morning for shooting lions, I hope.'

'Let me go get you your breakfast. Bram is by the Land Rover, which is on the other side of the yard, and he's sorting out the rifles and ammunition for you,' Jowidah said. 'Wait here and I'll take you over to him.'

Jowidah disappeared into the house, as Konner stood on the veranda looking out into the dark morning. The sun had not yet come up and the air was a little bit cooler this morning.

Within a few minutes, Jowidah arrived with what looked like a cool box and a bag over his shoulder. 'Let's go, Konner. I'll take you to where Bram is,' he said.

The two men walked across the yard, which was lit by a few dim lights around its perimeter. As they rounded the corner, Konner saw the Land Rover and Bram, holding a rifle.

'Morning, sir. This is your rifle for today. It's a Winchester Magnum with a .458 calibre. This will even stop an elephant in its tracks, so long as you shoot it in the right place,' he said, but Konner had already recognised the rifle as being the one that had been in the holder in the Land Rover on the way from the airport.

'A great gun — one of the best,' Konner said. 'I have a .338 Winchester at home to take with me to shoot grizzlies. But I know it has a massive recoil.'

'Yes, it's a man's rifle, that's for sure,' Bram said, almost in a mocking tone.

'I can handle it,' Konner responded, wanting to make sure this man didn't get the better of him.

'Did you speak with Dravin about those lions?' Konner asked.

'Yes, I did, and he has given me the go-ahead to venture onto our neighbour's land, but we'll need to be careful, though.'

'Why careful?' Konner asked, slightly worried as he watched the way Jowidah looked at Bram.

'Because I don't think he's got permission; he simply said that he had told you he knew of these large lions, and had promised you a 500-pound kill,' Bram said without looking at Konner, as he was readying the Land Rover for their trip under the dim light of the building they were next to.

'And if that's what he's promised, I have to go along with it, so get in and let's get going.'

Konner walked around to the passenger seat of the Land Rover and climbed in, expecting Jowidah to get in the rear of the vehicle, but he didn't. This concerned Konner, as he thought he would be coming, too.

'Are you not joining us, Jowidah?' Konner asked.

'No, I don't go on hunting trips, sir, but Bram will look after you.'

Konner wasn't convinced with this answer, as he got the impression from his discussions on the plane that he did go on hunting trips. Maybe it's the risk of going onto the neighbouring property, he thought.

Konner was so set on getting the largest lion kill he could, that even though he was a bit concerned about the destination, his urge to shoot a 500-pound lion was stronger.

Soon they were on their way. Bram drove a bit like a madman, with the vehicle bouncing across the rough terrain. Not much conversation was had between the two men as they made their way across savannahs, through wooded areas and at times followed the line of the Luangwa River. Within about half-an-hour into their journey, the sun was rising up over the horizon to provide another sunny day.

CHAPTER THIRTY-SEVEN

As Druker was waiting for Scott and Ken to get back, he remained in his office until Mulubwa called him to say that his lunch was ready. Druker then went out to the veranda, where he found the table set and an array of dishes with varying home-made treats, all laid out nicely.

He got stuck into his lunch and thanked Mulubwa for another wonderful meal, and she gave back one of her lovely smiles and replied, 'You're welcome, dear.'

He had kept his walk-talky with him at the table after Joshua had rushed over and told him that there were some tourists in the area. Druker had radioed to Scott to evacuate Smith back to base right away, and he was keeping the radio with him in case Scott wanted to speak with him again. Just as he was eating some home-made Nshima, which he was dipping into a chicken stew that she'd made, his radio sprang to life.

'We're on our way back boss. Over,' he heard

Scott's voice say.

'Did you find what you were looking for? Over,' Druker replied, not wanting to give too much away over the radio, in case others were listening in to their channel.

'Yes, we did, Druk. I'll tell you about what we found when we get back, which should be in about half an hour or so. Over.'

'Did you manage to find mark two? Over.' Druker questioned.

'Yes, we did, no problem, and we'll update you on this, too, when we get back. Over.'

'Okay Scott. I'm on the veranda having lunch right now, but I'll probably be in my office when you return. Over and out.'

He continued eating, thinking about his coded conversation with Scott and wondering just what they'd found out about Lane. He was sure it wouldn't be good news about their first mark and hoped that the tracking unit had not failed, otherwise it would cause a problem for his project. He was also pleased that they had found Smith, but he was interested to see what state the mark would be in when they arrived.

He finished up his lunch and sat for a few moments on the veranda, contemplating Scott's return. Whilst he did, he was thinking about his next trip, where he would be getting two new marks for his experiment.

Whilst letting his lunch settle for a few moments, he watched a couple of Vervet Monkeys playing in the trees next to the veranda. There was also a mother sitting in the tree, gently picking out fleas from the fur of her baby and eating them.

After watching them for a while, he returned to his office and immediately went to the tracking screen. There was still just the one dot showing, which represented Smith, which was moving fast and in the direction of base. This clearly showed Druker that they had Smith and that the tracker unit was working well.

He then heard the distinctive sound of the arrival of a Land Rover, which he assumed was Scott and Ken with Smith and possibly the remains of Lane.

He decided to wait in his office for Scott to come to him and explain what had happened, and within a few moments he was there standing in the doorway.

'Come in, Scott,' Druker said. 'So, tell me, what did you find of Lane?'

'Well, we looked in the area you sent us to, but we couldn't find anything other than what was definitely a fresh kill by a tree, as there were some blood stains on the ground. Whether this was Lane's blood, I'm not 100 percent sure, but it's likely,' Scott said.

'There were some hyenas in the area, and knowing them, they leave nothing of a carcase, so they'd have eaten every part of him, if it was them that had attacked,' he continued.

'What's also good, we saw some fresh rhino spoor near to where we found the blood, so we have a rhino on our land right now,' Scott added, which was his park ranger side coming out, 'but the other great news is that the rhino was a mother, and she had a calf in tow, so the rhino we have are breeding.

'It looked like, before he'd been attacked by the hyenas, he'd been chased by the rhino, and judging by the disturbance on the ground, he had also been attacked by her and probably mortally injured. Knowing rhino and how protective they are of their young, I would guess that Lane stumbled into her and the mother charged instinctively, to protect her young calf,' Scott said.

'In addition to seeing some hyenas disappearing off, there were plenty of their spoor around the blood-stained ground, so I'd say that they found his body and simply ate him,' he added.

'Hmmm. From what you say, I would almost guarantee that the blood stain was Lane's. So he didn't even last a day,' Druker said, then asked, 'How old would you say this calf was?'

'I would say around two to three weeks, judging by the size of its spoor, but I'd love to go out on a separate trip and take a look, if that would be okay with you, Druk.' Scott said. 'We also need to keep an eye on her, because if poachers get her, this new calf will not survive.'

'No problem, Scott, I agree, as we are all trying to help the rhino gain a foothold in the area, after the poachers killed them off before,' Druker confirmed, which also established his allegiance to the animal's welfare, which pleased Scott.

After they'd discussed both the rhino and Lane's demise, he then updated Druker on what had happened to Smith. He told him about how they'd just saved him from certain death from a pride of lions. He explained that he was in the cage on the Land Rover and in a bit of a bad way, but still alive.

'Put him into one of the holding cages for now, and I guess the best thing is that we leave him there until we return from the UK, as we are leaving the day after tomorrow. I don't want him out in the wild whilst you and I are away,' Druker instructed.

'Okay, no problem. Do you want us to feed him, though?'

'Yes, but feed him on that dog food I bought. Continue to treat him like an animal.'

'Will do, Druk. We'll put him inside a cage and go from there.'

With that, Druker nodded and Scott left his office.

CHAPTER THIRTY-EIGHT

As the cover was removed from the top of the cage, the sun bore down on Graham once more, but because he'd been under there for a while, he had to squint to allow his eyes to adjust to the sunlight. Whilst they were adjusting, he could hear the clang of keys and the bolt of the cage door open. Then, just as he was able to focus, he could see the huge man again, only this time he was joined by a very large black African, who was similar in stature to the younger of the two.

'Be careful, Joshua, his legs are covered in shit,' the white guy advised his colleague.

The large man put his hand inside the cage, grabbed Graham's bruised arm and pulled him out, almost like a rag doll.

As he did so, Graham yelped, 'Why am I being treated like a wild animal?'

He looked up then and came face to face with the black guy, whose eyes were dark with whites that were bloodshot, and who stared back at him without saying a word. He grabbed Graham's other arm and they jerked him upright.

'What the fuck are you doing with me and why am I here?' Graham demanded, but the two men simply ignored this question, just as they had his first question, and pushed him in the direction of some buildings off to his left.

These were concrete-built with metal corrugated roofs, so they looked more like shacks than somewhere that might be comfortable places to stay.

Graham's feet were very sore, but the men didn't give him a chance to walk carefully on his blistered soles, as they seemed intent on getting him inside and out of sight for some reason. Graham winced at each forced step he made, and as they approached the door to the building, the white guy let go, whilst the black guy grabbed harder on his other arm, to make sure he wasn't going to escape.

'You're hurting me,' Graham protested, but still there were no comments from either man.

The door was made of wood and was bolted across the top and the bottom. The white guy leaned down to pull the second bolt from across the bottom of the door, which made a loud metallic clang, and then undid the top bolt, which made a similar sound.

'This is more like entering a prison,' Graham thought. 'Where are you taking me?' he asked, as the door opened with a whining sound, its huge, rusted hinges seeming to protest at being opened.

They clearly needed oiling. There was still no response from either of the two large men, which angered Graham even more.

The doorway opening was dark and, as the light was bright outside, he couldn't see what lay beyond. He knew that he'd soon find out, though, as the white man joined his colleague by grabbing his right arm again as they dragged him inside.

Once inside, his eyes quickly adjusted to the change in light and he could see that the room had cages down both sides. The cages appeared to be empty, with one that had the door already wide open, so he knew immediately what was about to happen and where he was heading, which was soon confirmed. He was shoved into the small cage with the open door.

Graham shouted, 'I'm not an animal! I don't deserve this treatment!'

His protest was ignored by his two kidnappers, as the cage door was slammed shut behind him then bolted and padlocked. Afterwards, the two captors left the building and closed the outside door with a loud bang. Graham heard the two bolts slam into place once more.

There was very little light in the room, as he tried to adjust his eyes to his new environment. The floor of the cage was hard to the touch and was made from wood, and in one of the corners, it had a layer of straw. The ceiling of the cage was too low for him to stand up, so he had to either sit or lie down. The cage was about two metres square, so he was very cramped.

What light there was in the building was provided through the holes between the top of the walls and the corrugated roof line. His eyes became fully adjusted and he could see that there was a water trough attached to the side of the cage. Being extremely thirsty, he decided to drink the water straight away; despite its tepidness, he found it was better than the waterhole water he'd drunk earlier that day.

After he'd had his fill, he tried to survey his prison a bit further and began to think about how he could escape. He reached through the gap between the bars to test the door bolt and padlock, which from the way it had been closed earlier he knew was probably futile to try. The padlock was locked firm and would not open, despite him trying to shift it, and there was no way the door bolt would move either, as the padlock was preventing this.

Almost in despair and defiance, he shook the door of the cage back and forth, by holding two of the bars, like a caged monkey. Unfortunately, this only confirmed his plight, as the door was not going to budge, no matter how much he rattled it.

He sat back on the floor of the cage, knowing that he wouldn't be able to escape. The cage was secure and, even if he were let out for any reason, these men had guns and were far stronger than he was, so he was not likely to stand a chance.

As he sat there all alone in the dim light of his new-found prison, with his back against the cage bars, he thought back to his life in the UK, and he wondered what his family would be doing now. He was resigned to the thought that they wouldn't realise he had gone missing, as he was very much a loner, living on his own and not really interacting with people at all.

'It might be a long time before anyone notices I'm even gone, if ever,' he thought, which made him feel even more alone, if that were possible. Tears welled up in his eyes. He knew he'd wasted his life and not made anything of himself. But now someone had taken it upon themselves to punish him, or so it felt, for reasons unknown to him.

As he shifted his back against the bars of the cage to try and get more comfortable, he felt something in his neck. It was as if when resting against it, there was something between him and the cage bars. When he felt the back of his neck, he found that there was definitely something sitting just under his skin. The object, which he could move, was the size of a small stone or perhaps a bit bigger than a marble, and around where the object sat, was what felt like a small cut, which he was surprised he hadn't noticed before.

He had been wondering how the two men had found him so easily in their Land Rover, despite the fact that he'd walked quite a distance from where he'd been placed.

'Perhaps this is the answer; perhaps this is some form of tracking device they've placed in me,' he thought, and shuddered, feeling he'd been even more violated than before.

'Forget the fact that they placed me in danger and out in the wild with no clothes on, but these people have carried out a surgical procedure on me, without my consent, and now they're tracking me like some kind of wild animal.'

But then his thoughts were interrupted by voices just outside the building. Although he couldn't actually make out what they were saying, to him it sounded like there were at least three people, although he could be mistaken. He felt tense and waited to hear the outer door bolts open, worried what might happen next and what they had planned for him now.

CHAPTER THIRTY-NINE

Carly awoke to cockerel crowing, which was the sound of her mobile phone alarm. She snoozed the alarm, as she needed to take time to awaken, since this was always a bit of a shock to her system. This was unusual for her. She never normally set her alarm, but today she had an interview.

Her immediate thought was to have her morning cigarette before anything else, but she also began to think about her interview and how she would behave. She always acted in a way to put the person off taking her on, and she planned to do the same thing today.

She always made sure she hadn't washed for a few days, so that her personal aroma was unpleasant for the interviewer. Sometimes she'd throw in certain comments about how she'd lost her previous job, as if surprised that this had happened. But she invariably made sure the interviewer was left with the thought that she didn't make a good employee, especially if she thought there was any way the interview was going well. Usually, she would get strange looks. She secretly loved the way people reacted to her behaviour.

Not able to wait any longer, she sat up in bed and leant over to grab her packet of cigarettes. On opening it, she could see there were just two left. She also knew that there were no other packets in the house. Poised on the edge of the bed, she placed one of the cigarettes in her mouth. To light it, she opened the lid on her petrol lighter, but before striking the flint, she drew in the potent smell of petrol fumes.

This allowed her to drift off for a moment to think again about her father, a man who had always been under weight and who had never looked well. Her last memory before he'd died was him coming over to see her on her thirty-fifth birthday, when he'd brought her some flowers and a large box of chocolates.

Her dad had died of a sudden heart attack, which happened around two months after her birthday. It had been a real shock to her, as she had always loved her dad, but he had been a heavy smoker and did like his whiskey, too, so it wasn't a real surprise in some respects. He had always been kind to her, and ever since her mother had died when Carly had only just turned 21, they spoke to each other on most days. She had always been surprised that her dad had stayed with her mum, as she'd suffered badly with Borderline

Personality Disorder, with her mood swings making her always difficult to live with.

She'd always found it hard to deal with her mum's unpredictable moods; it could be the slightest thing that changed her from a loving mother to a devil woman. Carly grew up hating herself, with the constant belittling and put-me-downs from her mother too much to take sometimes, and since her mother's death, her father had tried to make up for it, as he had known the effect it had had on her.

On many occasions she would wake up to her parents having a shouting match, which would usually be accompanied by objects flying around. If the argument began in the kitchen, many of the pots and crockery would get smashed on the floor. She always remembered how her mother would take great pleasure in saying to her father he had to clear the mess up, always blaming him for whatever it was the argument was about.

Mostly, the fights stemmed from her mother not trusting him, and she'd make wild accusations about him seeing other women. She had hated her mother, although deep down she felt guilty about her death and blamed herself for it, as she'd often wished it on her.

It had been a warm, sunny day when it happened and it had been an awful morning. It was a Sunday and she'd awoken with a start, hearing a crashing sound coming from below her bedroom. Then she had heard the shouting — mainly, she had heard her mother's voice rather than her father's, which had been normal. Her father, as usual, had been trying to appease her mother, which usually consisted of him simply saying that he loved her, whilst she had continued to shout at him.

Her mum had always threatened suicide and mostly the threats had always been idle ones, which were really just for effect, but that day had been different. As Carly had got up to go to the toilet that day, she had delayed, as much as possible, to avoid having to go downstairs. But then she had heard the front door slam, which was quickly followed by the slamming of the car door. This had been followed by the over exuberant revving of the car's engine, and then her mum had disappeared down the road.

It had been several hours later that day, when the police had turned up on the doorstep, and both Carly and her father had instantly known what they were there for. But they hadn't prepared themselves for the news they'd been brought. It turned out that she had driven off the A138 and into the river Chelmer, smashing through the barrier on the Chelmer Bridge. It had been known locally that the bridge was in need of work or replacement due to decay, having originally been built in 1932.

Her mother had drowned when the car was submerged in the river. She had been knocked unconscious from the impact on the bridge structure.

Not long after the police had arrived, her father

had been taken to the mortuary to identify her remains.

Carly remembered sitting there on her own, as her father had just left without really thinking about her at all, but had been thinking about her mother instead. She recalled the mixed emotions she'd had, between the relief in some ways that she'd never have to suffer the wrath of her mother ever again, but realising also that this was her mum and that she should feel at least a bit of sorrow.

With the thoughts of her mother still floating around in her head, and with remnants of guilt over not having shed one tear since she died, Carly struck the flint on her lighter several times until it lit and guided the flame to the end of her cigarette. Then she drew in a long drag and tried to push the thoughts of her mother from her mind.

CHAPTER FORTY

'How will this all end?' Graham questioned in his mind. *'I was nearly killed and eaten by lions, but saved by the same men who put me in danger in the first place.'*

The voices grew louder as footsteps approached the building, then he heard the two outside bolts on the main door scrape back. When the door opened, the bright light pouring into the dark space made him squint. He tried to make out the silhouetted figure who walked in, followed by another man.

As they entered, the first man said, 'We'd better give him some food. He must be hungry by now.'

Graham thought, *'Finally, I get to eat something, but what will it be?'*

As he was thinking about what food he might be given, the first man went over to several bins sitting near the door. The bins were blue and round and didn't look like they contained any food that he would normally like to eat.

The man reached inside one container and pulled out a bag, which was clearly dog food, as the outside of the bag had the picture of a dog on it. Graham watched as he filled a bowl with some of this dried dog food. As he walked towards Graham, he said, 'You're joking! I'm not a dog! I'm not an animal! Why are you treating me like this and why are you feeding me dog food?'

He stared at the approaching man, who scowled at Graham and said, 'It's all there is for you, so you'd better eat it, you leech! And if you know what's good for you, you'd better be quiet!'

'I can't eat dog food! You can't feed that to me!' Graham protested.

Just as these words left his lips, the man threw the bowl and its contents at Graham. The bowl and the dried food hit the bars of the cage, making a clinking sound, as the pieces of food scatted everywhere. The bowl fell to the floor and shattered into several pieces, with some of the shards scattering into his cage across the floor.

'There you go, you little shit! Look what you made me do, you ungrateful moron!' the man said.

'Now you can go hungry or pick up the food from the floor, and you'd better be careful you don't cut yourself on that broken bowl,' he said sarcastically as he stared at Graham through the cage bars.

Graham stared back in disgust. 'I don't believe you guys! What the hell is wrong with you, treating a fellow human being like this? I've done nothing wrong!' he protested again.

'Nothing wrong?' the man said, almost spitting out the words.

'You mean you've done nothing right. You sponge off your government and laze around doing nothing all day, expecting everyone else to pay for you,' he said.

'You're a leech on society, so you deserve to be part of the little experiment we have going here.'

'Experiment? What experiment?' Graham asked incredulously.

'Hey, Scott, stop! Don't tell him anymore,' his colleague shouted.

Ignoring what the second man had said, Graham asked again, 'What experiment? What are you doing with me and why?'

But now Scott fell silent, walked away and left the building, leaving the other man to bark, 'Look, you leech! We offered you food and you dare to even question that. Just remember, only a short while ago you were out there in the wild fending for yourself without any food or water.

'You've got water now, and you'd better eat the food on the floor or else you will starve. There's no one to help you and we don't care. There are others to replace you in this experiment and there are plenty of others who simply failed to survive before you.'

With this Graham froze and stared at the man, as a shiver ran up his spine. '*Others,*' he thought. *'There must be other innocent people like me that these men have kidnapped and who they are experimenting with.'*

He didn't know that what the man had said was an exaggeration of the truth, which he had done for effect, when in fact it had been just one other so far.

'How many have you experimented with?' he asked the man.

'Look, you idiot! We've already told you too much, so shut the fuck up and eat your dog food! You'd better make the most of the food you have, or you'll go hungry. There's nothing else available for the likes of you!'

Graham looked down at the pieces of dog food on the floor and around his cage, and then looked up to the man who was still looking down at him. Then the man turned and, without saying another word, left the building. For a brief instant light streamed in again from outside, before the door was closed once more behind him and locked. Graham shuddered as he heard the metal-on-metal sound of the two bolts sliding into place.

Plunged into semi-darkness once more, he sat back to think about what he'd heard. He now knew that he was a part of some weird experiment, and it seemed as though it was directed at benefit claimants.

'Maybe I'm putting two and two together and making five, but I'm now sure that this is not just an experiment, but a survival experiment to see if we can survive in the wild,' he thought.

'There seemed to be a clue in the way these

two men spoke to me and their making reference to my getting government benefits. But that's back in the UK. Why would they care about my claiming benefits in another country?

'But how did they get me out here, and how did they get me on a plane without my knowing?'

With those questions in mind, he thought back to what had happened in England.

He was aware of waking up in a coffin-like box and glimpsing the blue-eyed man who had confronted him in his flat.

'Perhaps after they'd sedated me, they put me in that box — or was it a coffin? — in order to smuggle me out of the country on the understanding that it contained a body,' he thought.

'But that's a long time to be sedated for, and I'm now sure the sharp pain I felt when I was in my flat was an injection of anaesthetic.'

His thoughts returned to the blue-eyed man. *'Why does he hates people like me so much,'* he posited.

'I know that I've made nothing of myself and I know I've been cheating the system, but how dare this man play god like this with me and others!'

With these thoughts, he turned to look down at the dog food scattered across the floor of his cage together with the broken bits of bowl. He also remembered the comment by the one called Scott, how he'd blamed him for smashing the bowl and for the food being thrown on the floor. After staring at the dry dog food for some time, he decided to try it. But first, he carefully picked out the pieces of shattered bowl and put these outside the cage.

'Surely, this stuff can't be that bad,' he thought.

As he picked up the first piece of dog food and put it into his mouth, he recalled drinking the dirty water at the waterhole, and thought, *'Eating this food can't be as bad as that, and I'm surprised I wasn't really ill from drinking that water.'*

He tasted the piece of dog food and found it really dry with a bit of a combined fishy and chicken taste. The food was crunchy, and after chewing it, he forced himself to swallow. He then picked up a few more pieces of the dog food and ate these, too, making the most of the food he had, not knowing when he might be fed again or sent back out into the wild. The feeling of humiliation was almost overwhelming to him at this point, and this made him think again about how he'd led his life up to now.

'If only these men would give me another chance. Perhaps I can ask to see the man with the blue eyes and ask for his forgiveness. Then maybe he'll let me go free,' he thought in a positive way, the first time he'd done so for as long as he could remember.

CHAPTER FORTY-ONE

Joshua liked it when Druker went away; it meant that he could go off exploring on his own. He liked to track lions and he was keen to watch how the prides developed. He also was aware that their neighbouring owner hunted lion.

He showed more concern than even Scott, who he knew was into animal conservation, but more interested in the rhino population in Zambia. However, Joshua knew that lions were under more pressure these days, with their numbers dwindling.

He knew that to the south of their property there were three male lions, which he was surprised hadn't yet gone in search of their own pride, although he put it down to the abundance of game that kept them sated.

Joshua went to ask Mulubwa what she could rustle him up for a packed lunch for when he was out in the reserve.

'Good morning, Mulubwa, how are you this morning?'

'I'm good, thank you, how are you?' she replied, with one of her usual smiles.

'What could you put together for me for a packed lunch today, my darling?' Joshua said to her, as he returned the smile.

'Well, my sweetie, give me half an hour and I'll put together something for you. I have some freshly made Nshima for you.'

'Great, thank you. I'll just be outside sorting out the Land Rover and my rifle.'

'Where you off to, Josh?'

'Off to the south of the reserve to see if I can find the three lions. I like to make the most of the time when Druker is away.'

'OK, my sweetie, it'll be ready in half an hour or so and I'll bring it out to you.'

'Thank you.'

And with that Joshua left the kitchen to go and check on the mark beforehand, and to speak with Ken to make sure he would look after things whilst he was away.

CHAPTER FORTY-TWO

Druker arrived at his offices in Chelmsford, where he met with his secretary and receptionist, Felicity. After a few moments of idle chat, she confirmed his first interview was with a woman named Carly Prow in around half an hour. Felicity handed him her CV and at the same time told him that there were a number of things she needed to catch up on, once he'd settled in.

When Druker was in the UK, he referred to himself as Blake Caldwell, which was his real name. Peter Druker was a made-up name and was used to cover up what he was doing. Felicity had always referred to him as Blake and was not aware of his other name, nor was she aware of his African experiment. She did, however, begin to question the candidates he'd been seeing recently, as their CVs were not exactly great. Her questions led her to explain that she was worried about working with people like this, but Druker explained this away by saying that he was interested to see if there was any hope for people who up to now had been wasting their lives.

'The person you are seeing today, Carly Prow, if you look at her CV, there are huge gaps in it. She has now been out of work for over two years,' Felicity said.

'Okay, I'll take a look,' he confirmed, as he took Prow's CV from her.

'Also, the Jobcentre called last week following up on some of your previous interviews; there was David Lane and Graham Smith. I told them that you were still considering them,' she said. 'Is that right?'

'Eh, yes, that's right; let's see how we get on today, shall we?' he replied.

'I really don't know how these people get away with it for so long and continue to receive their benefits,' Felicity said disapprovingly.

'Nor do I, and that's why I want to see if there's any way of changing their attitude,' he lied, as in reality he was trying to find people who were sponging off the system for his experiment, which would certainly 'change their attitude,' all right.

He had always hated this behaviour and he felt that the UK had become too much of a nanny state. His hate had really been fuelled when he was holidaying in Barbados, where he'd come across a couple who were boasting about how they were receiving benefits whilst at the same time dealing in drugs. The couple had got very drunk one evening and Druker had overheard the conversation they were having with a small group of people. He had been surprised at how open they were, not just about their benefit fraud, but also about how they openly bragged about their cocaine dealings. They were telling these people how easy it had been to fool the agencies into paying them their benefits, despite living in a large home filled with an expensive kitchen, furnishings, and other luxuries, which were largely funded from their drug money.

It was very apparent that they lived the high life. They also bragged about driving around in Mercedes cars and he had seen that they each wore Rolex watches and other costly jewellery, together with designer clothes. He was still with his wife at the time and they were both holidaying at Sandy Lane, which was probably one of the most expensive hotels on the island, and despite the fact that this couple were claiming benefits, they were staying there, too.

At the time, Druker had felt really angry at how this couple were taking advantage of the government, and especially the way they had talked about it in such a dismissive way, whilst they blamed the authorities for being so stupid, rather than looking at their own scruples. He had always paid his taxes, and plenty of them, so he, along with every other honest, hardworking person in the UK, were unsuspectingly helping to fund this couple's lavish lifestyle. He could also see that the other hotel guests, who had been listening to this bragging pair, were not too happy with what they were hearing, but the couple were so drunk, they were completely unaware of how people were reacting around them.

The group of people with them had been Americans, so although it was apparent that they were disapproving of what they were hearing, it would be unlikely they'd tell the UK authorities about the scams these two were pulling off. Druker considered dobbing them in when he got back, but it was a couple of years later that he read about them in a newspaper, having been caught and sentenced to prison, which at the time brought a smile to his face.

At that time, he hadn't really taken his thoughts too much further, except for wondering what could be done about it. He even thought of writing to the prime minister about the issue. He wanted to urge the government to change the system in order to prevent this type of fraud from happening, but he realised it would be a waste of paper and time. It was only once he'd broken up from his wife and he'd begun to think about moving to Africa, that he thought about it in more detail.

The idea behind his experiment had been hatched whilst he'd been watching a program about lions on The Discovery Channel. It was at this moment he worked out how he could teach these people a valuable lesson in life, but he had also wanted to see if they could survive in the wild. If they didn't, he decided that they were wasting their lives in any case, so it didn't matter.

His plans began to come together after he'd

purchased his game reserve in Zambia, at which point he'd turned his mind to how he would choose his victims. This turned out to be more straightforward than he originally thought it would be, after he'd done a Google search on benefit claimants. Whilst doing his research, he discovered that they were all required to apply for a certain number of jobs in order for them to retain their benefits. He decided that the ones he would be particularly interested in were the ones that had registered at Jobcentres, thinking that these were more likely to be playing the system.

In order for him to discover more, Druker decided to use his property company, Hatton Property Developments, as a cover to interview his candidates.

He would ask the Jobcentre to send him the CVs of the long-term unemployed, explaining to them that his aim was to see if he could rehabilitate them and get them back to work. He would then set up an interview for likely candidates. He was convinced that he'd be able to distinguish between the ones who were genuinely unemployed and claiming benefits, over someone who was playing the system, by asking the right questions and by judging their body language. The CV of this Carly Prow seemed to fit what he was looking for and Felicity's reaction only helped to confirm his opinion.

'I think this is crazy, if you want my opinion, Blake, and sorry to be so bold, but I also think you're wasting your time,' she continued.

'We'll see, Felicity,' he responded, not really paying too much attention to her words because he was glancing through the post that she'd just handed to him.

'You've already interviewed a few, and so far they've all turned out to be useless, so I don't understand,' she said with frustration in her voice. As she looked at him, she could see he wasn't really paying any attention to her. She was also really struggling to understand this new project of his, as she'd worked with Blake for a number of years and what he was doing seemed to be in contradiction to what she knew about him.

'Look at it as a new challenge, and you never know, you may even learn something from this,' he said, trying to appease her mood.

'A challenge! I think that's an understatement. It will be a nightmare, and I can see it all now,' her mood unchanged by his tact.

'It's okay for you living out in Zambia. You'll only see them every few weeks, whereas I'll have to see anyone you hire every day,' she said, realising as she did it that she might have over-stepped her bounds and immediately regretted her words. Druker looked up from his pile of post and stared at Felicity. He didn't need to say a word, and she quickly apologised for her outburst and offered to make him a cup of coffee.

'I've some freshly ground coffee from a new delicatessen that's opened up near to where I live,' she said, knowing how much he loved good coffee and hoping that this might change the mood.

'That sounds like a good idea and the best thing you've said all morning,' he agreed, as he turned to go into his office.

CHAPTER FORTY-THREE

After smoking her cigarette, Carly looked at her watch and realised that she needed to get ready quickly and get on her way. The interview was at a property company that had made contact via the Jobcentre. The company was looking to recruit staff that would be making out-bound calls to prospects in order to sell properties.

She knew that she'd be no good as a telemarketer, but she also knew that it was essential for her to go for this interview, to avoid the risk of her losing her benefits. She was well-rehearsed in making sure that she didn't get the job at the interview, but even if she did get employed, she knew how to lose the job quite quickly, too.

The interview was a half-hour walk from her flat and was in about 40 minutes, so she hastily donned her interview clothes and set off. Her outfit included a pair of black trousers and an old purple and blue top that she'd not cleaned in years, so it had a distinctive, stale smell about it. This was one of her deliberate ploys to make sure her first impressions were never the best, as she knew people wouldn't want to work with someone who smelled.

As she left her flat and began to walk, it was colder that it had been for a while. There was a slight drizzle in the air, which made it feel even colder and made her shiver, as the damp air got through to her core. She pulled her coat tighter around herself and wrapped her arms around her body and began to walk a bit faster than normal, to avoid getting too wet, and within 10 minutes of leaving her flat, she was walking down Rainsford Road.

As she passed the Rose of India restaurant on her left, she could smell the aroma of freshly cooked Indian food.

Walking a few steps further, she now faced a blue door which had the number of the building etched on a window above it. To the left of the door were four buttons, as part of an intercom system, with the names of the companies written behind plastic covers.

She looked down the list of names until she saw the one she had come to see and then pressed the button. She heard it buzz a couple of times, and then a young-sounding woman answered with 'Hatton Property.' Carly identified herself, after which the door buzzer sounded and the woman asked her to come up to the first floor, so she pushed the door open and walked in off the street.

The hallway that presented itself to her was newly painted and the carpet looked like it had only recently been laid. The entrance had that newly decorated smell to it and it was obvious that the company had either recently moved in or they were keen to make a good impression on visitors.

Directly in front of Carly were a set of stairs leading up to the first floor, so she immediately walked up to the top, and as she approached the top landing, there were a couple of doors. One of the doors was marked with a toilet sign, which left the second door as the obvious place to go. It held a sign saying Hatton Property Developments Ltd in a simple, black font printed onto a white placard. The door was a modern, light-coloured wood, which to Carly looked very new as well.

She knocked on this second door and heard the same young voice invite her in. She opened the door and walked in to find another newly decorated entrance lobby, which had a small desk right in front of her. The smell of freshly brewed coffee hit her, as she entered. Behind the desk was a very pretty young lady who was probably in her mid- to late-twenties. She had long, blond hair and had applied enough makeup to make her look quite glamorous.

She gave Carly a big smile, and as she did, she showed off her perfectly white teeth, which were surrounded by perfectly shaped lips, which had what looked like newly applied bright, red lipstick on them.

'You must be Carly,' she said, and despite

Carly's obviously shabby appearance, she made no sign of a reaction to it. At this stage she wouldn't be able to smell her, though, but the aroma of her top would eventually drift across to her, and she would smell her for sure, as the room was quite small. She then introduced herself as Felicity and told her to take a seat. 'Mr Caldwell will be with you in a short while. I'll let him know you're here,' she said as she lifted the receiver on her phone and rang through.

Carly took a seat in front of Felicity and waited.

When suddenly the door to the office next to her opened, she was startled for a second, caught in the midst of thinking how she'd flunk the interview.

She looked up to see a stocky man with tanned skin emerge from the room. He looked down at her and introduced himself as Blake. He invited her to join him, so she got up and followed him into his office, which was yet another newly refurbished room. As she followed him, she got a whiff of his aftershave, which appeared to be a very expensive fragrance that struck her as being distinctive.

As she walked into the office, she saw what looked like a freshly painted single-sash window looking out onto Rainsford Road. The room had the similar newly decorated smell that the entrance hall had, with new carpet on the floor, too. The man walked behind his desk, as she waited beside two chairs that had been positioned directly in front of him. The desk looked brand new and was made of a deep, reddish-coloured wood, which had a sheen that made the surface look almost like glass.

She studied Blake, and, as she did, she noticed that the clothes he wore appeared expensive. She wasn't sure why, but perhaps it was something about the material they were made of, and how they sat on his more than average-built frame that made them look this way. There were no visible labels on the clothes to give away their designer brand, but she was convinced he was a man of considerable wealth.

She had noticed his shoes on the way into his office. They were clearly expensive and as shiny as when they'd been taken from the box they'd come in. The man's trousers sat perfectly on his shoes, making her realise that this man certainly knew how to dress.

Carly's mum had worked for a high-end tailor until she got sacked for upsetting too many customers, and she had learnt a lot about tailoring and men's fashion. Her mum would often point out to her the well-dressed men in the high street and would always explain the reasons why. She would always say you can tell a man by the shoes he wears and, looking at Blake, Carly could see that this man was very particular about his shoes.

'Take a seat, Carly,' the man instructed, as he himself sat opposite her in the lavishly styled leather chair that almost engulfed him. It was only when she'd sat down that she observed on the wall behind his desk a large picture of an African scene with elephants and giraffes on a wide plain. She thought the scene looked a bit out of place here in Chelmsford, and in this newly refurbished office, too. His voice was almost military like and not very friendly at all, which made her feel even more uncomfortable than she had when she'd first arrived.

Sitting in front of Blake with her legs close together, she clamped her clammy hands tightly and rested them on her legs, barely daring to look at the man in front of her. He was making her feel nervous, but she wasn't able to put her finger on why.

Instead, she decided that it would be safer to stare out of the window and onto the road below. She watched as a large, articulated lorry rumbled by, which sent vibrations through the building. This multi-ton vehicle was followed by a double-decker bus, which also inflicted its own vibration on the building.

Carly's gaze out of the window was suddenly broken by the man's voice. 'You seem very nervous, Carly,' Blake observed, as he gave her a firm look with his steely blue eyes. She could barely look the man in the eyes, as he seemed to represent everything that she hated, but she wasn't sure why, only just having met him.

'So you've been off work for quite some time now, I see,' Blake noted, 'and I see from your CV that, even when you manage to get a job, you don't seem to be able to hold on to it for very long.'

She was shocked at his approach and how direct he was being, and she was beginning to wonder why he'd even invited her to the interview. She was at a loss for words for once, whereas usually she knew just what to say.

'Are you looking for a job?' he asked.

'Yes, of course I am!' Carly exclaimed, but only after she'd said it, did she realise just how defensive she was being.

'I just haven't had much luck recently,' she continued, in a less defensive manner, trying to over-compensate for her initial approach.

'Not much luck? I'd say no luck at all, looking at your CV and track record,' he said with a touch of sarcasm in his voice.

The way he spoke to her made Carly shift uneasily on her chair. It was as if he knew exactly what she was up to, but she continued to wonder why he'd invited her for an interview.

'Perhaps he's investigating me,' she thought worryingly, before she replied, 'What do you mean?'

'Well, Carly, you have long periods of no work at all and, let me see, your last job was as a cleaner, which lasted for just four months, is that correct?'

Blake stared at her for a few seconds for the effect and to allow what he'd just said to sink in, then continued, 'So, what happened at Semicon for the job to end after such a short space of time?' He then looked at her intently, waiting for a response.

'I was sacked because I spilt bleach on the carpet in the board room,' she explained. 'It was an accident, though.' She found herself defending what had happened, for once, which she'd never done before.

'Why would it have been anything else but an accident, Carly?' he asked, as if he knew what she was thinking. Or was it he had noticed the tone in her voice?

This was a really strange experience for her. It was as if she was being tested rather than interviewed.

'*This man knows my game,*' she said to herself, as she wondered whether the Jobcentre set this up to see if they could find her out. She even cast a quick gaze around the room to see if there were any obvious hidden cameras.

Carly sat there still barely able to make eye contact with Blake, and she didn't really know how to answer his last question. No interview had ever been as difficult as this before, and she was always very adept at the game she played out, but this time it was different. She knew she had to be careful with what she said, and she even wanted to make sure that he was keen to take her on before she left.

'So, Carly, how are you on the phone? I assume you realise what this job is about and that you have actually read the job summary we sent to you,' he said, probing her a little bit more.

'Yes, I did, Mr Caldwell. I understand that I

need to call people about your property to sell to them,' she replied, relieved this time that she had actually read what the job entailed. She realised that had she not read the job description, this man would be able to see right through her game and she'd be found out right away.

'I'm not too good on the phone, though, as I get quite nervous when I speak to people,' she added.

'So tell me why I should give you the job over someone else, Carly,' he pushed, causing her to blush with guilt.

'Is my game up?' she wondered. *'What if I get found out and don't get this job — will my benefits be stopped?'*

She paused for a few seconds, thinking about how to answer his question, but not wanting to delay too much, as the silence was deafening. She could feel him staring right at her.

Eventually, after what felt like an eternity, she spoke. 'I'll work hard for you and I will do my best to make sure I please you,' which is all that she could think to say.

'Please you,' she repeated in her mind, *'what was I thinking?'*

'That's an interesting reply. Are you eager to please me, then?' He mocked her, picking on the two words she couldn't believe she'd just said.

'But why should I believe you with your CV reading the way it does, and why should I give you a chance?'

'I feel that this is the right job for me, Mr

Caldwell, and I will try my best to work really hard for you,' she replied.

'I know that I'm ready for this now and I really want to work for you,' she continued, trying to show a real interest for once.

'So if you are keen on this job, why is it that you dressed like that and I can smell your clothes or you or both, Carly? It's not good,' he told her. Her face flushed with blood again as she realised she had been found out.

'The job had also been advertised for quite a while before I asked the Jobcentre to contact you directly, so why didn't you apply yourself? If, as you say, this is a job you really want,' he pushed harder.

She sat there trying to control her emotions and began to think about how to respond to this latest dig. This all seemed wrong somehow.

Before she could respond, he said, 'that's all I need for now. I will let you know, as we have other candidates applying for this position. I would like you to leave now,' he said as he finished the interview.

Carly got up to leave, not quite sure what to say, but in the end she said, 'Nice to meet you, Mr Caldwell, and I look forward to hearing from you.'

She rushed to the door now, shaking with fear — or was it anger? — as she reached for the handle and left Blake's office. She almost knocked into Felicity as she hurried into the entrance lobby, quickly apologised, then set off down the stairs. At this point she was holding back her tears, whilst she was still in the building, but they soon broke as she burst out onto the street.

Carly barely remembered how she'd got back to her flat, as she had cried nearly all the way home, having been totally humiliated by this Mr Blake Caldwell. She sat in her small kitchen and lit up a cigarette, as, despite her emotional state, she had remembered to stop off on the way home to buy another packet at the local mini-market.

As Carly brought the cigarette to her mouth, her hand was still shaking from her experience and she was still questioning why it was that he had got to her so deeply. Yes, this man had been rude and he did question her in an unorthodox way, but she sensed that there was something more to it than that. She just couldn't put her finger on it.

'Is the Jobcentre on to me?' she thought again, as she sat in her kitchen smoking her second cigarette.

CHAPTER FORTY-FOUR

Druker began opening mail and, just after Carly left, Felicity came rushing into his office. 'What on earth did you say to her?' she said.

He looked at Felicity blankly, as she stood there in front of his desk. 'She nearly bumped into me and couldn't get out of here quick enough, so I guess you will not be employing her,' she probed.

'No, I won't be. Didn't you smell her?' he replied. As Felicity studied her boss, she was starting to see another side to him that she'd never seen before. She really didn't like this new side; it was beginning to make her feel a bit uneasy.

'So, where does that leave us on this project?' she asked.

'I'll call the Jobcentre myself to discuss further candidates and the ones we've seen so far,' he said to her to get her off his back.

Druker did call the Jobcentre and explained that all of the candidates he'd seen so far were not suitable for what he was looking for, but he requested more CVs. The Jobcentre then told Druker about another candidate, John Bowman, who they'd eventually got to complete an application form. However, they explained that he couldn't be seen until next week, at which point Druker explained to the Jobcentre consultant that this would be too late, but that he'd be in contact to arrange to see him on his next trip. Although he did ask for Bowman's CV to be emailed in advance for him to review.

After making a few more phone calls regarding his properties, he picked up the phone to call Scott, who would have been at the hotel where he'd left him earlier.

'Scott, I've just interviewed our next mark. Her name is Carly Prow and I think she's perfect. I know I really rattled her in the interview. It was obvious she had come with the intention to put me off employing her, plus her CV is terrible. She's another one that deserves to be taught a lesson,' he told his colleague.

'It's now 3:30 p.m. and the other mark, a Mr Bowman, has not yet arranged his interview, and it looks like from speaking with the Jobcentre that he's using delaying tactics. But I'll soon have his CV and he looks like another ideal candidate. So I suggest we leave this Bowman person for our next trip, as it's Friday and it's not likely I'll get a chance to interview him before we have to leave.' He clarified this with Scott, as he preferred to see all of his marks before he captured them.

'That's fine by me,' Scott replied.

'I'm going to see if we can arrange to leave on Sunday morning instead of Monday,' Druker said.

'Fine by me, Druk.'

'I suggest we do our reconnaissance on Prow's place tonight. So I'll finish up here at around 5:30 and come by the hotel and pick you up soon thereafter.'

'I'll be ready, boss.'

He hung up to continue with his other phone calls, then called Felicity into his office to go through what she needed to.

CHAPTER FORTY-FIVE

Joshua had his packed lunch and was happy that Ken would look after everything whilst he was out for the day. He'd been gone for two hours when he came across a herd of elephants. Joshua pulled the Land Rover over and turned the engine off to observe the herd.

The elephants were around 15 strong and he was pleased to see that there were a few young ones in tow. The herd were aware of his presence, but as he'd stopped his vehicle some distance from them and had turned his engine off, they continued to graze. However, the matriarch kept an eye on him, as there was a recently born calf among them.

As he sat there watching, the silence was shattered by the crack of a rifle. Joshua knew right away that the sound he'd heard was of an extremely high-powered weapon. The elephant herd jumped at the sound and made off in the opposite direction.

Joshua got out of his Land Rover, being

careful to remove the keys, and headed off in the direction of the gunshot. Before he set off he made sure his own rifle was fully loaded. Then he put his other rifle containing tranquiliser darts over his shoulder.

'Bloody poachers,' Joshua thought to himself, as he began to slowly walk towards where the shot had come from, seemingly a small group of trees.

Moving slowly through the trees, he soon came across their Land Rover, but no sign of the culprits. Joshua lent in and took the keys, which were still in the ignition, and then stood and listened for any voices. Nothing.

Looking at the ground to work out the direction of their travel, he saw signs of foot prints and an obvious trail they'd left. He decided his best move would be to hide and wait for them to return to the vehicle.

Joshua moved away from the Land Rover in the opposite direction of where he knew they'd walked, and hid in some bushes.

He didn't have to wait for long before a lone, large man carrying a rifle appeared from the opposite direction from where he sat. As he watched this man approaching his vehicle, Joshua brought his rifle up into a ready position, as he knew this guy would react badly once he found that the keys were missing from the ignition. As Joshua watched, being careful not to be seen, the man jumped into the Land Rover. As he did, Joshua made his move.

Joshua approached the vehicle from behind,

and within seconds of the man jumping into the driver's seat, he had jumped back out again and was holding his rifle. He immediately turned to face Joshua, who by now was only feet away from the vehicle, and just as he was bringing his rifle up to point it at Joshua, Joshua pulled his trigger and shot him.

The large man was flung back after the impact of the bullet hit him square in the chest. As he fell backwards, his rifle dropped to the ground. Joshua walked over to the man and leaned over him to see if he was still alive, which he was, so Joshua knelt down and said, 'Who else is out there?'

The man looked up at him, coughed and brought up some blood, and replied in a weak, croaky voice, 'You fucker, why did you shoot me?'

'I shot you before you could shoot me, as you were bringing your rifle up,' Joshua said, as he stared the man out and repeated, 'Who else is out there; are you alone?'

'I have a tourist game hunter with me, and he's by the kill in the bush,' the man said slowly, and then, 'you've fucking killed me.'

'It's called self-defence, and you are a poacher, as you are on our land,' Joshua said without feeling. 'What did you shoot?'

The man was struggling to keep his eyes open, and as he stared up at Joshua he said, 'It was a lion, he…' The man didn't finish his sentence, and Joshua confirmed by checking his carotid artery that he had died.

'*Fucking poachers,*' Joshua thought, as he stood up and switched weapons. He was now carrying the rifle that contained the tranquilisers.

He was certain that he'd be able to creep up on this tourist quite easily, and he was sure the guy would have heard the shot, but he was still convinced he'd be able to find him and tranquilise him without too much of a problem.

He set off in the direction the dead man had come from, whilst at the same time looking down and checking for obvious signs of his exact direction. Before very long, he came to a small clearing, and there in the middle of it was a large male lion, which was lying on its side next to a man dressed in khaki trousers and top, and wearing a cowboy-style hat. As Joshua broke through the cover of the trees, the man was looking in his direction, but he wasn't holding a rifle, as this was perched on the lion's head.

The man addressed Joshua: 'Who are you? I heard a gunshot.'

Before the man could say any more and without saying a word himself, Joshua shot the man in the stomach with a tranquiliser dart.

'What the fuck?' The man said, as he stared at Joshua before quickly dropping to the ground with a loud thud.

Joshua walked over and saw the tranquiliser drug taking effect on the man, who said again, 'Who are you?' And then he drifted off.

Joshua looked at the lion that he'd obviously shot as a trophy. He was sure it was the largest lion of the group of three that Joshua had been aware of and was hoping to see today. He was a magnificent creature and probably stood in at nearly 500 pounds, but now he lay there in the dirt with a large hole in his heart.

'*Bastards*,' Joshua said under his breath, as he turned and headed back to collect his Land Rover.

Before long, Joshua had both men in the back of his vehicle and was heading back to base. He couldn't wait for his boss to return and to tell him about his catch.

CHAPTER FORTY-SIX

Druker left his office at around 5:10, having managed to cover most of the phone calls he needed to, and he also managed to go through all the matters that Felicity had for him to deal with. After he'd had the interview with Carly Prow, Felicity had behaved differently. He decided not to say anything at this stage, as he didn't have time for arguments which might lead to him having to start interviewing for a new assistant.

To appease her mood further, he decided to give her a pay raise, which was a complete surprise to her. She was already on a very good salary for what she did, and the raise had changed her mood completely. Druker even heard her singing in the reception area whilst he was packing up to leave, which he knew was a good sign.

The drive from his office to the hotel was just over 10 minutes by car at this time of day, as there was quite a bit of traffic about, with people leaving work. He arrived at the hotel and called Scott from the car. He asked him to come down, as he saw no sense in going into the hotel, as this would waste time.

Scott came out right away, as he must have been in the lobby. He jumped into the passenger seat of the hire car, which was an Audi A4. When Scott got in, Druker was playing some classical music, which he wasn't too keen on himself, but he knew that his boss liked listening to it, so he wasn't about to say anything.

'So how was it at your office today?' Scott asked.

'It was good and I managed to get most things done, which I'm pleased about.'

'That's always good when you get things done.'

'So what have you done today, Scott?'

'Not much, really. I went to the gym as usual and then went for a walk into town and had lunch. I then came back to the hotel and watched some TV.'

'Never really been a big TV fan myself.'

'Me neither, I'd much rather be out on the African plain myself, but I ended up watching a day-time movie, which was okay.'

By now it was already dark and whilst they spoke, Druker had plugged Carly's address details into the satnav, which had indicated a journey time of six minutes from where they were. Druker followed the instructions of the lady's voice on the navigation system and they were soon pulling up outside her flat.

'Here we are. She lives in that converted house over there,' Druker said.

'Okay,' Scott replied. 'It shouldn't be too difficult to get her out of there. What floor is she on?"

'She's on the ground floor, which will make things even easier for us.'

'That's good. When do you plan to come and get her then?'

'I suggest tomorrow night, as I have a few things I need to do tomorrow morning. We should then be able to fly home first thing the following morning,' Druker said.

'It's good to be going home early. I miss Africa when I'm not there,' Scott replied.

'Yes, me too, I feel it is my home now, even though I've not been there for that long. I'm excited about my project, too,' Druker said.

After they'd done the reconnaissance on Carly's home, they set off back to the hotel.

CHAPTER FORTY-SEVEN

Carly had fallen asleep on the sofa and had awoken to the sound of someone ringing her intercom. She wasn't used to having visitors and it seemed very strange, as she couldn't think who it might be. She leant over and switched the lamp on, which was set on a small table next to her sofa.

She was still lying there, half awake, wondering whether the noise she'd heard was part of a dream, and then she heard the ring once more. *'Who the hell is ringing my intercom?'* she thought. *'I bet it's someone that's rung the wrong one.'* She was irritated that someone had interrupted her sleep and kept lying on her sofa, not wanting to move. Then the third ring made it certain that they weren't going away, and whoever they were, they were keen to get her attention.

She got up off the sofa and walked towards her front door and the intercom, but before she had even reached them, the fourth ring resounded. This time it seemed even louder. She wasn't sure how long she'd been asleep, but to her it felt like the middle of the night, especially as it was dark outside.

She pressed the answer button on her intercom to speak to the person who was ringing her buzzer and said, 'Who are you?'

'I'm a plumber and I've been asked to come and check your boiler,' a man's voice said at the other end. 'Your landlord contacted me and said there seemed to be a problem with a couple of the boilers in the building and we want to make sure yours is OK.'

The man had a strange English accent, which sounded a bit posh and one she wouldn't normally associate with a plumber.

'But I don't know anything about this,' she replied.

'Yes, I know, and your landlord asked me to apologise on his behalf for not contacting you himself, but it is important we check your boiler to make sure it's safe,' the man continued.

She could now hear something else in this English accent, and continued to question him. 'Is it unsafe, then?' she probed, becoming more agitated.

'It could be. The boiler you have in your flat is the same as the one in flat three and we had to change a part on that one only yesterday. We did knock on your door then, but you were out,' the voice said.

'That must have been when I was at the interview yesterday,' she thought. *'This man must*

be genuine, if he knew I was out and has been to flat three.'

The accent this man had was still bugging her, and yet despite this she pressed the button to release the latch on the main door to the building and told him to come to her flat, explaining that she was on the ground floor.

She undid the latch, but just as she began to open the door, and before she could open it fully, it was pushed hard by whoever was on the other side. She briefly caught sight of two masked people, as they rushed in, grabbed her and wrestled her to the floor.

Before she could properly work out what was happening, and just as she was about to let out an almighty scream, her mouth was covered by what felt like a gloved hand. Her scream came out as a very muffled sound. She tried in vain to make all the noise she could muster, but as she did, the hand around her lips tightened still further. All she could think was that the sounds wouldn't be heard by anyone. She then heard her front door being closed, as the two intruders pinned her to the floor of her flat.

As she struggled to set herself free, she felt something sting on her arm, and then she felt herself starting to drift off.

'Have I just been injected?' she thought as panic began to set in, but there was no more fight left in her.

Whatever had just been pushed into her bloodstream was having an immediate effect and rendering her useless against her attackers. But just before she passed out, whilst she was still conscious and aware of what was going on, she realised there was something familiar about one of the invaders — it was a familiar fragrance. Then she faded away.

When Carly awakened, she felt a bit groggy, and when she opened her eyes fully, she found that she was in some kind of a strange, dark room.

CHAPTER FORTY-EIGHT

As Carly tried to make out where she was, she felt the whole room move. It was as if it were floating somehow, but then all of a sudden dropped for what felt like a metre or so and stopped with a thud. Trying to steady herself with her hands, she realised that she couldn't move them. They were bound to her sides. Panic began to set in, as she remembered what had happened to her in her flat, where two intruders had pushed in and given her what felt like an injection.

She tried to move her legs, but like her arms, she could feel that her ankles were also tied together. She then tried to draw her legs towards her chest, but her knees hit something. Her panic increased, as she began to realise the darkened room she was in was really quite small and was more like a coffin.

It then struck her like a ten-ton lorry careering out of control and smacking into her head: *'I'm in a coffin!'*

The realisation that she might be in a such a place increased her panic levels even higher.

'Have I been buried alive?' she thought, adding, *'But why is the coffin moving?'*

Then it happened again — the whole box moving, as if it was floating in the air. *'Maybe I'm on the way to be buried or to be cremated,'* she worried, not knowing which would be worse, and then began to think about oxygen levels and how long she had been in this box and how long before the air ran out.

She tried to sit up, but her forehead hit the low ceiling, which confirmed that she was in a very confined space. Then she tried to roll onto her side to see if she could explore the container further, but again found there was little room to manoeuvre.

Her head was in a spin as she tried to pull her arms free. She pulled against the binding, but it was no good. As her wrists were also tethered to her body and her arms were by her sides, she had no leverage to pull herself away. Her heart was racing and she was now beginning to hyperventilate.

Her mind went back to her kidnappers, and how they'd forced their way into her flat. She then remembered the familiar smell; it was the aftershave she'd smelt when she went for the interview. It was so distinctive, and she remembered the man, Blake, being somewhat aggressive and it being a very different interview to any she'd ever experienced.

'Surely, this can't be a coincidence, but then, why would he go to all the bother of interviewing me first?' she questioned. *'What a strange, sadistic thing to do!'*

The prison box shuddered again, which brought her out of her thoughts about Blake and back into the present.

'Where the hell am I and what's going on?' she thought.

The shuddering that she had felt suddenly became more violent, after which came a hard thud, accompanied by what sounded like a small screech, almost like a tyre squealing on a road. She then felt herself being forced forward, as if there'd be a sharp deceleration, which would mean that she had been travelling in some form of transport. The vibrations she felt were now different; it was definitely as if she were moving across rough ground or an uneven road.

She began to scream and then shouted, 'Help! Help!'

As she shouted, and despite her being enclosed in a dark chamber, she felt a change in direction. It was almost as if her other senses had been enhanced somehow, with her ability to see having been taken away.

'I must be in a hearse,' she worried again. *'I'm about to be buried alive or, worse still, cremated.'*

She was then aware that the vehicle had come to a complete stop. Then she heard the opening of doors and the sound of voices. She couldn't make out what they were saying, but she was now aware they were getting closer. Soon she heard another door open, which was much closer to where she lay. Her coffin then moved, but this time it was more violent. She realised it was now being shifted.

Her heart rate rose again, as she began to panic about what was going on, which was completely out of her control. It then felt like she was being lifted and carried away from whatever the vehicle was that she had been transported in. '*But where to?*' she thought.

She had begun to shout 'Help me!' again just at the point where it felt like the coffin had been put down, when all of a sudden the lid was opened and a flood of light came rushing in. It was so bright she had to close her eyes to protect them from the sudden glare.

Despite being bound, she still tried to struggle to break loose from her bindings, but realised this was to no avail. Gradually, she opened her eyes again and found two men staring down at her. The first face she saw was not someone she recognised, but the second was very familiar — the tanned skin and the piercing blue eyes she couldn't forget. It was Blake.

Carly began to shout at the two men. 'What are you doing to mc?

No answer.

'Where have you brought me and why am I here?'

The men ignored her, and before she knew it, she saw one of them lean in to her box with a needle. She shifted as much as she could and tried to resist the inevitable, but it was futile. The needle was pushed into her left arm and she then felt the same feeling of drifting away begin again, the same that had happened only a short time before in her flat. Then she slept.

CHAPTER FORTY-NINE

As Graham sat on the floor of his cage eating dog food, he heard the bolts of the main door opening again.

Light flooded in and the same two men came in. They were carrying what looked like another person, who seemed to be either dead or asleep, as the body of this person was totally motionless. They placed the obvious victim into a cage adjacent to Graham's, but at this point he couldn't make out whether they were male or female.

He watched in silence as the two men first unlocked the padlock and then unbolted the door before opening it, with a metal-on-metal sound, as the un-oiled hinges squealed in protest. They were being extremely rough and took no real care over how they handled this poor person, who, like him, was naked. He then realised it was in fact a woman, as he could make out the soft curve of her breasts and the curved shape of a woman's pelvic area.

'My god, a woman,' he thought.

They almost threw the lady into the cage, then locked it and didn't even give her a second glance as they disappeared outside, closing the door behind them once more.

It was too dark and too gloomy for him to make out who this new person might be. He sat there and willed her to wake up, as this would give him someone to talk to and between them they could perhaps work out what was happening, maybe together find a way to escape.

He decided to try and rouse his new cell-mate. 'Hey you, hey you, over there,' he said in as loud a voice as he dared for fear of being heard outside.

There was neither sound nor movement from her, so he tried again, raising his voice a little higher. 'Hey, hey, wake up, wake up!' he demanded, still keeping his voice to more than a loud whisper.

There was still no sign of any life coming from the lady, despite his calls to her, so he sat back in his own cage to contemplate what to do next. As he lay there he suddenly felt the urge to go to the toilet, so he thought this would be a good opportunity to shout for help from the two men outside, and perhaps the shouting might awaken his fellow prisoner in the process.

'Help, hey, help, please! I need to go to the toilet!' Graham shouted, hoping that his kidnappers would actually hear him.

He sat there for a few moments. When he heard no footsteps and no sound of the door opening, he shouted again, but this time a little bit louder. He was getting desperate now, so he rocked from side to side in an attempt to make his desperation go away.

'Help, please, Scott, I need to go to the toilet!'
'Surely, they cannot expect me to go to the toilet in this cage like an animal,' he thought.

But then it hit him. *'That's exactly what they want. They have no intention of letting me out to use the toilet.'*

With this realisation he grabbed the bars with both hands and began shaking the cage — shaking it violently and shouting at the top of his voice. He was sure the men would hear him now and come to see what all the noise was about. But nothing. Even the woman lay still, not moving a muscle, despite all the commotion he was generating.

Although he was now at bursting point and his bladder felt so full it was getting painful, he still found it difficult to let go and relieve himself in the cage. However, in the end, the urge to go was so overwhelming, he simply had to give in. He tried to direct the urine to the outside of the cage, which would keep the floor of his temporary new home dry.

As he relaxed his bladder, he had a sudden urge for a bowel movement, too. This surprised him, as his body had let his bowels go automatically when he had been faced with the lions. Directing his urine out and away from his cage was relatively easy, but to do the same with his faeces would not be. He would have to do it to one side of his cage, so that he wouldn't have to touch it.

After he'd relieved himself, he felt totally degraded. The room smelt of his faeces and urine. Now he hoped that the person across from him wouldn't wake up, as he'd feel extremely embarrassed about what had just happened. Totally frustrated and angry, Graham decided to yell out, and the only word that would come out was 'Help!'

He kept shouting and shouting at the top of his voice, knowing that his kidnappers would eventually hear him. He didn't really care right now what they would do to him. And he was right: The door to the building shot open as he continued yelling, and in came both men he'd seen before.

They were holding a gun and another implement which he'd not seen before. As they approached the cage, one of the men shouted at him, 'Shut the fuck up!'

Scott was holding the gun, whilst his colleague was carrying a long, metal, pole-like implement. He continued with his shouting, ignoring what Scott was saying and stared at his kidnappers in defiance. Then suddenly the rod-like implement was thrust in through the bars of his cage and, as it touched his bare skin, he jerked backwards in pain. The implement was a stun gun, which shot out a huge electric charge.

Graham cried out in pain as the charge hit his skin, and then the man jolted him again, which resulted in him bouncing back and hitting himself on the bars at the back of the cage. 'Stop!' he cried.

'Please stop!' he pleaded, as he lay there in shock.

'Well, shut the fuck up, or we'll keep prodding you until you do, and I mean it, you little shit!' Scott snarled at him.

He cowered in his cage, looking up at the two men, as he writhed in pain from the two jolts of electricity he'd just received.

'Why are you doing this to me?' he said weakly.

Scott turned to his colleague and said, 'Blimey, he stinks! You get the hose, Ken, and I'll keep an eye on him to make sure he doesn't start shouting again.'

Ken handed the stun gun to Scott, turned away and walked towards the door of the building. Graham could see that he was walking towards a hose reel and watched as he grabbed the hose and brought it towards his cage. Within seconds he was being fired at with a powerful jet of freezing, cold water. The whole cage was being blasted. The food remains and dirt on the floor were flicked up onto Graham and then washed off again as Ken fired the jet at him over and over.

The water on the floor and all the effluent it carried was washed away into a small trench that ran across the back of the building. The two men were laughing and jeering as they fired the water at him. He huddled in the corner of his cage, covering his genitals with his hands so they wouldn't be hurt by the forceful stream of water. The ordeal seemed to last for an eternity. The two kidnappers enjoyed it every bit as much as Graham hated it. Although it was good to have his cage cleaned and his legs finally washed off, it wasn't how he would have wanted it to happen.

Finally, as the hose was turned off, Scott said to Graham, 'Now, let that be a lesson to you. The next time you start yelling, we'll not be so lenient. You got off lightly this time.'

The two men left the side of his cage. Ken returned the hose to its holder and then left the building, following his colleague, who'd already gone out. They closed the door behind them.

Once again, he was plunged into semi-darkness, only this time in a bit more pain and feeling chilly, despite the warmth of the building. He was shivering now and had nothing to dry himself nor to keep himself warm, so instead he wrapped his arms around his knees as he hunched up as small as possible. The emotions of anger, helplessness and frustration swirled around in his head, as he sat there in his cage, not sure what he should do next.

It was then that he heard the faint sound of a woman's voice: 'Hello, where am I?'

He realised the woman who had been brought in earlier had woken up.

Despite being wet and a bit ashamed of how he looked, he got up from his curled-up position and whispered, 'Hey, you! Are you awake?'

With the sound of his voice, the person in the other cage stirred and sat up, turning to see where the voice was coming from. Realising that she was totally naked, she covered her breasts and genitals as best she could and replied, 'Where the hell am I and who the hell are you?'

He replied in a whispered voice, 'We are in Africa.'

'Africa?' the lady exclaimed.

'Yes, Africa, and I'm a bit lucky, because they've already put me out into the wild, only to be rescued from being eaten alive by a pride of lions,' he replied.

'What are you talking about? Rescued from a pride of lions? Are you completely mad? I live in Chelmsford. I can't be in Africa. I only came home from the shops a short while ago,' the lady protested.

'*She lives in Chelmsford, which isn't far from where I live,*' he thought before replying.

'You might think that, but think a bit harder and you might remember something that happened just before you fell asleep. I have some vague recollections myself about what happened to me and how I got here,' he said.

The woman looked down to her bare legs. In the dim light she could see a large bruise on her right leg and, as she went to touch it, there were a few memories of a man in her house and her feeling frightened.

'So, who are you, then, and what are you doing here?' she asked.

'Well, firstly, we must keep our voices down, otherwise our kidnappers will hear us and they don't like us at all,' he warned.

'Why wouldn't they like us?'

'I'm not totally sure, but I know they really hate me and they have treated me like an animal or worse,' he replied with venom in his husky voice.

'Worse still, I tried to cry for help and they zapped me with this electric stun stick and then squirted me with a hose.'

'Yes, I remember hearing the sound of water, as I was coming to,' she said.

'So, what's your name?' he asked, pleased to have the company of this lady, even though they were both caged like animals. 'My name is Graham.'

She looked at him before replying, trying to summon up a little dignity.

'I'm Carly,' she said. 'I'm feeling really woozy and my memory seems to be a bit blank right now, but I'm also really hungry and thirsty. Do we get food around here?

'Well, yes, we do, but only dog food, and you get it thrown at you, if you're lucky,' he said.

'Dog food? What the hell is this?' she replied bluntly.

'I told you we are being treated like animals, and if you make a fuss then you will be in for it,' he responded.

'I really need a cigarette,' she said to Graham. 'I haven't had one for ages now and can't survive without.'

'You'll be lucky to get dog food, so to get a cigarette would be a miracle.'

'But I need one!' she said irritably.

Trying to ignore her plea for a cigarette, he began to tell her about the man with the blue eyes and how he remembered going to an interview and meeting him. He told her about how the same man had confronted him in his flat with another man who he thought had injected him with what must have been an anaesthetic. He also recounted his memory of waking up in what felt like a coffin and seeing the blue-eye man again, staring down at him.

Carly's memory was still very fuzzy, but with Graham mentioning the blue-eyed man, this brought forward a similar memory for her of an interview in a newly painted office in Rainsford Road. They gradually pieced together their memories, as they both discussed their similar experiences.

After their talk she got angry. She grabbed the bars of the cage and started to shake them vigorously, like a monkey possessed. The sound reverberated around the building.

'Shhhh,' he whispered. 'The men outside will hear you, and then you'll be in for it. They really aren't very nice. I found out the hard way,' he said, trying to protect her from what he'd been through.

'I don't care! Let me out, you bastards!' she started shouting, to his dismay.

CHAPTER FIFTY

Druker was in his office with Scott discussing the two new marks, one that they'd brought from the UK only yesterday, and Konner Hurley, who Joshua had found poaching on Druker's reserve the day before.

When Druker arrived home with Scott, Joshua had quickly told him about his catch and what had happened out in the bush. At first, Druker questioned him about what had occurred, but he reassured his boss that he'd buried the body of the man he'd shot and that the tourist was lying unconscious in what was called the round house.

Joshua also said he had gone through the hunter's wallet and found out his name.

Druker seemed to be pleased. His thinking was that this Konner guy would make up for only getting one new mark in the UK. He completely bought into Joshua's idea of using this tourist game hunter as another mark, and to put him out into the wild as a lesson. Druker was angry that they'd come onto his reserve and had shot one of his prized lions.

Then he'd stopped and thought for a moment about Joshua's report. It occurred to him that leaving the neighbour's Land Rover out there on his property could cause problems with the authorities later.

'Joshua,' he said, 'you and Ken take our Land Rover back to the scene of the lion's shooting and get rid of the Land Rover you left there. It's evidence we don't need coming back to haunt us. Drive it into a deeper part of the Luangwa River.'

Joshua nodded and went off to get the deed done.

Back in his office with Scott, he asked, 'Have we made the arrangements to put tracking devices into the latest marks' necks?'

'Yes, all arranged. We are just waiting for the vet to arrive later,' Scott replied.

'Excellent! We don't want to waste time because we haven't got trackers inserted in our marks,' Druker said.

'We want to make sure the next two are ready to go out as soon as possible, but let's get the new ones out before we put Smith back out in the field. Let him sweat a bit longer in his cage and worry about it.' Druker paused for effect. 'I bet he's really pissed off by now.'

'It'll be done, sir, don't you worry. The vet is due to arrive at 1:30,' Scott replied, and as he did, Druker was thinking to himself how he enjoyed treating these dregs like animals, even to the extent of using a vet instead of a doctor to insert the tracking devices.

'How is Konner now; is he looking any better?' Druker asked Scott, as it had turned out the dosage of tranquiliser that Joshua had shot him with was enough for an animal the size of a lion. Konner was not well enough to be put into the usual holding cages, so Joshua had placed him in a bed in the round house.

'Yes, he seems to be better this morning, and I've explained to the vet that we want him to look the guy over,' Scott replied.

'I hope he's okay to have the tracker fitted today and that he'll be fit enough to go out later on, too,' Druker said.

Fitting the trackers was a relatively simple procedure. Druker had even considered having one of his men do the task instead of a veterinarian, in order to limit the number of people who knew about his experiment. However, in the end he decided that he didn't want the operation jeopardised by a blunder on this front. He was determined to prove that if an urbane man or woman is put back into the wild, with nothing but their birthday suit, they wouldn't survive.

With years of being pampered by society, with food, water and shelter being so easy to get, even if you don't have a job, man had lost his ability to survive in the wild. So for his experiment to be real, he didn't want a stupid infection from a botched operation to jeopardise his live experiment; instead, he wanted nature to do its job.

In Africa, most things could be bought. If you offered the right amount of money, almost any person could be bribed. He had met Roger, his vet, in a bar in the local township of Kakumbi and got chatting about how in the UK there are so many spongers. He was explaining to the veterinary surgeon about how many benefit cheaters there were and how they needed to be taught a lesson.

He was pleased when the vet agreed with his argument, as he'd trained in the UK and then came to Zambia about 15 years ago. In the end he decided to risk telling him what he intended to do. At first he talked as if it were a joke and that it was something he would love to experiment with, but when Roger got really enthusiastic about the whole idea, he decided to tell him it was going to actually happen. The risk paid off, and after negotiating a tidy fee for each operation, the deal was sealed.

Each procedure, although only lasting around a half hour, cost Druker the equivalent of $50,000 US. The vet wanted the money paid in dollars, as this was a better currency than their local Zambian Kwacha. The funds were always transferred to an off-shore bank account, right after each operation.

The vet had been reliable by turning up when he was asked to and did a good job, but most importantly, he kept it to himself. He had only one simple request: He wanted none of the prisoners ever to see him, which Druker agreed to right away.

'You said the vet is arriving at 1:30, didn't you?' Druker asked,

'Yes, that's right,' Scott replied.

'I would like to get these two out this afternoon.'

'Okay, but that might be quite late, which means they will be out at night before they've had a chance to adjust to the wild,' Scott said.

'Mother nature never rests. She stops for no one,' Druker said. 'They'll need to learn that survival is a full-time job.'

'I guess so, Druk. I was just checking with you.'

The two men were suddenly interrupted by the sound of an alarm and a red flashing light on the desk. Both men looked at the flashing light and then at each other.

'You had better go find out what that's all about, Scott!' Druker exclaimed. 'And report back to me immediately with what you find.'

'No problem, sir. I'll get right on it and see what the issue is.'

With that, Scott hurried from Druker's office, leaving him looking at his computer screens.

CHAPTER FIFTY-ONE

Scott joined Joshua, who was the one who had raised the alarm.

'Hey, Scott, the new girl in the front cage has woken up,' Joshua said in his deep South African accent. 'She's making a huge amount of noise, too.'

'Then we'd better stop that right away, Josh, and I have just the trick,' Scott said to his colleague, as he grabbed the stun gun.

If the truth be known, Scott quite enjoyed the idea of using it on the marks. This model of stun gun, when turned up to full power, produced 5,000,000 volts. When it was used, a focused electrical charge would fire through the body. The prongs on the end of the stun device deliver a shock that causes the loss of balance and muscle control for the victim.

The device works by dumping electricity into the muscles, which causes them to overwork very rapidly and depletes the blood sugars needed for energy. The assailant can be out of commission for anywhere from five to 10 minutes and can be totally confused and disoriented after being hit. The effects are not long lasting and usually no permanent damage is done, except if the victim falls over after being hit with the voltage, and 'secondary damage,' as Druker would call it, occurs. So he had advised his staff to use it with caution and be careful not to damage the marks too much.

Most stun guns, especially those producing one million-plus volts, are designed to cut through clothes to ensure the assailant gets a full charge of electricity. However, as the captives were naked, the lower-powered guns were enough, meaning they would feel the full force of the electric shock.

Joshua was a broad-shouldered man who clearly worked out. He had the face of a man most would not think about messing with. He wore khaki trousers and a green singlet showing off his rugged body. His muscular arms showed off large biceps with well-defined cephalic veins. Both his arms were covered in tattoos, which ran into his shoulders, and he had a large tattoo of a fighting bull across his wide back. His face was clean shaven and it looked like he'd been out in the sun for the most of his life, as his skin was very dark and weathered.

Both men left the radio room, led by Joshua, and approached the main door to where the captives were being held. The door was double padlocked from the outside, and Joshua put the key into the first lock and pulled the padlock free, then slid the bolt back from its loop. He then did the same with the second lock before opening the door.

The two men walked in, this time led by Scott, and as they did the smell of urine and faeces hit them, like a wall of chemicals eating away at their sensitive noses.

'Damn, these fuckers stink,' Joshua grunted to Scott. 'They're worse than fucking pigs.'

'And that's even after we washed Smith down with the hose,' Scott added, grimacing when the smell hit his senses.

The room was dark, as although there were windows in the building, these had been deliberately boarded over. The room they had entered not only smelt bad, but it was also very warm. There was not much ventilation, and the metal corrugated roof acted like a huge radiator. This warmth created a humid atmosphere, which only added to the stench.

The central floor was made of concrete. Down each side there were cages, which were all empty except for the two that were occupied. It was these that the men moved towards, but in particular the one with Carly Prow in it, who was screaming at the top of her lungs.

Scott approached her and raised his stun gun.

CHAPTER FIFTY-TWO

Within what seemed like just seconds from when Carly had begun shouting, the prisoners heard the bolts being unlocked and the outside door bursting open, letting in shards of light. They both squinted as they watched two men rush in from outside.

'Ah, you've woken up have you, and you'd better stop that noise, you stupid little bitch,' Scott barked at Carly, as he wielded the electric prod stick. He then poked it through the bars to her cage and, as it touched her skin, she yelped in pain.

'You fucker you, what the hell are you doing with me?' she shouted at Scott, who pushed the stun gun against her for a second time, as she seemed to be defiant of his commands. The second charge of the stun gun threw her back against the rear of the cage, where she fell motionless and silent.

'There you go, you fat bitch! That'll teach you

for yelling and making a noise!' Scott yelled at her motionless form.

Then he turned to stare at Graham and snorted, 'What the fuck are you looking at, you pervert? Take a lesson from that, too, if you're thinking of doing anything about it.'

Graham averted his gaze from Scott and from Carly, who lay still with her head against the bars in an awkward position. The rest of her body was lying flat and her legs splayed apart, revealing her privates.

As Scott turned to walk out, Graham asked in the politest voice he could muster, 'Please, can we have some more food? Carly was just saying that she was hungry and I'm hungry, too.'

'No, you little shit, you don't deserve anything, and as for this little bitch she can continue to starve until we set her free in the wild,' he snarled at Graham.

'Surely, you could give her something, and, come on, you can't let a lady out in the wild,' Graham protested.

With this, Scott turned and headed towards Graham's cage, whilst the other man watched intently. As he did so, Graham pulled back as far as he could into the cage. He cowered, as he knew what this man could do and he didn't want to be prodded by the stun gun a second time.

'Look here, you have no idea who this bitch is and what she has done. She deserves to be here just as much as you do, so I'd be quiet if I were you, or you'll be first in line again,' he barked at

Graham.

'But surely we haven't been that bad, and certainly not bad enough to be treated like animals,' he dared to protest once more.

With this, Scott poked the stun gun through the bars of the cage, as Graham tried to recoil even further back. But the stick was too long and caught him on the sole of his foot. His foot jolted up and his knee hit him square on the jaw, which in turn knocked his head back, causing him to hit his head on the bars behind him. Then it all went very hazy and he blacked out.

CHAPTER FIFTY-THREE

Scott returned to Druker's office and updated him on what had happened. He explained that, due to the way they were behaving, he'd stunned both of the captives.

As they were talking, they could hear the distinct sound of a Cessna plane overhead, and immediately knew that this would be the vet arriving. Both men walked out of the office, with Scott following his boss to the front door. As they looked out they could see the small aircraft on its final approach to the runway, so they made their way to the nearest Land Rover.

Before they headed off, Druker shouted, 'Hey, Josh! You and Ken get Prow out of her cage and to take her to the operating room. The vet has just arrived.'

Scott automatically jumped into the driver's seat, Druker got in on the passenger side, and the Land Rover jumped into life when Scott turned the key. He spun the vehicle around, pressed the accelerator and headed in the direction of the airstrip. As they were driving, Scott added a bit more detail about Carly, telling Druker how he thought she'd knocked herself out when she was thrown back onto the bars of the cage.

Druker looked straight ahead as Scott was telling him about Carly, then said, 'We don't want that to impede what the vet is about to do, now do we? I did tell you to use that stun gun with caution, as we want our marks to be fit for release.'

'I'm sure she'll be okay,' Scott reassured him.

As they approached the airfield, the Cessna was taxiing back down the runway towards the hanger that Druker used to house his own plane. Scott pulled the Land Rover up to a convenient position, so that as soon as Roger got out of his plane, he could get straight in and they could get him back to the house.

The small aircraft stood for a few seconds, whilst Roger let the engine run, in order to do his final checks before shutting it down. Druker had got out of the Land Rover in readiness to greet him, and walked towards the small plane.

The door opened and Roger stepped out. He was a tall, skinny man in his fifties and had a full head of grey hair. His face lit up when he reached Druker, who gave him a huge smile. The two men shook hands and Druker invited him to get into the Land Rover for their short trip back to the house.

Roger always carried his bag, which had all

the equipment and solutions required to perform the procedure, which included the anaesthetic injections needed to put the patient out. The trackers were purchased by Druker and were held on site and he always hid them away in a cupboard in his house.

During the short drive, Druker explained about how the project was going and how he now had three marks. He explained that one had already been out in the wild, but had been brought back because of tourists. He told him about the two new marks, and in particular about the one in the round house. Druker was keen to see whether they would be able to have both tracker units fitted today. He also hoped to get them both out into the field.

Scott pulled the Land Rover up in front of the house and all three men got out.

'Would you like a coffee, Roger?' Druker asked.

'Yes, please, that would be lovely, with a biscuit if you have one. Or a piece of Mulubwa's cake would be even better, if she has made one,' Roger replied cheekily with a smile.

Druker looked at Roger, smiled back at him and, affecting a military stance, said, 'Coming up! No problem, sir! And I'll see if we have any cake for you, too.'

Turning to his chief aide, he said, 'Scott, whilst I organise that, will you take Roger to the operating room?'

'No problem, Druk. Come on, Roger, she

should already be there waiting for us,' Scott responded.

The two men walked off as Druker went into the house to get a coffee and a biscuit or cake for Roger.

CHAPTER FIFTY-FOUR

Druker joined Scott, Joshua, and Roger in the operating room where Carly was lying on one of the two tables in the middle of the floor. The room was brightly lit with fluorescent tubes and had been set up as a sterile unit under the guidance of Roger. The operating tables were made of aluminium and were really designed for animal operations. Whenever Druker entered the room, the clinical smell always hit him, as it was cleaned on a regular basis and the chemicals used would linger in the air.

Carly had already been sedated by Roger in readiness for the small procedure, and, as he arrived, Joshua and Scott were turning her over so that he could access the back of her neck.

Roger's vet bag was open and he was taking out the necessary tools to carry out the operation, and was waiting for Druker to bring the tracker unit for him to insert.

'Here you go, Roger, still in its packet ready to

go,' Druker said, as he passed him the new tracker unit.

By now Roger and the other two men were masked up and Scott handed out a further mask for Druker to put on. He opened the packet containing the tracker and before he sterilised it by immersing it into a cleaning fluid, he sorted out the battery and tested the unit with the tester it came supplied with. He then proceeded to clean the area on her neck, in preparation for the incision, covered it in iodine and then proceeded to carry out the small operation to insert the tracker.

'Good job, Roger,' Druker said to the vet, as he finished sewing up the very small incision with dissolvable stitches.

'Okay to send her out into the wild, Doc?' Druker asked, almost impatiently.

'I don't see any real reason not to, as I know you like to have them asleep when you put them out there, so yes, okay,' Roger replied.

'You said there was another one, Druker?' Roger asked, as he began to wash up and collect his tools.

'Yes, he's in the round house. I'll take you to him right away,' Druker replied.

Roger closed his bag and they all left the operating room together. The place where the other mark was being held was across the courtyard. It was a small, stone building with a thatched roof and was circular in shape. The door to it was made of a dark wood and the building had a number of small windows, which were all framed in the same dark wood. Each of the windows had a blind, which prevented any one from looking in.

The four men approached the building with Scott leading the way, as he was the one with the key to unlock the door, which he proceeded to do. He opened it and they all trooped in.

In the centre of the room was a bed with a naked man on it, with his arms and legs bound. The man had a blindfold covering his eyes, together with a mouth gag, so that he couldn't shout out. Joshua had put these on him earlier that day, firstly so that he couldn't see the vet, but secondly the mouth gag was to stop him from shouting, as he'd woken up earlier that day and begun to shout at the top of his voice, for all to hear.

The vet went over to the man and, as he stood by the bed, he opened his bag to get his sphygmomanometer to measure his blood pressure, together with his stethoscope to check his heart rate.

The man on the bed was now writhing and trying to escape. Noises of protest were coming from his gagged mouth, as he was now aware of the men in the room. Roger ignored these protests and asked Scott if he could restrain him, in order to take his blood pressure.

'It's a good sign that he is struggling like he is. There can't be too much wrong with him,' Roger explained, as he unfolded his sphygmomanometer and placed it around the man's right arm.

The man heard what Roger had said and, now that Scott and Joshua were holding him, was protesting even more, but he was no match for the strength of these two men that had no trouble in holding him still.

'If you don't stay still, I'll have no option but to inject you,' Roger told his patient.

With this the man settled down, but he continued with his verbal sounds, which no one in the room could understand, as he had the gag over his mouth.

After the vet had checked the man over, Roger indicated to Druker that he was fine. 'His blood pressure is a bit on the high side, as is his pulse rate, but then that's to be expected with what he is experiencing right now.'

'Thank you, Roger, so you think he is okay to have the procedure?' Druker asked.

'Yes, I don't see any reason not to, and it makes sense whilst I'm here. What I'll do is give him a sedative whilst he's here and then if we can get Scott and Joshua to transfer him to the operating room, I'll get straight to it,' Roger replied.

On hearing this, the man started to squirm even more, and made extra mumbling sounds through his gagged mouth.

Despite the man's movements and his mumbled protests, the vet prepared the injection to sedate him, and within seconds of the needle entering his skin, he went limp and fell quiet.

Scott and Joshua transferred him to a nearby trolley bed and then wheeled him to the operating room, whilst Druker and Roger followed on behind.

'I'm just going to get the other tracking device from the house, Roger,' Druker said, as the two men followed the trolley bed.

'Okay, Druker, no problem, I'll get started with the patient in preparing him for the insertion for when you return,' Roger replied.

Druker split off and went to the house to get another of the tracking devices. Each device cost Druker around $6,000, as they were the latest technology in miniature tracking. These small tracking devices could be put under the skin, and were still able to receive a GPS signal.

He went to his office to retrieve the next tracker and then headed back to the operating room. He was feeling pleased with himself about how his experiment was going, even though the first mark hadn't lasted long at all, but after the tracker had been fitted to Konner, he intended to get Scott to take both him and the woman out into the field right away.

When he arrived at the operating room, Carly was still lying on one table and was thankfully still unconscious. Konner was being prepared on the second operating table, with Roger and the other two men having masked up. He had already put the iodine on the area of skin on the back of Konner's neck, in preparation for the incision to insert the tracker.

'Ah, Druker, just in time. He's all ready to receive the tracker unit, once it's been sterilised, but please put your mask on again, before I start,' Roger said.

The small operation on Konner took no time at all, and soon Roger was stitching him up and finishing off.

'How long do you think they'll be unconscious for now, Roger?' Druker asked.

'Difficult to say for sure, but at least another half an hour I would say, but before I go I can top them both up with another small injection if you wish,' Roger offered.

'Yes, that would be good, as I don't want either of them to come around too soon. I want to get them out in the wild right away, before either of them wakes up,' Druker responded.

Roger got another syringe from his bag, and administered an injection to Carly in order to keep her asleep for at least another hour. He then took a slightly smaller dose for Konner and injected him too. After that he packed his things away ready to leave.

'Right lads, we're all done here,' Druker said. 'So get to it and take them both out, but make sure they are far enough away from each other as we dare, but not too far to cause us a problem should we need to evacuate either of them. May I suggest Area Two, away from Area Three where we evacuated Smith from yesterday.'

The men knew what to do and Druker left them to it, whilst he escorted Roger out of the operating room and back to the house.

'I can't stay, Druker. I have another visit I have to get to right away over at Mfuwe, so I'd better be off,' Roger explained.

'No problem, Roger. I'll get you back to your plane right away and then when I've done that, I'll pay your monies over right away,' Druker replied.

'Thank you, very much appreciated,' Roger said, as they both walked towards the Land Rover.

Druker waved Roger off at the air field and got back into the Land Rover to return to his house, whilst thinking, *'this is all working out just right.'*

As he arrived at the house, Scott and Joshua were just setting off with the two marks in the back of the other Land Rover. Scott waved at Druker as they disappeared in a cloud of dust.

CHAPTER FIFTY-FIVE

Graham came to, after what seemed like seconds to him, but when he did, Scott and his colleague had gone. His jaw and head were throbbing from the jolt he'd received from the stun gun. He gradually got up from where he lay. He wasn't really sure if it was the electric shock of the stun gun or the blow to his head that had knocked him out.

He looked over at Carly's cage, but she was gone. He knew where she might be and shivered with fear, knowing all too well what she would be going through right now.

'Oh, my god!' he said out loud. 'She's out there with the lions and other wild creatures.'

Night was drawing in, as the little light that filtered in through the small gaps between the wall and the roof lessened until he was plunged into complete darkness. He was surprised at how quickly the sun went down. As he lay there he wondered how he would ever get out of this situation and how he might escape. He also began to think about Carly again and what it must be like for her being out there in the dark. It was scary enough in daylight.

The air in the building was chilly now, so it had gone from one extreme to the other, as during the day it was very warm, but now he was feeling a bit cold. Being soaked earlier hadn't helped. There were no blankets and all he had was a hard, wooden floor to lie on and nothing for comfort.

'At least they could have given me a bed of sorts,' he whispered to himself.

He needed to go to the toilet again and had no choice but to do this in his cage, but he tried to keep it to one corner. After relieving himself he tried to curl up into as small a ball as possible in order to keep warm and to try to get some sleep.

As he lay there trying to fall to asleep, he heard a vehicle, which sounded like a Land Rover, draw up outside. The distinctive sound of the two diffs on the four-wheel drive vehicle came to a halt, and he then heard voices and the two doors slam shut, with the hollow metal sound of an open top vehicle.

He struggled to hear what they were saying, and managed to pick up a couple of words within the sentences, which confirmed that they had indeed left Carly somewhere out in the wilderness. He wondered if it was in the same placed they'd left him. He heard one say, 'I give that little bitch just twelve hours and she'll be eaten alive.' That was enough to know exactly who they were talking about and what they had done with her.

Graham shuddered with the horrible thought of this poor woman being out in the wild like he had been earlier, but at night. He couldn't think of a worse thing to happen, and he could only imagine how she must be feeling, having experienced this himself in the day-time.

CHAPTER FIFTY-SIX

After the two men returned from putting the two marks out into the wild, Scott immediately went to Druker's office, where his boss was looking at the tracking screen. The screen was showing two new dots that represented Prow and Hurley.

'So how did it go?' Druker asked.

'Well, we dropped Hurley off first and then dropped Prow off after that, and at the time they were both still out of it, but I don't think it will be long before either of them comes to,' Scott said.

'We put Hurley in the open area just outside Area Two, so he's actually just in Area Three. And we put Prow within the trees near where that small river leads into the Luangwa River,' he explained.

'Where we've put her, we noticed there was a large troop of baboons, and they caused a big commotion when we arrived,' Scott added.

'That will be interesting,' Druker reflected.

'Baboons have been known to attack larger animals, especially if they feel threatened and their territory is encroached upon.'

'Let's see what happens. She'll probably be awake now and will probably be really pissed off, as she is a bit of a feisty one,' Scott said.

Druker paused for a moment, then said, 'My suggestion is we wait until one of these two croak it and then send Smith back out right after that, but this time let's put him in the cave where we put Lane, in Area Two.'

'I think that's a good idea, boss,' Scott replied. 'It will be interesting to see if either of them survive the night, though.'

'Yes, they'll both be working very hard right now, as there's no let-up in the wild. There are no days off, no holidays. Nature respects no one but the strong,' Druker responded in a profound tone, which Scott had never observed him using before.

CHAPTER FIFTY-SEVEN

Konner awoke to a strange sound above his head. As he came to and opened his eyes, the sunlight blinded him. He squinted towards the bright sky, thinking, *'I must have fallen asleep, but how strange. The last thing I remember was being in some kind of round-shaped building.'* He then recalled a man coming in and gagging him to stop his shouting; he also remembered having a mask placed over his face.

When sat up, in order to work out where the noise was coming from, Konner realised that he was still totally naked. As his eyes final adjusted to the bright sunlight, he looked around to discover that he was in a field — or what appeared to be a field.

'How long have I been here for?' he thought.

The noise that he could hear was coming from some strange-looking birds that were circling over his head. A few of these birds had landed on the ground and were gathered around him. Startled, he then realised that these ugly birds, with their featherless heads, were vultures.

He considered for a moment why so many of these scavenging creatures might be around him. He then got it — vultures always gather at the site of a dead or dying animal. Quickly, he looked around to see what they might be interested in, but there was nothing. Then it came to him in a scary flash: *'Oh, my god, they are here for me! They think I'm dying or that I have died!'*

With this thought, he jumped to his feet, and although his only audience was a crowd of vultures, his modesty instincts made him cover his manhood with his hands. With him standing, the vultures took to the air, many letting out loud squawking noises at the same time. The vultures continued to circle in the sky above him.

'What on earth is this?' he wondered.

Then he thought back to what had happened. He remembered some men coming into the building where he was being held. At the time he was blindfolded, so he wasn't sure just how many men, but he remembered hearing a few different voices. He recalled them talking about a procedure and taking him to an operating room and then he remembered they'd injected him.

The bed he was in was in a round room with a number of windows, all of which were covered over. He recalled that within minutes of waking he had begun shouting for help. It was at this point that a tall, muscular man had come rushing in to tell him he'd better shut up or there'd be consequences, and then proceeded to stuff a gag in his mouth.

Konner recalled his futile resistance to what this man was doing and he'd continued his shouting until his shouts were muffled by the gag. There was not much that he could do, as his arms and legs were restrained at the wrists and ankles. He then recalled that this same man then put a blindfold on him, so that he was no longer able to see what was going on, either

As he looked down at his wrists, he could still see where the restraints had been, as the ties had left him bruised. There were similar marks on his ankles, too

'What is this?' he questioned out loud. 'What the hell is going on?'

As he surveyed the savannah, he still felt woozy, as some of the drugs continued to flow through his veins.

'Am I awake or is this one huge nightmare?' he questioned, and then pinched himself. *'Have I gone completely mad.'*

Suddenly he realised something. *'The man who gagged and bound me was the same man who shot me in the bush.'* Then he recalled his hunting trip with Bram and his shooting the lion. He remembered seeing the three magnificent creatures for the first time, which had all disappeared into the bush when they saw the Land Rover.

He recalled getting nervous when Bram had pulled the Land Rover up in the wooded area, especially when he'd told him to get out so they could then track the lions on foot. He remembered seeing the three lions in the clearing, with the larger of the three standing looking back at him and Bram.

Bram had whispered to him to take aim and to shoot, telling him to aim for its chest. This he had done without any questions, not wanting to miss the opportunity of his first lion kill – the lion had dropped immediately, as his bullet pierced its skin, entered the chest cavity had punctured its heart.

'Why the hell have they put me out here on my own?' he thought.

The ground under his bare feet was hard and it hurt him as he started to walk. He chose to walk away from the sun, which was beating down on his bare back. He no longer had the factor 50 sun cream he'd brought with him. So unless he could find some shade, his back would soon become burned and blistered.

The plain he was on seemed to stretch out for many kilometres and it was scattered with a few umbrella-shaped trees. He decided first to walk to the nearest one and sit under its branches. This would at least afford him a reprieve from the sun's rays whilst he contemplated his predicament and collected his thoughts.

As Konner approached the first acacia tree, he could see a herd of various large plains feeding animals. With the heat haze it was difficult to determine what the animals were, but he soon realised that where there were herbivores eating grass, there would usually be carnivores looking to eat them, too.

As he reached the acacia tree, his bare feet were already feeling extremely sore. The grass here was not a complete blanket like it was in his garden at home, but rather a patchy growth, between which was hard dirt and stones.

Thankfully, there was a bit of shade under the tree, so he decided to sit there for a while.

He settled down on the ground, but it wasn't at all comfortable on his bare skin. He had to get up again and brush away small stones and debris from the ground where he wanted to sit to minimise any discomfort. He then slowly lowered himself to the cleared area and thought to lean his back against the tree, using this as something to lean on. However, the bark, which looked a bit like a patchwork of peeling paper, was uncomfortable. It took him awhile to find a spot that didn't aggravate the skin on his back.

Whilst he was manoeuvring himself to find a place of comfort, he became aware of something in his neck. Reaching around, he found a small lump at the nape. He felt a small cut, which he didn't remember being there before. As he touched the lump, it moved, as if there were something under the skin like a small stone. He shuddered with the thought that he'd been through some kind of operation, and without his consent.

'Maybe this is what they were referring to when they talked about a procedure and the operating room, but what have they done to me?'

He looked apprehensively around where he sat

and wondered whether there might be some cameras watching his every move.

'But how could this be? They couldn't know which way I'd go after waking, so to have cameras in all directions is not realistic,' he concluded, but still kept looking around to see if he could see anything that resembled a camera.

'Perhaps they don't actually care where I am, so they aren't watching my every move,' his thoughts continued, *'so I might be stuck out here forever.'*

As Konner sat there he realised he was really thirsty and he scanned the plain for what might reveal a place where he could find water. He decided to wait under the tree until the sun had gone down in the sky, and only then would he make the effort to find somewhere to quench his thirst.

'Those bastards! But will I survive this ordeal?' he said out loud.

He could hear the herd of animals in the distance and recognised the sounds of both zebra and wildebeest. He remembered watching a wildlife program on the African plains and remembered the sounds they made. These made him feel very alone out here. The bleats and brays were not friendly, although he knew the beasts would not hurt him, but they made him feel extremely vulnerable and very far away from the safety of his apartment in New York City and his life there as a dentist.

He was more worried now about how he was

going to walk the distance to find water, not knowing which way to go. How far this might be was a problem. He considered for a moment what animals he might encounter on his way. He was sure these wouldn't only be the feathered kind he'd awakened to nor the herbivore kind he could see in the distance. He already knew there were lions in the region, but where were they in relation to the one he'd shot?

Just as he was having these thoughts, he caught some movement in the grass to his right.

CHAPTER FIFTY-EIGHT

Carly awoke with the sound of running water next to her ear and felt what appeared to be a rough bed beneath her. As she came to, she knew instantly that she was naked from top to bottom. As this realisation hit her, she sat up and looked around.

'Where the hell am I?' she said aloud to herself.

She felt extremely self-conscious, as she was not used to being naked, especially out in the open.

Confused and a bit dazed, she thought, *'What's going on?* She then shouted, 'Help!'

As her mind was beginning to clear, she recalled speaking with a naked man named Graham in a cage, whilst she was also caged and opposite him. She remembered him telling her that they were part of an experiment and that they were in Africa. She also recalled how she'd reacted in complete disbelief, thinking that this man was mad.

'Maybe Graham wasn't so mad after all. But in Africa?' she thought, as she looked around at the scenery.

She was suddenly aware that what this man had said was very likely true; it looked like she was now out in a wilderness, and if it was Africa, then that would also mean dangerous animals could be around, too.

She then recalled what had happened when she was in the cage — that a man told her to be quiet, but that she had panicked and ignored him. That he'd prodded her with a stun-stick. That she'd been thrown back against the cage, and must have blacked out. Now she found herself waking up here amongst the trees.

With these thoughts, she felt the back of her neck, which was still very sore from her ordeal. As she felt her nape, she could feel a lump there. The lump was not like a bruise, which is what she expected, but was different; there clearly was something under her skin the size of a large bean. Maybe this was as a result of hitting the cage bars, she thought to herself, but it did seem a bit strange, as it moved in her fingers under the skin like there was a foreign object there.

As she was remembering as much as she could about what had happened to her and realising that she was probably part of some kind of sick experiment, Carly's feelings of anger came back.

'Why me? Why have they brought me here? How dare these men treat me in this way! What

have I done to be caged and then put out into the wild, and without my clothes?' she ranted to herself in disgust, as she began again to crave a cigarette. Her usual habit of smoking twenty-plus cigarettes a day was going to be a huge challenge for her, as she wasn't going to be able to satisfy that need.

Feeling helpless, she tried to get to her feet, which she found a struggle, as she was just coming around from her ordeal and the effects of the anaesthetic she'd been given for the operation. The episode with the man prodding her with the stun gun in the cage only seemed like moments ago, but now she realised it could have been quite some time ago.

'They've managed to get me out here whilst I was knocked out. But how far am I away from the place with the cages?' she wondered.

Feeling helpless and extremely vulnerable, she began to walk. As she did, she realised that her feet were also bare. The ground where she was walking was hard and the stones dug into the soles of her feet.

She stood in a wooded area, which was next to a small river, trying to decide what to do next. She was thinking about the man with the prodding stick, feeling angry and at the same time wondering how to get to help. *'Surely there must be someone nearby to help me,'* she deliberated.

Despite being naked she didn't feel cold; instead, it felt unusually warm. As she looked up, she could see that the sky was a lovely blue colour, with not a cloud to be seen.

She returned to the memory of waking up in a coffin-like box. She remembered the men looking in when the lid was taken off, with the man called Blake being one of them. This was the man she'd met at her interview only a few days ago.

'They injected me. How dare they?' she said to herself indignantly, as she recalled what had happened.

She thought back to the interview and remembered the picture of the African plain with the elephants and giraffes behind Blake's desk. She also began to reflect on her interview again and what a strange experience it had been from beginning to end. She also thought about how she'd known instinctively that there was something wrong, a sixth sense perhaps of what was to come.

It was too late to change what had happened, but she wished she'd not gone to the interview at all.

Her thoughts turned to where she found herself and she thought again about how warm it felt.

'This is definitely not English weather. Maybe Graham is right about it being Africa,' she thought.

She then thought again about the coffin experience and how it felt like she was floating. *'So maybe I've been in an aeroplane, but how did they get me through the airport?'* she questioned.

Walking was difficult, as the ground beneath

her feet was rough. She wasn't used to having bare feet. She glanced down at her bare, white skin and stopped to look at her more than ample breasts, which had now begun to sag.

Her stomach was also bigger than it should be, which obstructed her view of her female parts and her bush, which she'd never taken care of and had simply let grow.

Her stream of thoughts was suddenly broken when she heard a sound and realised she was not alone. There was movement in the trees on her side of the river. The sound was a bit like a barking dog, but surely there were no dogs out here.

Carly froze to the spot; her heart was in her mouth and the adrenalin in her blood raised her heart's rate to what felt like an alarming level.

CHAPTER FIFTY-NINE

After having dinner with Scott, which had been a large T-bone steak with fries and all the trimmings, Druker returned with him to his office. The pair went straight to the tracking screen to see what was happening with the marks.

The dot representing Konner had moved some distance, but then it had come to a complete stop. The one with Prow's name attached to it had also moved from where it had been to begin with, but not as much. However, it had moved enough for Druker to know she was awake and experiencing the wild, which is the part he loved about his experiment.

'One down, three to go,' Druker said.

'That one is a bit feisty, believe it or not,' Scott said, pointing to Carly's dot.

'Yes, these fuckers sit around all day on their fat arses and then when you bring them out here, they get all righteous and fight for themselves,' Druker snorted.

'Yes, I know; they still feel like they're owed something for some reason,' Scott replied in his mixed English and South African accent.

'Why don't we let Smith out again, as he's been a bit of a pain like Prow?' he asked.

'As I said earlier, let's wait until one of these is terminated, and then we'll put him out in the cave,' Druker replied, adding, 'I think having two marks out at a time is more than enough for us to track. If we had three out and some two-bit tourists came wandering along, as they often do, getting three of these suckers back would be a bit more of a challenge.'

Druker took another swig of red wine, which he'd poured after opening a new bottle of Château Lafite Rothschild.

'Hurley seems to have stopped for quite a while now, whereas Prow has kept moving. Night will be setting in soon, so I wonder if something has happened to him.'

Scott thought about this for a second, then replied, 'It seems quite soon for him to have been attacked by something, but I guess it's possible, as there are lions and those hyenas about where he is.'

They both watched the screen intently as just one of the dots was moving very slowly, whilst the other remained in one place.

CHAPTER SIXTY

Konner soon realised that he'd observed a cheetah moving slowly through the grass, and following behind were a couple of her cubs. Not really too sure whether this was a dangerous situation or not, he remained as still as he could, hoping that the cheetah wouldn't see him and continue walking by.

Fortunately for him, the cheetah either didn't see him or wasn't too bothered by his presence, and walked off into the distance with her offspring in tow.

By now the sun was getting lower in the sky. He was still surprised at how quickly it began to set, which was totally different to where he lived in America.

As the sunlight dimmed, he got up from his resting place to continue walking. He decided to go in an easterly direction, knowing that the sun set in the west. He had no idea if this was the right or wrong decision, but he had to walk somewhere, otherwise he'd simply die of dehydration by remaining where he was.

Before he had made very much progress, a spectacular sunset began to appear. Ordinarily, he might have appreciated such a wonderful scene, but in the circumstances, it was very difficult to enjoy all the colours.

However, Konner did decide to turn and watch the sun finally disappear below the horizon. He could almost visibly see it move towards the distant ground, turning the sky above it into a beautiful palette of deep oranges and reds spread out across the African sky. He watched a flock of birds fly across the scene, then the hues of deep colours finally gave way to a dark night sky. It was as if someone had switched the lights off, and he felt the night suddenly close in on him.

In the dark, the crickets came to life, as if someone had also flipped a switch on a huge, ratcheting machine. Each cricket rubbed its legs together, as if to outdo the others in a noise battle. The sound didn't comfort him at all; instead, it reminded him about how exposed he was in the dark in the middle of an African plain.

As he looked at the night sky, he was amazed at how bright the stars were. They were all so vivid! Konner had never seen a night sky like it, but he understood that the phenomenon he was witnessing was due to the absence of any light pollution.

Knowing why the stars were so vibrant made him realise just how far away he was from any civilisation. There were absolutely no people or houses nearby to create the type of light pollution he was used to around where he lived, so although he stood in amazement at the wonder of the sight before him, he was feeling a bit lost with what it represented to him right now.

He knew about how to find the North Star, though, so he looked for the 'Plough,' which he knew was an easy way to identify the group of seven stars that he thought looked more like a saucepan.

Once he'd found them, he could simply look along what are known as the pointer stars. These were the stars that made up the far edge of the saucepan. The North Star lay about five times the distance between these two pointers in the direction they pointed, and north lay directly under this star. So he simply needed to keep the North Star on his left shoulder. So even though he wasn't sure if this was the right way, at least he'd be moving consistently in one direction.

Walking carefully now, the darkness around him seemed oppressive. There was no moon to light the way, so the ground in front of him was hard to see. His eyes had adjusted to the dim light as much as they were going to, but he still couldn't really see where he was going. Quite often, he found himself treading on stones and what seemed like thorns, which made him wince.

Despite this pain and discomfort, he knew that he had to keep moving. He was now even thirstier than before. The anxiety he felt — something he'd never felt before — was made worse when he was unsure whether the direction he was walking was the right one.

In the distance, he heard the sounds of wild animals — sounds that were unfamiliar to him but that were too close for comfort. And, to his horror, he realised they were straight ahead of him.

Konner immediately stopped dead in his tracks. He felt his heart rate jump to a level he'd never experienced before. The night was impenetrable. No matter how much he stared in the direction of the sound, he was not able to see a thing — although he wasn't too sure if he wanted to see what he'd heard.

Not feeling safe going toward where the sounds had come from, he changed his direction. His biggest fear now was that some huge creature would suddenly appear out of the night and jump at his throat.

Although he was in an expanse of open plain, he felt somehow like he was in a dark and enclosed room. His senses were at an all-time high. His hearing seemed to be heightened, and he was more alert than he could ever remember being.

His heart was pounding, as the adrenalin flowed freely through his veins. 'Please, God, forgive me my sins. Please help me get through this,' he whispered.

Sensing movement to his left, he heard an animal in the grass. He strained once again to look into the dark, trying desperately to adjust his eyes to see what he'd heard. His heart thundered to another level, so he could even hear the sound of his blood pumping around in his head, as the arteries and veins around his ear drums sounded out the rhythm of each cardiac beat.

The next thing he heard was like an old man laughing in slow motion, another sound he had never experienced before. He was being stalked, but he wasn't quite sure why they hadn't attacked.

'I'm easy prey, but maybe they don't know that yet,' he thought.

He dared to continue his slow walk. And then he heard the sound of the slow laughing sound again, as if he were being taunted by a group of bullies. But it wasn't the laugh of a person he heard — it was some kind of animal, which appeared to be mocking him. The next sound he heard was similar to a screeching bird, but he was sure they weren't birds. Whatever they were, they seemed to be closing in on him.

Stubbing his foot on a rock, he stumbled and fell to the hard ground. His bare skin was cut as he hit the African dirt, but he quickly got up and looked around.

As he stood, he could still hear the sound of these strange creatures, followed by a loud growling, which was even closer than any of the other sounds so far. He was convinced that this was a lion. He froze to the spot. If it was possible, another full dose of adrenalin pumped into his blood stream to make his already fast-beating heart beat even faster. Even more than before, it felt like his heart was about to jump out of his chest and present itself as a ready meal for these creatures of the night.

As he strained to look around, trying to work out where the first attack might come from, directly in front of him he could just about make out a tree, albeit a very vague shape in the dark.

Thinking, '*Climb the tree. Get away from these creatures and sit out the night.*'

CHAPTER SIXTY-ONE

As Carly stood next to the river, she couldn't see what was moving the trees, but it wasn't too far away and now she was scared. All she could think to do was to scream at the top of her voice to try and scare whatever it was in the trees away. It seemed to work, as the movement stopped for now and it didn't bark again.

She was painfully aware of how thirsty she was, so she fumbled towards the river's edge and dipped her toes in the water, wondering whether it would be okay to drink.

The water didn't look very clean. *'What if it's contaminated?'* she thought, as she had no idea where she was or where the river came from.

The need for a drink was more overpowering than her logical reasoning of whether it was okay to drink or not. Her mouth was parched, which had been the case ever since she'd awoken.

She leaned down to the water's edge, cupped her hands, and took a drink. The water was cool, and although it tasted a bit strange, it was refreshing to her parched mouth and throat.

When she got up from the river's edge, she began to get more concerned, as it was beginning to get dark; she could see the sun starting to set.

'I can't believe that I'm out here in the jungle naked and all alone and it's getting dark,' she thought. *'I must find somewhere to hide for the night.'*

Hobbling across the rocks and ground next to the river, she began to make her way downstream, searching for a likely place to hide. All around were tall trees. Previously where she had seen blue sky through their gaps, this had changed to a darker blue. She could see the orange of the sunset coming through the trees ahead.

To her right, Carly spotted a small clump of bushes, which were closer together than any of the other bushes around. She made her way over to this area, as she thought she could use this as shelter for the night.

She knelt down and crawled into the bushes and lay on the ground, trying to conceal herself as much as she could. She managed to break off a few of the branches to put around her, which would help to disguise her position from any passing animals.

She was surprised at how quickly it had gone dark, which caught her out. In the UK, night came much more gradually than this. All of a sudden she was under an African bush in the dark and all alone, with her heart racing. Suddenly she could hear the sound of crickets that were all around her. It was as if someone had flicked a switch for them all to come alive as soon as it went dark. She couldn't see a thing, so even if an animal were stalking her, she wouldn't be able to see it coming.

The ground where she lay was also very uncomfortable. She knew that she wouldn't get very much sleep, if any at all, as her fear would probably keep her awake.

Then she could hear a high-pitched squeaking sound, which was very close to where she lay, and then there were other unfamiliar noises that seemed to come from all directions. It was as if the woods had come to life, simply because it had gone dark. It seemed as if the darkness was closing in on her, too, so she tried to curl up into as tight a ball as she could. She even put her hands over her ears to block out the sounds, but this didn't work very well. She lay there terrified and alone.

CHAPTER SIXTY-TWO

Konner was still frozen to the spot for an instant, switching his stare from one direction to the next, not really knowing where to go from here. Climbing the tree seemed the best option right now, but that meant moving again.

He finally gathered the strength to move towards the tree, and just as he reached the trunk and stretched up to climb it, he caught a glimpse of something running across in front of him. He very quickly grabbed the branches above his head, as the shape of the creature could just be made out in the darkness.

His worst nightmare had become a reality. A large, maned lion was staring up at him. As the huge creature suddenly made a fast move towards him, he also heard something move directly behind him.

He was surrounded by a pride of lions. *'I'm being hunted!'* he thought.

As he grappled to move higher in the branches,

he sensed the lions surging forward. Then he reached up for the next branch above his head and slipped back. The bark on the tree was sharp on his hands and on his already cut feet.

Its roughness was tearing into his broken skin, but the fear of being eaten alive kept him pushing forward. The adrenalin helped to anaesthetise the pain his cuts would ordinarily have caused. He regained his hold on the branches and managed to get a good footing, as he heard one of the lions at the base of the tree.

He heard the sound of claws against the bark below him, as one of the huge creatures stretched up, trying to catch his legs. He reached up further into the branches of the tree, but suddenly felt a sharp pain in his leg, as the lion's claws hooked him from below. Fortunately for him, the lion couldn't manage to get a good hold, as it was also struggling to climb the tree at the same time.

When the big cat let him go, he managed to move this leg further up the tree, and was able to climb higher into the branches. The fear of being chased was almost too much, as he grappled to get up and away from the what he realised was an attacking lioness.

The thorns of the tree spiked into his skin, too, as he lifted his body up and his head was forced into the foliage and the hard thorns above him.

The thorns, which were there to discourage animals from grazing on the leaves, pierced his bare skin like pins being stuck into a pin cushion. His white flesh began to ooze dark, red blood from each of these pin-prick holes.

He paused for a moment to feel his skin where he'd been stabbed, and he could feel the blood oozing from his wounds. His hand was now wet with his own fresh blood, which he was sure the lions would smell from below. This realisation spurred him to keep climbing, even though he was scared of heights.

Ever since he was a boy, he had never liked to climb ladders and didn't even like tall buildings, but his fear of what lurked below far outweighed his acrophobia. All he wanted to do was to escape.

As Konner worked his way up and into the safety of the branches above, he kept telling himself, *'Lions can't climb trees.'* He would be safe up here for now, he hoped, although every time he stopped to check his footing, he could hear the noises of the lions below, growling with frustration and scratching at the bark of the trunk.

Finding it difficult to see where he was going, and not too sure how high the tree was, Konner struggled on, actually unsure whether lions could climb or not.

The dangers lurking below seemed so far removed from his normal routine at home. And he'd been out here only a few days to shoot at these lions, so it felt surreal to him. It was as if he'd been placed into some weird movie, in which at any point he'd spot the camera and the director would shout 'Cut!'

His head continued to bash into the thorn-covered branches above him. The more he pushed on and up the tree, the more his body was being cut to shreds.

He could never imagine climbing a tree as a kid. His friends would always tease him for being a wimp as they climbed for apples and he didn't. So how he'd managed to get to this point was a bit of a surprise to him.

Konner pushed further and further up into the branches of the tree, trying to find a safe stopping place. He pushed his back against the narrowing trunk and peered down. He could hear the lions in their hunting frenzy below, but couldn't see much at all, which only added to his fear. He imagined suddenly seeing the piercing eyes of a lion making its way up the tree, and he could see the face of the lion he'd shot, as vivid as if it were real.

'Surely, if I can get up high enough, I'll be safe,' he thought. *'Lions can't climb trees,'* he kept trying to convince himself.

'Maybe if I get to a safe point in the tree, someone will find me tomorrow and help me get away from here.'

As he had this thought, he felt the lump in his neck again. He was now convinced that it was something they had placed under his skin, and was what they had referred to as 'the procedure.'

'They've put a tracking device under my skin,' he thought.

CHAPTER SIXTY-THREE

Carly tried various positions under her temporary bush-covered bed, but there was not one that made it any more comfortable than another.

It was so dark that she could hardly see a thing, but her eyes had adjusted somewhat to the night and she could now just about make out the bushes above her head, so she decided to try and gather a few of the leaves for temporary bedding.

The few that she could gather, she put on the ground around where her bottom was sitting. This helped a bit, but she now wished that she had managed to get some grass to lie on, but it had gone dark so quickly that she didn't have time. Not only was it too dark to see where the grass was now, but there was no way she was going to start walking around out there, either.

She knew that this was going to be a very long night. She continued to listen to the various animal noises, with each new one making her jump. Her heart rate continued at a high level, as adrenalin was being pumped though her body.

Right now she thought that a cigarette would help calm her nerves, and she was struggling with having had this luxury taken away. *'How dare they treat me like this,'* she thought.

Then she remembered Graham again, the man in the cage next to her who had tried to fill her in on what was going on. He had seemed kind. For a brief moment, she fantasised that they could get together when this ordeal was all over and be friends.

'Maybe we'd meet at the Railway Tavern in Chelmsford for a pint,' she thought. *'I'd tell him my story and offer him a cigarette.'*

But as she lay there, she could still feel her heart. She worried whether it would be able to cope with beating at such a high rate for such a long time. She didn't think that it would be possible to sleep at all, with this heightened level of anxiety. She began to wonder how animals ever managed to sleep, with the constant fear of an attack.

'How on earth am I going to continue with this?' she thought. *'This is my first night, and if I don't get any sleep tonight, what about tomorrow?'*

It was only now that she began to have a realisation about her own life back home. *'I've never really appreciated what I have, nor how easy I have it,'* she thought. *'Perhaps this guy Blake is trying to help us see a way forward, and at the interview with him, he was testing me. I know that now.'*

'I need to find this guy and appeal to his good side. I need to speak with Blake, and tell him that his test has worked on me.'

Then her thoughts turned back to reality. *'I need to get through the night. I need to somehow survive this.'*

Out here alone and in the dark, she also began to think about her dad and how she missed him. As she did, tears began to flow and then she began to sob uncontrollably. Her sobbing was interrupted by the sound of something out in the dark, a new sound.

'What was that?'

Her heart rate suddenly rose, as a fresh load of adrenalin flowed into her veins. She lay there waiting to see if she could hear the sound again, but all was quiet, except for the noise of the crickets.

Trying to see into the darkness, she stared in the direction of the noise she'd heard, but actually hoped that she wouldn't see what had made it. She was scared that, whatever it was, the animal was stalking her and would suddenly pounce out of the darkness to eat her alive. The seconds ticked by and turned to minutes. It seemed like hours to her, yet there were no further sounds.

She tried to get herself comfortable again, but she couldn't relax, as she had to stay alert just in case something appeared out of the blackness. She tried to imagine what animals might be out there, and to visualise what creature might have made that last sound, which was a bit like the gruff rumble of a dog, but, like everything else, it was also unfamiliar to her. And the likelihood of there being any dogs out here was remote. Even if there were, they'd probably be wild and unfriendly. Her eyes were wide open and she dared not close them, for fear of falling asleep and being attacked whilst she slept.

'Please, please help me. I don't want to die,' she said out loud. 'I'll do whatever you want,' she said, hoping that some human might hear what she was saying.

Then the sound came again, but this time it was much louder and nearer to where she lay. She sat up and looked out into the dark. Her heart was now pounding again and she was convinced that she was being stalked by whatever this animal was. She decided to scream at the top of her voice, hoping this would scare it away.

Her screaming stopped and all went silent — or what seemed like silence, after she had screamed so loud. Her screams had not had any effect on the crickets, which continued with their night-time concert, irrespective of what was happening around them. This frustrated Carly, as it made it more difficult to listen for other sounds, like a stalking animal.

'I'm a sitting duck,' she thought, *'and there's nothing I can do about it.'*

She had no idea what time it was, nor how long she'd been under the bush since it had gone dark, but it felt like hours. She sat there with her heart palpitating and wondered how long it would be before she would see the sun rise.

'What if I never see the sun again?' she thought. *'I just want Blake to give me a chance and to see that I'm willing to make changes in my life.'*

All she could do was huddle and wait and listen for more animal sounds, but time ticked by so slowly, and she knew that even if she were to survive, it was going to be a very long night.

CHAPTER SIXTY-FOUR

Konner was by now up in the higher branches of the umbrella tree. He was as far up as he thought he could possibly get, but he could still hear the lions below. He pushed himself hard against the bark of the main tree trunk again, which dug into his bare flesh. He spread his legs apart onto two separate branches, giving him as much balance as possible, should he need to kick out at his attackers.

The deep, echoing growl of the huge male lion sent a shiver up his spine and made him wish he had his rifle right now. He reached his arms behind his back and gripped hard to the tree trunk. He looked down again, relieved in some part that he couldn't see the ground below. But he had created an image of lions in the dark, slowly climbing the tree.

As he looked harder and peered through the branches, he could just make out the shapes of lions circling the base of the tree — there seemed to be about six in total, but he couldn't be sure, as the dark made it difficult to get an exact count. They were looking up at him with their deep, piercing eyes.

Then he saw a lioness lurch at the trunk of the tree, putting her huge claws on the bark, and he began to climb higher once again. He gripped tighter to the trunk behind him and pushed his feet into the branches, as his heart pounded.

Using her claws like grappling hooks, the lioness's muscle sinews rippled as she tried to cling on to the tree. She was desperate to get to what seemed like an easy meal.

Knowing that her prey was up in the branches, she worked her way up the trunk bit by bit, whilst he watched in horror, seeing for the first time that lions actually can climb trees.

'Surely, they're not built for this,' he thought, as in all the animal programs he'd watched, there wasn't one he'd seen showing lions climbing trees.

'They must be extremely hungry.'

His legs were shaking violently and he thought he might lose his footing, or that his legs might collapse. The branches where he'd got to were beginning to get a lot thinner, so he daren't go any higher for fear of them giving way. But the lioness was making slow progress towards him.

He looked up to survey the part of the tree that was above him, and as he did, he got a glimpse of the starry night sky. The sky was the deepest black and the stars appeared even closer and brighter than he'd ever noticed before. It seemed ironic that he'd be looking at a beautiful night sky, whilst he had a pride of lions in a frenzy below, all waiting to feast on him.

Each pinprick of light that represented a star was millions, if not billions, of light years away. A seeming impossibility that he could see these stars so far away, and as he looked into the blackness and the almost abysmal feeling of the African sky, it made him feel vulnerable and alone. It was a feeling so deep that it made him suddenly go spacey, and have what felt like an out-of-body experience. It was a sensation that he'd never felt before, and as he was now a bit unsteady, he held on even more tightly to the branches around him.

It was the sound of the lion's claws against the bark below him that suddenly brought him back to face his grim situation. The lioness crawled even higher, as she gripped the flaking bark of the tree. She used her powerful back legs to push herself higher still.

She had now reached a split in the tree and was getting much too close for comfort. The lioness had fixed her gaze on him with a determined look of predatory meaning. This terrifying look sent a primal shiver down Konner's spine, a feeling he'd never experienced before — a feeling that must in some way be an almost daily occurrence for the local wildebeest and other wildlife living out here. It was a feeling that was lost on modern man. He knew this look, though, but the last time he saw it was when he had been peering through the telescopic sight on his rifle only a few days ago.

The lioness was just starting up the next set of branches towards where he sat, when she lost her footing and fell backwards. One of the larger branches broke her initial fall, but as she tried to get her balance, she spun and fell the rest of the way to hit the hard African ground below. As she reached the bottom, she was met by the growling pride, as if they were disappointed in her failure.

He stood with his back against the tree, watching intently, as the lioness that had struggled to get to him, was now pacing around with the rest of the pride at the base of the tree. Relieved to see her fall, he was also surprised she got up and shook herself off, without any obvious signs of injury.

He hadn't realised it, but he'd been holding his breath and now started to breathe again. His heart was still pounding away inside his ribcage, pumping his adrenalin-rich blood around his more than tired body.

The lions were still circling like vultures, as if watching and waiting for their meal to die on the plain. He could still make out a couple of the pride, walking with purpose, around the base of the tree. Every now and again, one would lurch up at the tree with its front paws and look up through the branches at Konner. Each time they did, he would hold his breath, hoping that none of them was a good climber, and he hoped they would eventually move away.

After what seemed like an eternity, and still

frozen against the tree, he stared down at the ground, gradually seeing fewer and fewer lions. Finally, he could no longer see them at all. It looked like they were giving up on their meal — for now.

He felt a slight sense of relief as the lions decided to move away and off into the dark. This whole ordeal seemed to drag on for hours, but since he no longer had his watch, as this had obviously been taken away from him at the same time as his clothes were removed, he had no way of knowing how much time had passed.

Even though the lions appeared to have given up, he was sure that the pride would still be lurking around nearby. So he wasn't safe yet. His predicament was still extremely precarious; he was still stuck up in a tree and still surrounded by wild animals. He now hoped that they had gone searching for one of their more traditional meals of an African evening.

Konner new he was dehydrating and soon would become very hungry. As he stayed propped in the branches of the umbrella tree, he knew that it was going to be a very long night ahead, and he was unlikely to get much sleep.

He did move around to make himself a bit more comfortable, whilst trying to avoid the thorns that were everywhere, but this was difficult to do in the dark.

He knew he would have to spend the rest of the night where he was, rather than risk climbing down. He would wait until it was light, when he would be able to see if danger lurked, if the lions were still nearby and ready to pounce. He also worried that if he did manage to drop off to sleep, he might fall from the branches.

The sounds of the animals were all around him and seemed to make an empty space appear enclosed and claustrophobic, if that were possible, in what was one of the most open spaces in the world. He was not sure how far his trek across the plain had taken him, nor whether in the morning he'd be able to find water and something to eat, but he would now make every effort to move during the day instead of at night, and to find somewhere safe to hide before darkness fell. Also, he was still hopeful that tomorrow he might be able to find someone to help him.

A night full of demons and a place where he was no longer safe seemed to bring up primeval feelings from deep inside, feelings he'd never known he could have. They seemed to be coming from a place that had lain dormant in his body, waiting for a moment like this to stir and come forward. He knew now that he was a part of the food chain, not at the top. Instead of being the hunter, he'd now become the hunted.

The safety of home and being able to walk down the street feeling secure seemed like a long way away, a place he wasn't certain he'd get to see again. The very slim chance of being mugged whilst walking the streets at night, which he did worry about on occasion, paled in significance to being on the food menu out here on an African plain.

As he began to reflect on what had happened to him, he thought again that perhaps there might be someone watching him from a camera, some weird, sadistic person waiting to see how and when he got eaten by a lion. He then touched the lump on his neck. *'This has to be some sort of tracking device they've inserted in me, so they know exactly where I am,'* he thought once more.

This made absolute sense. Otherwise, it would be virtually impossible to find him again — assuming they would want to find him, that is. In a very small way this actually made him feel slightly safer, as he knew that, although these men were obviously crazy in some way, someone could know where he was. It also meant that perhaps if he could survive for a couple of days, they might well come and pick him up, and then he would have a chance of escape.

With these thoughts and, as he sat in the tree knowing he was safe for a while, the adrenalin levels in his blood abated. He began to become acutely aware of the pain in his body, mainly from his feet after walking across the plain, but also from the gouge in his calf caused by the lion. Added to this were the numerous scratches and holes in his skin from the umbrella tree thorns.

He began to worry about whether his wounds might get infected, especially the one from the lion's claws, although he knew in some ways this was the least of his problems.

Since he also knew there was no way of

disinfecting his injuries out here, his feelings of worry soon turned to anger — anger at his kidnappers, people he hadn't even seen except for the face of the man who had shot him with a dart.

CHAPTER SIXTY-FIVE

He was exhausted, but after what seemed like an eternity, he eventually fell asleep on the hard floor of the cage. When Graham awoke, not quite sure how long he'd been out, he could see light coming in though the corrugations along the roof line, so he knew it was morning.

He wondered how Carly was doing, having spent a night out in the wild. *'I wonder whether she is still alive or did an animal get her in the night,'* he thought.

He'd woken up hungry, as he'd not eaten much at all yesterday, but he didn't dare ask for anything to eat for fear of being hit with the stun gun again. So he sat there in his cage and waited.

After he had sat there for what felt like an hour or so, he heard footsteps approaching the building.

The bolts on the door, which were now familiar to him, sounded and the door opened. The man who entered went over to where the dog food was kept, and, as Graham's eyes were adjusting to the new light coming in, he could make out that the man was Scott, who grabbed a food bowl and filled it with the dry food. He brought it over to his cage, whilst Graham watched, not daring to mutter a word.

'So, do you want it smashed on the floor again or are you going to be a good animal today?' Scott tormented.

'Animal, he called me an animal,' Graham thought and wondered how to respond.

In the end, he said nothing, just stared at Scott and waited for him to give him the food. Instead of giving it to him, though, he put it down outside of his cage and said, 'You stink again, so you need hosing down.'

'Please, no, I hate that, please!' Graham pleaded, as Scott walked off towards where the hose was kept.

He returned with it, turned it on and pointed it towards Graham and his cage. The water was warm to begin with, but then turned cold, as he was blasted with a powerful jet of water. As he tried to move out of the line of fire, Scott moved the nozzle to wherever he'd moved, so Graham closed his eyes to avoid getting water in them. After a few moments of firing water directly at him, Scott did eventually redirect the jet and clean the cage floor, so that the urine and faeces were washed away into the channel that ran across the back of the building.

'There you go, clean again,' Scott said in a sarcastic voice. 'Now, do you want your food?'

'Yes, please,' Graham said begrudgingly, as he sat there dripping wet.

Before he gave him the food, he filled the water holder with the hose, then wound it back onto its reel.

Scott returned to the side of his cage and stood there for a moment. To one side of the cage and next to where the water holder was, there was a smaller access designed for passing food through. As Scott put the food bowl through this access hatch, he said, 'There you go. You'd better eat this all up, as I doubt whether your girlfriend and the other man we set free yesterday will be alive this morning, then it'll be your turn again.'

'My turn. Why are you doing this to us?' Graham dared to question.

'Because we enjoy it,' Scott said, as he turned and walked away.

Graham was left hanging with this last comment. He shook his head and wondered how someone could be so unkind to a fellow human being. *'What makes someone like that?'* he thought, as he looked down at his dry-looking breakfast of dog food and began to eat.

CHAPTER SIXTY-SIX

Night eventually gave way to light, and Carly saw the sky turning blue again as the sun began to rise. She had not slept at all the whole night, and her bottom was very sore from sitting in one position for so long. The few leaves she'd managed to put under her hadn't really helped at all.

She stood up and moved out from under the bush where she'd spent the night and began walking very slowly back towards the small river. She never walked particularly fast, anyway, but now this was made even harder because her feet still hurt from their ordeal yesterday.

Carly was thirsty and, despite the discolouration of the flowing river, the sight of the water this morning was a good one. It looked refreshing as she tried to work her way down the riverbank, being careful where she put her feet.

She reached the water's edge and placed her left foot slowly into the water, which was cool to the touch and soothing. Then she stood there in her bulky birthday suit letting the water soothe both feet for a while.

Tears began to run down her face as she realised how vulnerable she was. She looked around at the landscape she'd never seen before, except on TV nature programs, and began to realise the enormousness of her situation.

She looked down at her feet, which were completely immersed in the dirty-looking water, then looked out across the undulating surface and wondered what creatures might lurk beneath the surface and further down.

'Are there any crocodiles?' Carly pondered with dread, and with this thought, her heart jumped.

Still feeling thirsty, she decided that she had no choice but to drink. Even though it was river water, it hadn't done her any harm the day before. Her mouth was dryer than she'd ever known, so she knew she was dangerously dehydrated and had to drink as much as she could.

Carly crouched down to drink, but as she did, her left foot slipped and she fell backwards into the water.

The fall was so unexpected, she let out a loud scream and then felt the impact on her side of something hard on the river bed, an object that dug into her naked skin.

Lying in shock in the river, she struggled to get up, but as she sat up, her more than ample bottom remained in the river mud, with water swooshing around her as it continued its journey downstream.

She looked down at her side, where she had hit the hard object, and, sure enough, whatever it was had broken her skin. Bright, red blood flowed out from the gash and down her side. As it entered the water, it turned immediately light red, but within seconds the colour had dissipated and merged into the river water.

Carly sobbed, as she now realised her predicament had just gotten worse. She already knew she wasn't built for an African experience, but now with cuts and bruises down one side, she might get infected, too.

As she sat there in the water, which was actually quite soothing, she cupped the water and washed it over herself, washing away the surface blood that was now running down her bare skin. As soon as she washed the blood away, more appeared from the deep cut. The skin around the cut was already starting to bruise badly and beginning to turn red, with other areas changing to a dark blue.

Tears flowed now, as she was so distressed and in such pain, without any real hope of rescue. She also began to fear the smell of her blood might attract predators, since she had no idea whether there might be animals out there already aware of her predicament.

Her parched throat reminded her that she still hadn't drunk any water. So, despite the pain she was now feeling, she cupped her hands to drink the life-giving liquid.

It was difficult to keep her hands together to get much water to her mouth, as they were trembling so much. As she drank the first palm full, the earthy taste she remembered from yesterday returned. But it was refreshing and it wasn't too unpleasant, so she cupped her hands yet again to drink more.

Finally, having satisfied her immediate thirst, Carly decided to get out of the water, but as she moved again she realised how painful her cuts and bruises were. She dared not stand up fully in the river, for fear of slipping once again, so she semi-crawled in an arched position, with her feet and hands feeling their way along in a crab-like motion, until she'd reached the relative safety of the riverbank.

As she reached it with her hands and then her feet, she climbed out and onto dry land and stood up. She turned to look back at the river, relieved that she'd managed to get out.

As she was watching the water, she saw something moving in the muddy flow. She froze to the spot when she realised what it was — a large python, its head above the water as it meandered downstream. And it seemed to be looking at her.

'Oh, my god!' she thought.

She had a real phobia of snakes and to see one so big was terrifying.

'As if it wasn't already enough to be dumped in the middle of Africa, I now have to contend with a snake.'

Her heart started to pound even harder than it

had during the night, as the very thought of snakes in the water she had just drunk from was overwhelming.

'What if it had swum by when I was sitting in the river?' she thought and shuddered.

Suddenly, Carly felt even more alone and vulnerable. She watched as the snake swam off into the distance until she could no longer see it. She stood there for a few moments, not daring to move, just in case it came back or she saw another one.

Then, as she began to walk slowly along the side of the river, with her eyes now riveted to the flowing water, she wondered if she'd wake up and discover that this had all been a big nightmare.

Just as she was thinking that, something caught her eye. A huge creature was blocking the path directly in front of her!

She stared at the animal and it stared back, as if it were weighing her up. Its golden-yellow eyes were fixed on her. Instantly, her heart was in her mouth and pounding away again.

CHAPTER SIXTY-SEVEN

Konner looked out into the dark from his tree prison, hoping to see some glimmer of light — perhaps there might be a house in the distance or someone with a fire. But nothing. The only lights were the stars above him, and as he looked up in wonder at the millions of sparkling lights, he once again realised how alone he really was.

Had it not been for his situation, he might have been able to appreciate the wonder and beauty of the scene above him. Instead, he could only worry about what he would do when the light returned in the morning.

Time seemed to stand still. Minutes seemed like hours, and hours felt like days, as he perched in the tree, not daring to move. He could still hear the sounds of animals, none of which was familiar, in the dark night around him, but every sound made him feel even farther away from home.

Tears welled up in his eyes, as he considered how helpless he felt. '*What am I going to do in the morning?'* he thought. *'Sure, I'll be able to see again, but the animals will still be out there and waiting to eat me.'*

Thinking about what to do to quench his thirst and satisfy his hunger, he thought about eating the leaves in the tree. Not knowing whether they would be poisonous or even if it would help much, but realising that if he had nothing to eat or drink he'd die anyway, he reached out, grabbed a few leaves and put them into his parched mouth. The smooth surface of each leaf crunched as he bit through its hard, outer coating.

The leaves tasted somewhat like iron and they were quite hard to chew, but nonetheless he could taste their moisture as he crushed them between his teeth. Not the best meal he had ever eaten, but at least it might provide some fluids until morning, when he hoped to go looking for a river or lake. He knew it was the beginning of the rainy season here in Zambia and that the rains had begun to fall, so there should be water in the rivers, if he could manage to find one. He just hoped that where he'd been dropped was near to a river.

Looking down to the ground, he could make out a large creature moving past the trunk of the tree. He could almost feel the adrenalin pumping back into his veins as his heartbeat increased once more. He hoped that the animal would not get a whiff of his scent.

His relief that the animal walked off into the dark was short-lived, as seeing it had only served to remind him of his predicament and how dangerous it was. He kept wishing he would wake up from this nightmare and find he was in his bed at home.

Finally, despite what seemed like an eternity, the sun eventually started to rise and the starry night gave way to a blue, cloudless sky.

As the morning sun lit up the ground, Konner scanned around near the base of the tree and looked through the leaves and branches, as far as he could, to see if there were any animals lurking nearby.

He worried that the pride of lions might be still around, waiting for him to climb down from the tree. *'But surely these animals don't have that level of intelligence,'* he thought, hopefully. *'Yeah, right.'*

Now that it was light, he was able to assess the damage to his body and could see the cuts he'd suffered from the night. He could see the gouges in his leg from the lion's claws, where the bleeding had now stopped. He also checked the soles of his feet and could see that they were both cut and blistered from his walking on the hard African ground.

After studying the scene around him once more, he decided his only option was to climb down from his night-time prison and make tracks to find water, maybe some food, and possibly even eventual rescue.

Trying to ignore the pain, he looked at the way down. His fear of heights became his next big obstacle, as he froze against the tree, only now realising that he was up quite high. Last night, with a menacing lion on his heels and as it was dark, he had managed to get up the tree without giving too much thought to his acrophobia. However, in the cold light of day and being able to see the ground clearly below, this fear struck with a vengeance.

He began to shake almost uncontrollably, but despite that, he still managed to slowly move his left leg to the next branch down, being careful not to lessen his grip on the trunk. His back was still against the rough bark, and as he slid down it cut into his bare skin. When he placed his full weight on the branch, it moved, which sent another shiver through his body.

He realised the only way to proceed was to turn and face the tree, not look down and take it a step at a time. So he slowly turned, being careful to look at the branches and leaves directly in front of him. Feeling his way carefully step by step, switching from one leg to the other, eventually he managed to get to the ground.

He resumed walking in yesterday's easterly direction, leaving the refuge of the tree behind him, not knowing whether in fact this was the right way to go or not. On high alert, he proceeded cautiously, worried about whether the lions were still in the vicinity or whether any other wild, meat-eating animals were about.

Feeling totally parched now and beginning to feel the heat of the sun on his bare skin, Konner looked across the plain to his left in the direction of the sun and could see some animals in the distance, including the very recognisable zebra. The others looked like wildebeest. They all appeared to be on alert, too. Was it because they'd spotted him, or was it that they had spotted some other predator that he couldn't yet see?

Making progress was difficult, as the ground was really hard on his feet. He knew that his only chance of survival in this seemingly endless, waterless zone was to keep going and to ignore the pain.

But faced with his extreme situation, he recognised he had found something deep inside himself, a primal determination to survive. He even began to think about what he might do if he managed to get out of it alive.

As he had those thoughts, he realised that only a day or so ago he was safe and out here shooting these same animals that were now his biggest fear. He was able to go to the fridge and get a cold beer. Whereas now, he wasn't sure where his next drink — or any drink — was coming from.

As Konner walked across the short, dry grass, he scanned the distance to see if he could see anything that might resemble a river or a lake. Over to his left he could see that the land dipped away and, as he continued to walk, he could see there appeared to be more trees and greenery.

This was a good sign. With the ground dipping away, not quite as deep as a valley, it encouraged him to think there might be a river in the distance, which was likely to be the Luangwa. If it was, he knew that it would have water in it, as it always did during the rainy season. However, he also knew that it harboured some very dangerous creatures, including crocodiles. With renewed vigour he pushed on, whilst trying to ignore the ever increasing pain from his blister- and cut-ridden feet.

Looking from tree to tree and from almost every patch of grass to the next, he scanned for danger, hoping to find, if not the river, at least a waterhole. Suddenly, from that direction he heard the sound of an elephant trumpeting.

'Oh, my god!' he thought, *'how do I deal with an elephant?'* That was a question he had not had to worry about before when he was with guides and armed with a rifle.

As he walked he began to notice more and more what appeared to be well-trodden pathways, which all seemed to lead to where he was heading. *'This must be the right way to go!'* he thought.

He chose to follow a winding mud path, which was a whole lot smoother on his feet than the ground on either side of it.

Suddenly, he caught movement to his right behind the trees. He froze to the spot, not knowing what it was or how big it would be.

'Is it dangerous?' raced through his mind.

His heart rate soared once again. And then the animal showed itself. As it did, Konner felt a warm sensation running down the inside of his legs.

CHAPTER SIXTY-EIGHT

Not daring to look down at what he realised was his bladder emptying, Konner stared at the animal now standing directly in front of him. It was a huge, bull-like creature with heavy horns across the top of its head.

He recognised it as a buffalo. Its enormous back was almost as tall as he was, with its shoulder height rising around two metres from the ground.

'*That thing must weigh nearly 2,000 pounds,*' he thought.

The buffalo's huge head was carried slightly lower, with the top of its horns located just below its back-line. The beast stood there with its front hooves in a wide stance and looked menacingly at him. The stance the buffalo had was needed to support the huge weight of the front part of its heavy body.

The animal had a dark brown coat and whitish circles around its eyes. Its horns were fused at the base, which seemed to form a continuous bony shield across the top of its head. Rising out from the base, the horns curved down and then smoothly curved upwards and outwards towards the tips. The span of these horns between the ends was at least a metre wide.

The buffalo was raising and lowering its head in an aggressive manner, and then made a move towards him. He stepped backwards away from the animal, not knowing quite how dangerous this beast was. He was taking no chances, and his primal body functions were taking over automatically. His sympathetic nervous system, which he had no conscious control over, was part of his fight-or-flight response.

Without realising it, his bladder had relaxed to void excess weight and fluids, readying his body for flight, and his stomach and upper-intestinal action were being slowed down. Inside Konner there was a constriction of many of his blood vessels in certain parts of his body, whilst at the same time there was dilation of other blood vessels that supply the flow of blood to the main muscles used for flight or fight.

Other changes were happening in his body, including the relaxing of his anus, so he now felt a trickle of warm faeces running down the inside of his legs. Konner felt like time had slowed; everything was happening in slow motion and all his senses felt heightened; his hearing seemed to be less and his vision had tunnelled, and he was no longer aware of his peripheries.

The catecholamines, or 'fight-or-flight' hormones, were being released into his blood stream by his adrenal glands in response to the stress that now confronted him. Without knowing it, the human body's most abundant catecholamine, epinephrine (adrenaline), had been released in large levels together with norepinephrine (noradrenaline) and dopamine, all of which are produced from phenylalanine and tyrosine.

The buffalo then made a lunge towards Konner, lowering its head and huge horns towards the ground. He hesitated no more and turned to run; his muscles seemed to be stronger than he usually remembered them to be; his lungs and heart were pumping stronger than he'd ever known. As he fled, he could hear the buffalo behind, thumping its hooves on the hard ground and snorting loudly. He ran for his life, as fast as he could, jumping over the small bushes and instinctively dodging back and forth between the trees.

His lungs were now burning and he was desperate to stop running, but he pushed on. He had a body that was not designed to run and he could feel his stomach wobbling each time he placed a foot on the ground. Not certain the beast was still behind him, he continued to run through the trees and bushes.

'The buffalo could be almost on me, as I'm sure despite its bulk, he'd be able to out-run me any day,' he worried as he began to slow with

fatigue.

Daring to look behind, he couldn't see the animal anymore, so he stopped running. He continued to walk quickly, though, wary about where the buffalo was or whether he might run into other animals in the bushes. He couldn't let his guard down at all.

Exhausted from his encounter with the buffalo, he took a moment to sit down on a raised bit of ground in the shadow of the nearest umbrella tree. The shadow was almost directly under the tree, as the sun was high in the sky and, as he sat there in the shade, he looked out across the plain at the herd of wildebeest and zebra in the distance.

The ground was already heating up from the sun, and heat haze rose up from the grass like a huge, steaming pot, making the distant animals appear like apparitions. Even in the shade of the tree, he felt hotter than he remembered, and he ached from head to toe.

The deep-seated primal feeling he'd got when he was up in the tree during the night returned. It was a powerful desire to survive, like what radiated from the wildebeests and zebras. It sent a shiver down his spine, whilst spurring him on even more to find water, which he was certain was nearby.

He forced himself to his feet and moved out from the shade of the tree. The sun beat down relentlessly, burning his sensitive, bare skin. His back was already red from the day before, so this heat was like being in front of a blow torch. Not having sun cream to protect him, blisters were beginning to form on his back from the relentless rays of UV light.

Yet, despite his pain and discomfort, he pushed on through the bushes and trees in the direction of the sloping ground, ever watchful for signs of more danger. He already knew there could be elephants at the waterhole, having heard them earlier. His heart was still racing and now he wondered whether his heart could take much more of this pounding. He felt that he was very close to a heart attack every time he was faced with danger; his senses had never taken such a bashing before. He thought about the adrenalin rush that he got when he was shooting the animals out here, but that was nothing compared to this.

Finally, he came through a clearing and saw the water, but instead of being clean, it was a brown colour. There was a herd of several elephants lying and playing in it, stirring up the mud below.

The waterhole was a bit of a walk from the trees and the clearing he'd come through, and he found himself out in the open plain once again, which made him feel uneasy. He had no choice but to move on. He continued to walk towards where the water was and what appeared to be an abundance of life.

As he got closer, he could hear the slurping sounds of the animals drinking from this one huge life source, all seemingly trying to satisfy their thirsts as quickly as possible to avoid being there for any longer than was necessary. There were other animals around the waterhole, too, which included birds. There were several smaller birds which had perched themselves on the backs of many larger animals, and these darted and pecked at insects and flies that they found on their moving smorgasbords.

There were also a number of slightly larger white birds stalking around at the water's edge, seemingly looking for food in amongst the muddy ripples. They moved between the hooves and feet of the zebra and wildebeest. Every now and again, they'd fly up, as one would get too close.

All the animals were wary of Konner, except for the elephants, which were absorbed in playing in the mud and in covering their wrinkly skins with copious amounts of the brown liquid. It seemed as though the elephants took priority over all the other animals at the watering hole. There was a little group of antelope, which moved away from the water's edge as they saw him approaching.

These small creatures were very twitchy. As they considered whether Konner was a danger to them or not, they sounded off to one another with warning cries. There were a few zebras drinking at the water's edge, too, a bit further away from Konner than the antelopes, but they also moved away as he approached. The birds nearest to him on his side of the waterhole took to the air and escaped to the other side, feeling they were now safe from this strange-looking, white-skinned creature.

The area was a hive of activity, and the ground nearby had been trodden by thousands of hooves and paws. He moved around to the far side of the waterhole, trying to get away from where the elephants were playing, in order to find a part of the water that was less muddy. His heart pounded away; he felt so vulnerable in amongst this mass of activity.

The zebra neighed in their strange donkey-like fashion as they trotted away from the waterhole completely when he'd got too close for their liking. It was a strange feeling for him, as he was even more scared than ever, and yet these animals were frightened of him.

'*If only they knew,*' he thought.

Not having drunk from a natural water source before, he wasn't sure if this stuff would be safe to drink, but seeing its colour, he knew full well that these huge creatures probably also used it as a huge toilet facility. He wasn't completely sure what might happen to him if he drank it, but, as it was sure to contain urine and faeces, it was likely to give him an upset stomach at the very least.

The alternative to drinking from what looked like an oxbow lake was to drink from the main river, which he was sure was nearby, but as his guide had explained to him, there were a large number of crocodiles living in the Luangwa River. He didn't want to risk this. His guide had also explained about the large population of hippos there, too, and Konner knew they were known for defecating in the water, so the filthy water issue would be the same, but with the added risk of attack.

He really didn't have a choice — either drink the water that he had in front of him, die of thirst, or get eaten alive drinking from the river.

Konner approached the edge of the water slowly, and soon he could feel the mud squeezing between his toes. The squelchy goo was cooling on his feet, and for a while relieved their pain. He knelt down and leant forward to put his mouth to the dirty water and pursed his lips to drink. As he took his first mouthful, the taste was foul. The combination of mud and faeces was overpowering and he felt like vomiting, but at the same time the cool water was taking away the huge thirst he had, which was an even stronger urge, as he knew he had to drink or die.

This was a whole new world to him, one that was bewilderingly frightening and full of impossible choices. A world where courage is as important as strength and where actions have life-or-death consequences. What he was experiencing now was what wild animals experience every day of their lives, staring danger in the face and taking every chance that life offers.

As he drank, he kept an eye on what was going on around him, and he also glanced behind to make sure there was no danger lurking there either. Whilst doing so, he remembered watching a wildlife program and seeing wildebeest and antelope looking very twitchy, whilst drinking. He felt exactly the same, and he could now understand why these animals would take so long before taking a drink.

The foul-tasting water quenched his thirst for now, but with each mouthful he took, it made him wretch. He worried that later he might bring it all up again, as the bacteria contained in it would likely be rejected by his stomach.

After he felt he'd drunk enough, Konner got to his feet and took a look around. The elephants were still wallowing in the mud and stirring the water up into a muddy froth. Looking across to the other side of the pool to where he had arrived, he noticed to his horror a group of lions on the mound leading down to the water's edge.

His heart jumped and began to pump at an increased rate yet again, remembering his being chased up a tree. He wondered whether they were the same lions and if they might remember him or his smell. They did seem to be relaxed and not too interested in any of the animals around the waterhole, but nonetheless he still began walking back across the open grass area until he reached the bushes and trees, out of sight of the lions.

The next life-or-death problem he faced was finding food. Not having been in a survival situation before, he had no way of knowing how to catch food, nor did he know how to cook it or make a fire. If only he had his rifle, things would be different!

'What can I eat?' he wondered.

As he walked within the cover of the trees, he

knew that the buffalo he'd encountered earlier might not be too far away. Also, there were likely to be other animals, all equally eager to kill or attack him.

Since his drink, he was beginning to feel sick and his stomach was beginning to churn. He walked slowly through the bushes in search of a place to sit and rest — if rest was something he could do in a place like this. At least he could get off his feet, which were extremely sore.

Seeing a tree ahead of him, Konner approached carefully, knowing there could be an animal lurking behind every bush or tree trunk. He could see no immediate danger, but he still felt very uneasy and extremely tired now, not having slept all night and from his walk to the waterhole in the heat.

'If only I could find a cave or some other refuge,' he thought. *'Maybe I could build a protective barrier.'*

He reached the base of the tree and looked around once more to see if there were any predators. There were none to be seen. So he sat down with his back to the trunk, hoping that if any creature were to come along, he would be able to see it in time to climb into its branches. The bark of the tree was rough on his back and the ground wasn't exactly comfortable on his naked backside, either, but at least he could rest for the time being.

As he sat there, he began to think about home and how he missed his New York apartment and his life in the city. He would give anything to be there and not here, living in constant fear.

As he sat for a while, he started to feel very weak and extremely nauseous. Then, without warning, his stomach brought up all the water he'd drunk just a few moments before. He couldn't suppress it and continued to vomit violently. He then became really concerned at the noise he was making, but he was unable to stop until his body had rid itself of the foul water and the bacteria that it contained.

When the vomiting stopped, Konner leaned his back against the tree, completely drained. He was now concerned, as all the fluid he'd drunk had all been brought back up, plus more. He started to feel dizzy, as all the energy in his body drained away, and the world around him began to spin. He fell over on the ground, fainting from exhaustion.

Konner was abruptly awakened from his fainting spell by a sharp pain in his leg. As he opened his eyes, he realised what the pain was — an animal was tearing at his calf muscle. Horrified, he found himself face-to-face with a pack of wild hyenas, each one as eager as the next to be the first to rip into his tender, white flesh.

When he'd first woken and had seen the creature that had begun the attack, the hyena stepped back and stared at him with brown, unfeeling eyes. Another hyena then darted in to take its place, sinking its dog-like jaws and teeth into Konner's kneecap on his other leg, which caused him to let out a scream of agony. The first hyena that had attacked turned, snarled, and then bit the neck of the second hyena, which let out a loud squeal and turned to fight its rival. Then all of a sudden all the hyenas began to squabble and fight each other, whilst Konner tried to get up and move away from the clan.

With his movement, the first hyena turned and grabbed at Konner, not allowing him to get up. Then another of the pack joined in, as a third animal sunk its teeth into the soft flesh at the side of his stomach. Konner tried to push the creatures away, but there were too many of them, and they were coming at him from all angles. He was now starting to loose blood, and the pain was excruciating. He tried to get up again and began to shout at his attackers in an attempt to scare them away, but he was almost completely devoid of energy. These gory creatures had already tasted blood and were not about to give up now.

Konner turned onto his front and tried to crawl away, pulling himself with his arms and hands, but the hyenas were pulling him back, sinking their teeth into his flesh and tearing away the skin to reveal muscle and bone beneath. He could feel them tearing away at both of his calves, then one moved to his thigh muscle, whilst another sunk its teeth into his lower abdomen, ripping the lining and exposing his intestine.

Still another one of the pack tugged at his arm, and he quickly realised his fate was sealed. He was to be eaten alive by hyenas.

More of the animals turned to the soft flesh of his stomach. Before too long their sharp teeth had pulled out his intestines and other internal organs, including his liver. As the creatures tore at this vital organ, Konner's blood spurted and he blacked out, his last thought of his abductors and why they'd brought him here.

The animals had smelt the vomit and zeroed in on Konner. Now they gorged themselves on his flesh and bone, like they did with any other helpless plains animal.

CHAPTER SIXTY-NINE

Druker returned to his office after he'd had his lunch on the veranda again. Today Mulubwa had cooked him goat curry, which was one of his favourite dishes.

He looked at the tracking screen and the dot for Prow was moving slowly, but the Hurley dot had just disappeared right in front of him.

He went to his computer and checked the information of the tracking system and it showed that Konner had been still for a while. There didn't appear to be any problems with the system, especially as Prow's tracking unit was still showing on the screen.

He picked up his radio and called for Scott to come to his office right away. Within a few moments, in his usual compliant manner, Scott appeared in the office doorway.

'Hi, Scott. It looks like we've lost Hurley, as his tracking unit has just disappeared,' he said. 'It disappeared right in front of me only a few moments ago.'

'Well, he lasted the night, then, and it looks like Prow has lasted, too, as I see her tracking unit is still moving,' Scott replied.

'Yes, and maybe this feisty one will last longer than the rest,' Druker countered.

'So what do you want me to do?' Scott asked his boss.

'This time I'm sure the tracker unit is not at fault, like we thought last time, so I think it's time we put Smith back out there, don't you?'

'I agree, and is it okay that I use the tranquiliser gun on him this time?'

'I think that's a great idea! Treat him just like we would an animal that we were about to take out into the wild,' Druker said with enthusiasm.

'Okay, consider it done, Druk. Then I'll go and check on the site where Hurley was last recorded, if you could let me have the coordinates.'

Druker looked up Konner's last position on the system and gave these to Scott, so that it would make it easier for him to track him down, although Scott knew that he would likely be looking for a blood stain once more.

'I'll go get the tranquiliser gun. Then Joshua and I will put Smith back out right away,' Scott said and left the room.

CHAPTER SEVENTY

As Graham sat there not making a sound for what felt like an eternity, he heard footsteps and voices approaching from outside. The bolts on the outside door were released and then the door itself swung open. As he looked towards the entrance, bright sunlight streamed in, causing him to squint.

A dark figure approached, silhouetted by the light behind. As he approached his cage, he was sure it was Scott again.

As his eyes adjusted, he could see that yes, it was Scott who had come in, and that he was carrying something in his hands.

'Is it a gun or is it the stun gun again?' he though worriedly.

When Scott pointed it at him, he realised that it was in fact a gun. He was poking it through the bars of the cage and aiming straight at him. Graham looked into the whites of Scott's eyes and saw that there was no feeling there.

He recoiled in the cage and tried to get as far

away as possible.

'Why have they decided to kill me?' he wondered.

'Stop, Scott! Don't shoot me!' he shouted.

'Shut the fuck up,' Scott growled as he lined the gun up on Graham.

As Graham pushed himself back as far as he could, he heard the crack of the gun and almost simultaneously felt pain shoot up from his thigh, which is where the bullet had hit.

'Why are you doing this? I've done nothing wrong,' he whimpered. 'Why have you shot me in the leg?'

But as he looked down to where the pain was coming from, he realised that he'd not been shot with a bullet, but instead there was a large dart poking out from his thigh. As he looked at the red-coloured dart, he instinctively leaned down to remove it, but suddenly felt woozy. He then blacked out and collapsed to the floor of the cage, with images still in his head about what had just happened and why.

CHAPTER SEVENTY-ONE

Graham came around from being shot with the tranquiliser and, instead of seeing the bars of his cage, in which he'd lost consciousness, he found that he was in a more open space, although it was still quite dark. Feeling sluggish, he sat up to see where he was and found to his surprise that he seemed to be in a cave. He had been lying on something a bit softer than his hard, wooden cage floor. It was straw.

Looking towards the entrance of the cave, he sensed that he was no longer close to the relatively safe haven of the building with the cages. At least he had known whilst he was there that no wild animals would be able to attack him, and he had water and food — albeit dog food — to eat.

He felt his thigh where the dart had hit him. The dart was no longer there, but a red mark and a bruise from the impact remained. He realised it must have been a tranquilliser they shot into him; he didn't remember a thing about being moved out of his cage and back out into the wild again. The chemical had left him feeling a bit lightheaded and nauseous.

He wondered where he'd been taken this time as he slowly got to his feet and, still feeling woozy, walked slowly to the cave entrance, wondering to himself what time of day it was.

As he approached the aperture, not sure what animals he might see, he was very cautious. The sun was bright and he could smell the dry grass and open plain of Africa once more, which reminded him of when he had first awoken a couple of days ago, only in a different area.

There was a large open space with grasslands and a few trees scattered about and, in the near distance, he could see some grazing animals, which looked like wildebeest and zebra. He then heard the unmistakable sound of a zebra, with its unusual neigh that didn't really sound like a neigh at all.

He knew quite well that where there were plains animals, like wildebeest and zebra, close by there would also be lions like he'd encountered before and other predators. Although it was really quite warm, a shiver ran up his spine. He remembered how close he had come to being eaten alive by a pride of lions, and all those primal feelings came rushing back to him once more.

'Maybe I'm being watched, and as soon as I get into danger they'll rescue me,' Graham thought, then dismissed the idea as he remembered the lump under the skin in his neck. *'This could to*

be a tracker, but that's not going to let them see me, though.'

Graham then thought about Carly, who was also out here somewhere, and that maybe he might be lucky enough to find her.

'Perhaps as two we might stand more of a chance of surviving and of escaping,' he thought.

He soon decided, though, that their kidnappers were unlikely to place them anywhere near each other out here.

'We are likely to be too far apart to find each other — that's even if she's still alive by now,' he worried.

He knew that he'd been extremely lucky before, having tourists in the area. *'But I wonder how Scott and the others knew they were there?'* he wondered.

'It might be that I'll be found, perhaps this time not by the people who kidnapped me,' he thought, trying to be a little positive. *'Surely they can't be everywhere, but then perhaps they do have cameras.'*

Graham started to have a look around, to see if he could see anything that resembled a camera, but there was no evidence of this, but he decided he would continue to look. *'There's obviously something they have in place to enable them to know when tourists are around,'* he thought.

He was now really hungry and his stomach was churning. He was also starting to feel thirsty, too. Last time he was lucky enough to find the elephants and follow them to the waterhole, but he doubted that he'd have similar luck this time. As for food, he questioned whether he'd find anything to eat out here.

His feet were still really sore from his previous time in the bush, not having had time to heal. So with the ground being really hard, he hobbled around, but kept as close to the mouth of the cave as he could, not daring right now to wander too far. His skin was also sun burnt, so he was reluctant to go out for too long in the sun. In a bizarre way, he was thankful that they'd placed him in this shelter, rather than right out in the open like last time.

He realised, though, that his only chance of survival was to venture out onto the open plain once more. His search for food and water carried the risk of meeting up with lions or other predators again, but this would also give him the added chance of being found.

Graham surveyed the ground around the cave. Above the cave the land rose up to some rocky outcrops covered in small bushes and trees, and as he looked up, he saw movement and froze to the spot. Not knowing what he'd seen, he squinted and leant forward to see what had moved.

'What would live up there in the bushes? Am I being stalked already? Is it a predator or is it a smaller creature that was frightened of me instead?' he questioned, as his heart rate jumped to the levels he remembered from before, when he'd encountered a wild animal.

He edged closer to the cave entrance as he

focused on the crop of bushes where he'd seen the movement, but there was none now. Feeling really uneasy, he also looked behind himself at the plain that stretched out into the distance. He could almost feel the adrenalin pumping through his blood yet again. He wondered whether the body had a limitless supply of the stuff, as he'd certainly used up his fair share of it over the last few days. His heart was pumping and he could feel the sweat on the palms of his hands.

In the end, he decided to retreat back into the cave for now, not wanting to face the demons of the open plains just yet. He sat back down on the straw where he'd woken up a few moments ago.

Tears welled up in Graham's eyes as he began to wish he'd done much more with his life instead of sponging off the state. He knew he was intelligent enough, but he also knew that he was really lazy and couldn't be bothered. He had rebelled against the system, ever since he was at school, then followed his parents' sponging ways, too.

Tears ran down his face, now, and he felt really sorry for himself. But as he sat there, he became aware of the sound of dripping water coming from somewhere back in the cave. He turned his head and tried to focus on where the sound was coming from. If he could find this water, he could at least quench his thirst.

But as his eyes tried to adjust to the dim light of the cave, the sound of the dripping suddenly took on a sinister tone. He started to imagine creatures at the back of the cave waiting for him to approach, only to pounce on him and devour him alive. His heart was in his mouth, but his thirst drove back his fear of the dark. He forced himself to get up and move slowly deeper into the cave.

He could sense that the roof of the cave was getting lower as he moved further inside. He hoped that he would be able to get to where the water was before the height became a problem. He felt along the top of the cave with his hands as he ducked along, feeling the jagged edge of the rock. The surface of the rock was cold to the touch and somewhat rough on his fingers. Soon the decreasing height forced him onto his knees to crawl, but the rocks on the floor of the cave dug into the skin on his knees more than it had on his feet.

The sound of the dripping was ever closer, but now he was so far into the cave that very little light reached him, and he had to feel his way inch by inch. He didn't know what the water would taste like, but he was sure that it couldn't be any worse than the foul waterhole stuff he'd had before.

Reaching out with his left hand, he was feeling for obstructions, as he moved further into the small space. Then he hit his head on a jagged edge of rock. The immediate pain was excruciating. Cursing under his breath, he cupped his head in his hands to wait for the pain to subside.

The throbbing seemed to go on for ages. Being in the dark and on his knees somehow made it worse. *'Damn them! Damn those kidnappers!'* he thought.

He started forward again, this time lowering his head still further and holding one hand above him to gauge where the roof-line was. As he got closer to the sound of the water, he had to assume an almost crawling position, as the roof of the cave was getting lower and lower.

Then Graham realised that the floor of the cave had changed — it was now wet, very slippery, and colder to the touch than before. Reaching out in front of him to see if he could feel for any pools of water, all he felt was more damp rock. He had to get onto his stomach now and crawl crab-like, as the cave was now too low to even kneel. This was strange, because the dripping sound seemed as if water were falling from much higher than the distance between the floor he lay on and the ceiling of the cave.

'There must be a deep pool ahead of me and the cave must open out,' he thought hopefully.

He put his arms out to either side of him, one at a time, and could feel that the cave tapered out, both to his left and to his right, so there was no height there, either. The rock was hurting his bare skin as he crab-crawled along the cave floor, using his left hand every few centimetres to feel for the height of the ceiling to avoid hitting his head again.

Soon he realised the cave was getting almost too low for him to fit. He could still hear the dripping of water ahead and he was fast becoming aware that he might not even be able to reach it. The rock above him seemed to be extremely damp, so he thought it might be a good idea to turn onto his back and lick its surface for moisture. He accomplished this turn with difficulty, but was even more uncomfortable on his bare back, which was blistered from sunburn. The rock around his buttocks and lower back dug in, too, but he managed to reach up with his head to lick the rock surface.

The rock tasted bitter and earthy, but there wasn't enough moisture there to quench his thirst, so he struggled back around onto his belly again. He moved further into the gap, inching his way along the hard surface, which seemed to be putting dents and scratches in his skin. Finally, as he reached out into the dark in front of him to see if he could feel any water, it seemed as though the cave ceiling was getting higher.

This encouraged him to edge forward still further, hoping that eventually he would find the water he so desperately needed. Thoughts of what animals might be lurking in the cave were also going through his mind; he worried that his hands might stumble upon something that moved. His heart was in his mouth more than ever as he moved further into the dark. The entrance of the cave was too far way to illuminate this section of the cave.

But, yes, the cave ceiling definitely seemed to be rising and the area around him was wider still. The sound of the dripping water was louder now as it echoed around the opening in the cavern. He reached up to feel the roof of the cave and at this point he could only just reach it with his fingertips. He then sat up cautiously so he could shuffle along on his bottom, but being careful not to hit his head.

What Graham didn't know was that the water in this cave had percolated through the ground and rocks for many miles, hitherto being forced up through the surrounding rock formation, before appearing on the surface and then dripping into a large pool at the back of his temporary shelter.

The water that now dripped into the hidden pool was many years old, having fallen as rain a long time ago in a distant place before being soaked up by the ground and disappearing, only to collect via a natural underground filtering system. At each rainfall during the rainy season, this underground reservoir would be topped up and would push the water along bit by bit until it reappeared in other places, sometimes, as in this case, hundreds of miles away.

Now that he was sitting up, Graham raised his hands to guide himself along the ceiling, but after having moved only a short distance, he could feel the roof of the cave getting higher still. He managed to get up onto his feet, whilst cowering to avoid hitting the roof of the cave. He inched forward on his sore feet, feeling his way, carefully putting each foot ahead of the other, whilst feeling for sure footing on the damp, slippery rock.

Then his sixth sense started to kick in. He

suddenly knew he was not alone in this dark space, and stopped to listen. His heart pounded as his senses told him there was definitely something else occupying this cave. Not only was he certain he had entered an area where there was another animal or animals near him, but he was suddenly aware of a strange smell, too.

CHAPTER SEVENTY-TWO

Now confronted with a large predator, Carly's automatic fight-or-flight system kicked in. She felt warmth running down the insides of her legs, as she realised that her bladder had given way, with her body's need to prepare for the situation.

'Fight!' she thought. *'But with what and how?'*

In front of her stood a huge leopard bearing its teeth and snarling, with sinewy muscles showing through its skin and fur. The fur around its nose was creased, as the sides to its mouth were drawn up to show its complete set of yellow teeth. The pink-coloured tongue in its mouth was drawn back and lay between the lower two canines. Its eyes were squeezed slightly into narrower slits, which were glaring right at her.

Facing the leopard, with her heart pounding harder than she'd ever remembered, she wasn't sure what to do next.

She had a primal fear rising up through her

body. It was a fear she'd never experienced before, but despite this, somewhere from within the depths of her, she found the courage to wave her hands and scream at the top of her lungs at the snarling leopard.

The huge cat that stood in front of Carly snarled even more menacingly, in reaction to her behaviour, but fortunately for her this leopard was either not hungry or as surprised to see her as she was to see it. The huge cat then darted away into the low-standing undergrowth.

Now she began to realise how bad her predicament was and wondered why she'd been put in this situation, *'Why? Why me?'* she questioned angrily again.

With her heart still in her mouth, she was looking in every direction and continued to hobble along the path next to the river.

'What other animals are lurking in the bushes and trees? What if that snake comes back?' she thought.

Having now walked for a while and more than she'd walked in a long time, she was getting really tired, so she sat down to rest. Where she sat, the river opened up into a large basin area, where another much larger river entered, forming one big river.

The water in the combined rivers was muddy, and there were fewer trees along its banks. She could see across to the other side, where there was a huge plain. On this expanse grass grew, and she could see a few sparsely scattered umbrella-like acacia trees.

In the distance she could see a herd of animals. She was not entirely sure what they were, but to her they looked like wildebeest and a number of unmistakable zebra, too. Gazing at the far river bank, she could see crocodiles basking in the sun. She had to take a second look and suddenly realised how dangerous this place was. *'Oh, my god!'* she thought, *'crocodiles!'*

Looking slightly down river, where it really opened out and the flow slowed down, Carly saw the heads of hippos. She couldn't help but think she was living in a David Attenborough program.

As she sat there catching her breath, looking in total amazement at the animals before her, the river directly in front of her suddenly exploded. As the water came to life, she jumped and rolled backwards away from the edge of the high bank.

Just below where she ended up standing, a huge burst of sound and bubbles morphed into two very large bull hippopotamuses fighting for territory. Both powerful animals had their mouths agape, baring their massive, tusk-like teeth.

Frozen to the spot, she watched the scene unfold before her, not knowing what to do next. The two creatures suddenly disappeared again into the muddy depths of the river, so all went quiet for a brief moment, except for the mooing of the other hippos she could hear.

Then the first hippo came to the surface again, quickly followed by the second one. Both had their huge mouths wide open and interlocked.

Each hippo was trying to get higher out of the water than his counterpart, whilst the other was trying to score a blow with his teeth, as each one vied for supremacy and the right to the harem of female hippos nearby.

As the fight between the hippos raged on, she watched mesmerised. The water became a mass of waves, whipped up in mud and bubbles. Each hippo gapped its huge mouth showing off its tusk-like teeth. The tips of the mouths touched as each one tried to gain position. The water around the two fighting hippos was stirred up into such a frenzy that all the other hippos moved further away to avoid being involved.

By now there was blood showing on both animals, where they'd been caught by a tusk, and as she watched the two hippos fight it out, she began to feel extremely exposed. This was something she was more used to watching from the comfort of her arm chair at home, rather than being right there as a part of it without any clothes on.

Carly's nudity made her even more sensitive to her vulnerable situation. There was nothing at all to protect her. Having no clothes made her seem somehow equal to all the other animals around her — except in strength, speed and endurance. Such equality, despite its magnificent setting, she would gladly trade for the safety of her dingy flat back in Chelmsford.

CHAPTER SEVENTY-THREE

Graham's heart was pounding hard, but he was still not sure what it was that told his senses that he was not alone in this cavern. As he reached up to feel his way along the rocky ceiling, he touched something furry. Then all hell broke loose. The cave came alive with frantic screeches and what sounded like flapping wings.

Then he realised what was happening. The cave was full of bats! They all raced around his head, making panicked noises in their leather-winged frenzy. Now he knew what that smell was — bat guano. He edged forward with his hands covering his face as bats kept bumping into him. He was surprised that they were hitting him, as he knew they had a high level of sonar-like tracking for flying in the dark, but the space was obviously quite small to accommodate so many bats and, with him there, it was difficult for the creatures to avoid him.

As he took another step forward, one foot went

from under him and he slipped on the wet floor. He fell forward with a crash, hitting the floor of the cave with a thump, with the ribs on his right side taking the full force of his fall. Then all of a sudden he found himself under water.

He had slid into the pool, which was deep enough to swallow his whole body, and he suddenly found himself fighting to get to the surface for a breath of air. He was in total shock. The initial fall onto the rocks before he landed in the water had winded him, making it painful to breathe when he surfaced and tried to draw in his first big breath. The horror of his predicament was made worse by the fact that he was in almost total darkness, so it was difficult for him to see the sides of the pool to find a way out, as he thrashed around with his arms and legs, trying to keep his head above the water.

His feet didn't reach the bottom, which made him panic and caused him to kick his feet in a frenzy, until his left foot hit a jagged edge of rock on the pool wall.

'Fuck!' was the only word that came out, as the pain from kicking the rock spread out over his foot.

'Help me, help me! Someone please help me!' he shouted, struggling to keep his head above the surface as he thrashed around in the cold water.

Graham realised that in reality there was no one to help him, but he was now panicking and it was almost an automatic reaction to his situation to cry for help. He then reached out to the side walls in an effort to stabilise himself and to catch his breath, but the walls were slippery and he couldn't find any handholds. It was too dark to see what he was doing, then he disappeared below the surface again, before rising once more to fill his lungs with air. With each breath, his ribs hurt, too.

The water was deep and he wasn't sure how far back the pool went into the cave, but he knew he didn't want to go further in, so he began to use his arms to swim closer to where he knew the front of the pool was. It helped that he could just make out some rocks glistening from the feeble light that came in from the distant entrance.

As he got closer to the side, his knees hit the sharp rocks that formed the pool, but he managed to grab hold of the edge and lean forward. He held on to the rock while gradually catching his breath and looked around in the dark, trying to decide how to proceed.

The bats continued to fly around above him and occasionally he'd feel the draft from their wings as they flew past his head.

His immediate problem: How to get out of the water. He couldn't see what he was doing, but he could feel his way around, and at least the glimmer of light gave him a bearing on where he was in the pool. Holding on to the side, he tried to get a foothold, but it was difficult, as he needed to get his balance by leaning forward, which was also hard. The sides were more or less vertical and very slippery, too.

He decided to work himself around the outside

of the pool to see if there were any better sections where he could get out, but he didn't really want to find somewhere on the opposite side to where the entrance lay, for fear of being stuck inside this cave forever.

The water was very cool and, as there was no heat this far inside the cave, he began to feel cold. He realised he needed to get out of the water soon, or he might get hypothermia. He gradually worked himself around the edge, feeling to see if he could find a way out, whilst at the same time he used his feet to feel for footholds that might help him boost himself up.

'I'd prefer to be back in that cage than be stuck and drown in this pool,' he thought. *'What a way to go.*

'It might have been better to have been eaten by the lions yesterday. At least that would have been quick.'

CHAPTER SEVENTY-FOUR

With all these wild animals surrounding her and as she watched the fight between the hippos, Carly began to cry. Her total helplessness was now too much for her to take. Her mind was in total confusion and she had no idea what to do next; all she could do for now was to look across at the crocodiles on the far bank of the river and to watch the fight that was still going on below her. Finally, though, she decided to get moving again.

She remembered watching a film on the wildebeest migration, and how the crocodiles would wait patiently under the water and pounce on unsuspecting beasts. What was dawning on her was that she had become a part of this wilderness; she had been taken right back to nature— not just because she was naked, but because she was also right in amongst wild animals, without anything to help her. She felt immersed in the struggle for life and death, with the constant fear of where the next attack might come from.

With her physique, she was certainly not capable of fending for herself, and she had no survival skills whatsoever. Despite this, she started to think survival — where was she going to get food and what about drinking water? There was no way she could drink from this part of the river, as the water was not only dirty, but also full of dangerous and deadly creatures. She might have frightened off a leopard earlier, but this might not work with another animal, and another one could quite easily sneak up on her, too.

Carly decided to walk back for cover in the trees where she'd been before, as she felt even more vulnerable out in the open with all these wild creatures around.

As she turned to walk back to the trees, she heard a huge crashing sound, almost like there was a bulldozer ploughing through the brush in front of her. Whatever it was, it was coming her way.

The crashing sound was accompanied by the sounds of something that sounded familiar to her. Not knowing which way to turn and not knowing whether to try and run or to stand her ground again, she stood frozen to the spot with her heart pounding. She had nowhere to turn — to her right were hippos, crocodiles and a snake-infested river; to her left was an open plain of grassland; in front were trees and cover, but an obviously large creature coming right at her.

The crashing sounds were getting ever closer and she couldn't move. She daren't go any further into the tree-covered area and found herself looking desperately around at the savannah behind her, too.

Then she saw what was making the deafening noise, and it was coming straight at her.

CHAPTER SEVENTY-FIVE

Continuing to fumble around with his hands in the dark, Graham reached up to find a handhold on the slippery rock. As he was moving across the rock, his feet hit something hard below him. He kicked his legs and then his left ankle knocked against the same hard surface, which made him recoil in pain.

He managed, though, to put his two feet on the hard rock below him, which brought him out of the water by less than half a metre or so. He then began to feel around in the pool with his left foot a bit further, to see if he could find a slightly higher point which he could use to push himself up and out.

He found a slightly higher rock ledge, but this was further to his left and away from the direction of where the entrance was, but he had no choice. He put his left foot on the underwater ledge and pushed himself up still further, using his hands to stabilise himself. He was still waist deep in the pool and still had quite a distance to lift himself to get free.

He then reached up higher to see if he could find purchase on any of the rocks, whilst he leant forward and pushed with his feet. His large stomach was crushed against the craggy rock face, which dug in to his skin, and he was sure that he'd be left with yet more scrapes. The adrenalin running through his veins seemed to null the pain to a degree, but he knew that he was being cut quite badly.

Still leaning forward, he raised his left leg to try and push himself up, but it was difficult finding any small piece of rocky outcropping to leverage his heavy body with. As he fumbled with his hands trying to discover a viable pathway, he suddenly felt an above-water ledge that appeared to lead in the direction of the cave entrance.

He couldn't see how big the ledge was, and whether this would be wide enough for him to walk around and back out of the cave. Soon he had managed to pull himself out of the water and onto the flat surface, which was just about wide enough for him to lie on. Now that he was free of the pool, he crawled along the edge. Being careful not to fall back into the water, he moved towards the faint glimmer of light coming from the entrance.

He then realised that, despite having fallen into a huge pool of water, he had not drunk a drop. As he lay there on the ledge, he reached down with his right arm to the water to try and quench his terrible thirst.

He cupped his single hand to try and get a small amount of water, and brought it up to his lips. It was difficult to get much water into his single hand, but he didn't want to fall back in again. The water tasted bitter and a little metallic, but it was refreshing and tasted much better than the water he'd drunk at the waterhole a few days ago.

He cupped his hand again and again to get more water, to drink as much as he could. Most of the water in his hand dripped out before it got to his mouth, but at least he got some each time.

When he had finally had enough, Graham continued his crawl over the rough rocks towards the light, staying low to avoid falling back into the water and to avoid hitting his head on the cave ceiling. The cave's height increased again, as he moved closer to the entrance and back into the light once more.

Finally, he could stand on his sore feet. He walked carefully to the light at the front of the cave and stood naked in the entrance, looking out across the wilderness. He wondered what to do next, knowing he must find some food somehow, somewhere. He welcomed the warm air from outside, as he was still feeling cold from his plunge into the pool. He moved out into the sun to warm up further. Despite the fact he knew the sun's rays would burn his skin, the heat was needed right now.

As he looked over the savannah, a light breeze

hit his face, bringing with it the pure smell of nature, which helped to remind him exactly where he was — as if he needed reminding.

He surveyed more closely the area around the cave. The entrance was surrounded by light, greyish rock, which was interspersed with plants that had managed to root in its small crevices. Looking up further, the rock disappeared behind more plant growth and small bushes and trees. He studied them for movement again, but all was still at the moment.

The wild scene made Graham feel more lost and alone than ever, and he then felt tears rolling down his cheeks. All he knew was that all through his 32 years of life, he'd given up on everything and anything he had done. Would this be the last thing he'd give up on, or could he really survive the test?

'Is this a test? Or did these men simply want to leave us out here until we are killed and eaten, perhaps even putting bets on us?' he thought.

He had never been as hungry as he was right now and there was no prospect of finding food for a while, and even if he did, what sort of food would it be?

'Would it be like on the show "I'm a Celebrity Get Me Out of Here," where they eat grubs?' he wondered.

'But where am I going to begin looking? I haven't had any training in survival and don't know the first thing about what I can and can't eat,'

With these thoughts, he began considering where he might find these types of creatures here in Africa.

'Would I have to dig a hole? Would I find bugs in the trees and, if so, would they be poisonous?'

As he surveyed the landscape, wondering where he might find something that resembled food, he decided his only option was to begin moving. He knew he couldn't stay where he was and hope to survive, although he did feel safer keeping near to the cave and its supply of clean water to drink.

His tears had stopped, but his feelings of loss and fear were as high as they'd ever been. He felt like his life could be taken away from him at any moment. Gone was the feeling of security and comfort of his flat in Chelmsford and, although it was relatively small and not very tidy, it was home and it was safe. He knew that no matter what happened each week, he would get his social security money to buy food and stay in his council-paid residence.

The worst dangers he'd ever come across or worried about at home were gangs on the street or getting run over by a bus. But out here, danger seemed to lurk in every direction. A shiver went down his spine, as he remembered his encounter with the lions and how he'd been saved by his kidnappers just seconds before he was about to be eaten alive.

'Maybe I'd be better off dead. If I hadn't been saved, my misery would be over.'

He felt like a real mess, with cut feet and bruises all over, not only from his ordeal out here, but also from the bullying he'd received in the cage. He then looked down at the foot that he'd smashed when he was in the pool, which was cut and swollen. He could also see that his knees had been cut too, from when he hit the side of the pool, and that his stomach was also grazed from crawling along on the rocks. On top of all that he was also sun burnt.

Despite his battered body and the danger he might face, he walked down the slope and away from the relative safety of the cave. He headed towards the plain in front of him and the distant trees. His thought was to see if he could find some food; there might be some bugs in the trees to eat. He could also make out what he thought looked like the line of the river, which he assumed was the same river he had been next to before, although he was worried that by going there again he might encounter the lions once more.

With his feet still sore, the going was tough on the hard ground, plus his left foot made it even more difficult with the cut and bruise it had received in his earlier ordeal.

'It must be close to mid-day,' he thought, as he looked up towards the sun, which was very high in the sky. It was extremely hot.

He was on high alert — more focused than he'd ever been before or even thought possible.

He suddenly realised he should also consider making a weapon. Although he had no knives or cutting tools, he thought at the very least he should be able to find a stick to help protect himself from an animal. So this would now be his priority — to find some form of weapon. He hoped that where he was heading there would be some sticks that he could use for this purpose.

The African plain he was crossing was extremely open, and because of this, he felt even more vulnerable than before. He felt as if there were hundreds of evil eyes watching his every move, although right now he couldn't see any animals. He was sure that there would be animals lurking in the bushes somewhere, though.

The reality was that Graham knew what was out there, so it was only a question of time before something appeared.

Still, he kept alert every second as he looked around from left to right, in front and behind, whilst at the same time trying to make headway towards the distant trees.

CHAPTER SEVENTY-SIX

Druker was still in his office dealing with some paperwork relating to a new property deal he was working on in Cambridge.

He paused for a break and got up to refill his wine glass with some more red wine, and as he did so, he took a moment to look at the tracking screen. He noticed right away that the tracking dot that represented Smith was no longer on the screen, leaving the one which represented Prow still showing.

'That's another one to bite the dust, then,' he thought, as he opened up the program to see where Smith had been just before he'd vanished.

When he opened the data screen, it looked like Smith was still inside the cave, just before his tracker dot had disappeared, which Druker found to be a bit strange.

'What animal would go inside a cave?' he wondered.

He radioed Scott immediately to get his

opinion on the situation.

'What's up, Druk?' Scott questioned as he arrived in his office.

'Smith has disappeared from the tracking screen.'

'When did that happen?'

'Well, he was there when I last looked, but then when I checked the data, it would appear that his last position showed him in the cave. He went missing about 15 minutes ago, meaning that he didn't leave the cave.'

'Interesting,' Scott responded, as he looked at the screen to confirm what his boss had said.

'What could have got him in the cave, though?' Druker asked.

'Well, when we went there the other day to track Lane, we found lion spoor around the cave entrance, but I must admit I didn't check to see if they had ventured inside,' Scott replied.

'So do you think they might have gone in and got the poor bastard before he even ventured outside?'

'It certainly looks that way, doesn't it? So do you want me and Ken to take a look?'

'Yes, I guess so, as we need to find out what has happened and to confirm whether he has been taken out by an animal, as opposed to a tracker unit malfunction.'

As Druker spoke, the tracker dot representing Smith suddenly reappeared, showing his position was still inside the cave. They both stared at the screen and then looked at each other.

'You don't suppose Smith went so far inside the cave that the booster unit I put on the outside lost connection?' Scott asked.

'That's possible, and I suggest you hold fire for now. Let's wait and see what happens.'

'No problem, Druk. I'll be in the radio room with Ken. Just call me again if you need me.'

'Thank you, Scott. I'll keep an eye on things here, and I think you could be right,' Druker said, as Scott left him in his office looking at the tracker screen and sipping his wine.

CHAPTER SEVENTY-SEVEN

With a loud trumpeting sound, a huge, male elephant with enormous tusks broke out from the trees. Behind him were a number of other elephants of differing sizes. The massive creature stopped directly in front of Carly, rearing its head in an angry and threatening manner.

Once again she found the inside of her legs warmed by her own urine, as her bladder released what little fluid it had left from earlier. She had never been so scared in all her life. Her heart was racing so fast that she thought it would explode.

As she looked up at the grey monster that towered above her, she was frozen to the spot like a rabbit in the headlights of an on-coming car.

The bull elephant aggressively asserted itself by raising and lowering its huge tusked head, as it moved towards her and sounded off. What she soon realised was that the elephants wanted to get to the water and she stood in their way. Her position on the riverbank made that difficult, and all that she could do was to raise her hands above her head and scream at the creature, like she had done earlier with the leopard.

With this aggressive reaction from her, the elephant charged. With its huge head and trunk, it hit her squarely in the chest and knocked her back towards the river. She fell to the ground with the wind knocked out of her and was sure that the blow had probably cracked a few ribs.

Horrified, she realised the elephant had not given up yet after this attack, but continued to push her towards the river. She felt the blows to her hands and legs, as she'd curled up into a foetus position, instinctively trying to protect herself. Pain ran through her body, as she was taking a real pounding.

With each blow from this huge creature, she was being pushed closer and closer to the edge of the river. The elephant was using a combination of its trunk and its pillar-like legs to bulldoze her fragile body. The elephant was also showing its domination by letting out very loud trumpeting sounds.

She had her eyes tightly closed and her arms and hands over her head and face, so she was not aware of exactly where she was in relation to the river. Then she suddenly felt herself rolling down the slope. As she gained momentum, her arms came away from her face and she opened her eyes just before she hit the water.

The water was cooler than she thought it might be, and also deeper than she imagined, as she found herself getting completely submerged. As she surfaced, panic set in. She could see the male elephant and its family on the river bank watching as she floated away — triumphant at winning their 'battle' with this strange, white creature.

The flow of the water caught her and Carly felt herself being carried along. She became submerged once more under the brown, flowing water, then came to the surface again and found herself floating towards where the hippos had been fighting. Strangely, this was not worrying her the most — what was going through her mind was whether the crocodiles had seen her fall into the water.

She flailed around, trying to get herself back to the bank of the river, but to no avail. Her overweight body gave her the advantage of helping her float, but this was no comfort as she found herself carried away from the riverbank and into the centre of the river. She had no idea what lurked below her in the murky water, but she knew what was around her. She felt like one of the helpless wildebeest crossing the Mara River, easy prey for waiting crocodiles.

She had to find a way of getting out of the water before she found herself a victim of an attack, but with that thought she was hit from below. The pain was excruciating as the hidden attacker plunged her under the surface once again and she found herself not in the grip of a voracious crocodile, but in the mouth of a huge hippo. Massive tusks scored her torso and cracked more of her ribs, as she was tossed around in the river like a rag doll. Despite her own large size, the hippo made her look like a five-stone weakling.

Desperately trying to get to the surface for air, she punched and kicked for her life and got a reprieve — the hippo let her go. She continued to float along the top of the river, then, with her head dipping in and out of the water, as she struggled to keep afloat, to catch her breath and stay conscious.

But then Carly felt a hard thud to her back and again was pushed up and out of the water by another hippo. She disappeared below the surface once more, swallowing water as it went in her mouth and up her nose. It tasted fowl, with a muddy flavour combined with a taste of urine and faeces.

She broke to the surface and managed to catch her breath before being pushed down again. By now she was quite a long way from where she'd been attacked by the elephant, but was quite close to the river's edge.

*'Where are the crocodiles?' s*he suddenly thought.

Unbeknown to her, several of the deadly reptiles had already slipped into the water at the time she had been pushed off the riverbank by the elephant. As she had splashed around in the murky river water, their instincts had kicked in. Seeing the chance of an easy meal, they had headed towards the stranded 'animal' in the middle of the river.

At first, the crocodiles held back, as the second hippo tossed Carly about, waiting patiently for their time to move in. Also, they had not wanted to get caught up in the earlier hippo fight.

She had now passed through the hippos and their onslaught, which gave her the chance to swim to the bank, which she could see was not too far away. Lucky for her, none of the hippo rib wounds had punctured a lung or damaged any of her other internal organs.

What she wasn't aware of, though, as she drifted away from the hippopotamus clan, was that strange, dark lumps with eyes were silently closing in on her from all sides.

CHAPTER SEVENTY-EIGHT

As Graham reached the trees on the other side of the plain, he began to worry even more about what animals might be hidden among them. Watching carefully and listening for any sounds, he moved slowly, whilst still keeping a keen eye for a stick that might be usable as a weapon.

The trees were similar to the ones he'd seen before, when he was being chased by the lions. The trunks were covered in dry bark and the leaves were a dull green. The bark was ridged and many of the trees had thorns, which would make a good weapon if a small limb containing them could be broken off.

He continued to walk with his heart constantly in his mouth, looking at every single tree and every blade of grass, turning every few seconds to see if he was being followed. He was exhausted, not only physically, but also emotionally.

Ahead of him he saw movement in the grass and heard a loud rustling sound, which made him freeze to the spot. What was it? He stopped for a moment and listened harder, straining to hear what he'd observed, whilst at the same time he was focusing his eyes on the area where the movement had occurred.

Nothing more happened, so he continued walking very slowly, but putting as much distance between himself and where he'd seen the movement as he could. As he started on his way, the grass moved again, but this time slightly further away, which relieved him somewhat, as it meant that whatever it was, it was frightened of him and trying to get away, too.

As he continued to move cautiously, feeling as scared as ever and totally vulnerable, his thoughts turned to the people behind his predicament.

'You knew what you were doing when you put us out here naked,' he thought angrily at them.

'Being put in a wild environment was one thing, but having no clothes, too, made each of us feel even more vulnerable. Well, it worked, you bastards! That's exactly how I feel!'

Then he wondered what Carly might be thinking right now, if indeed she were still alive.

If it wasn't already mid-day it must have been getting close, as the sun felt really hot on his back and was very high in the sky. He felt around to his shoulders and could feel blisters rising on his back from the exposure. They were now extremely painful.

Something in the sky caught his eye, and as he looked up, he saw the distant contrail behind a high-flying jet. In a strange way this made him feel even more isolated from home. Although the jet represented civilisation and people, it was at such a height that he'd never be seen by its occupants. This made his predicament seem so totally hopeless it made him feel like giving up.

As he watched the jet disappear, he thought about how he had given up on life too much. He'd give anything to be rescued and returned to his simple life back in the UK, and he would even consider working and making something of himself, which was a route he had never really thought about taking before.

'Why work when the government is stupid enough to pay you to sit on your backside?' was how he ordinarily thought.

He then wondered about what it was that Carly had or hadn't done, and how many other people had been kidnapped in the same way. He recalled how the man who he thought was named Ken had said, 'There are plenty of others who simply failed to survive before you.'

'This is like a game to them,' he thought. *'Someone has to stop this blue-eyed bastard from catching any more innocent people and playing his cruel experiments. The man is clearly psychotic and needs to be locked up!'*

Tears began to run down his cheeks once more.

But with these thoughts came the conclusion that giving up was no longer an option. No, he must make every effort to escape and, despite being really thirsty again, he must try as hard as he could to find help or a way out. He wanted to get help to Carly and any others who had been locked up, but also to somehow stop this man and his heartless crew from the horrendous, inhumane things they were doing.

CHAPTER SEVENTY-NINE

As the crocodiles approached the white-looking, flailing animal, they slowly circled, not knowing whether this creature could kick out at them or had some other more effective means of defence. They moved in deliberately, but with steady caution, eyeing up their prey as they did.

Oblivious to the oncoming danger, Carly swam as fast as she could towards the river bank, which was seemingly not getting any closer.

There were now 10 to 15 crocodiles approaching her, with just the tops of their heads showing above the water as they closed in.

Suddenly sensing the danger, she looked behind her and could see the bumpy heads of several crocodiles only a short distance away.

Panicking, she turned and thrashed her arms more rapidly and kicked harder with her legs, until she suddenly felt the bottom of the river. As she touched it and stood, her feet sank into the soft mud. What with the resistance of the water and her sinking into the river bed, her progress was painfully slow. She glanced behind her and could see a few more heads moving towards her at speed.

She was now near exhaustion and battered from her ordeal with the hippos, but despite this, she pushed on. One by one she lifted each leg out of the soft mud. Bit by bit she got closer to the river bank. With every few steps she made, she checked to see how close the crocodiles were, finding the first one in the pack was only a few metres away, gliding through the water with relentless ease.

With a final last push and an adrenalin-filled energy boost, Carly reached the river bank and gradually struggled out of the water and onto harder ground. She knew that this close to the water's edge she was still an easy target, because she knew that crocodiles are capable of either coming out of the water or leaping out to attack. As she looked back, they were almost upon her. Within seconds, they'd be climbing out of the water, too. She turned back to look up at the river bank in front of her, which seemed like a mountain right now — an impossible mountain to climb with her depleted energy level.

'Perhaps I should just let them get me and give up right here,' she began to think, as she saw them drawing near. *'I'm probably going to die anyway. This might be a quicker way to go.'*

As she tried to gather the last of her strength, she could see that the lead crocodile had almost

reached the spot where she had first touched the bottom of the river. That changed her thinking:
'No! They're not going to get me! I don't want to die that way!'

With that, she renewed her efforts and finally worked her way up the river bank and away from the impending danger.

Once she'd got to the top of the bank, she sank to the ground and lay there exhausted.

Eventually, she sat up from where she had lain and inspected her battered body. There was a huge gash across her torso where the hippo's tusk had cut into her, which was oozing blood. This wasn't the only cut she'd suffered from the horrific ordeal with the hippos. She considered herself lucky to have escaped with her life, plus now she'd managed to get away from the crocodiles.

She was aware that all her cuts were covered in dirt and that the water she'd just escaped from was full of filth and bacteria, so if she didn't get to a hospital soon, and if another animal didn't kill her, she'd likely die from her injuries and infection.

Despite her battering, she amazed herself by somehow managing to get to her feet. She looked over to the trees where she'd come from earlier and it appeared that the elephants had moved on. So she felt that this was the best place to go for now, whilst she decided what to do next.

She walked slowly towards the trees. Looking down to the river, she could see the crocodiles slowly moving away, and, as she looked across to the other river bank, she could see a few climbing back out and into the sun.

It was a long, agonising walk, but eventually she reached the cover of the trees. She decided to return to where she'd spent the night and, as she was approaching the spot, she heard the same sound as she had before — a dog-like barking, which came from the branches above her. She instantly froze, not knowing what animal had just made this noise, as she'd been unable to see it in the dark.

Her heartbeat jumped to the high rate she'd experienced before, as she feared the worst. She looked up into the trees to see if she could spot what had made the sound this time. On the other hand, she wasn't too sure if she really wanted to see what it was.

Shaking with fear and still in pain from her ordeal in the river, with blood still seeping from the deepest of her cuts, she hobbled away to find cover in the trees. As she sat down on a higher piece of ground, the trees above her moved and the creature that had made the sound made another, but much louder this time. She wasn't too sure if it was closer now than before, but either way it was too close for comfort. And it seemed to be focusing on her.

She pulled her knees up under her chin and crossed her arms around her legs in a foetal type position, hoping to somehow make herself feel a little safer. She was now shaking uncontrollably, as if she were cold. She realised that she'd gone into shock from her recent ordeal, but was now absolutely terrified of what might be in the trees above her head.

It was then that a large, dog-like creature dropped to the ground. The animal in front of her opened its elongated jaw to reveal large, canine teeth, and just as it did, more similar-sized creatures came out from the bushes making dog-like barking sounds, too.

The first creature rushed at her as she jerked backwards from where she sat, but as she did so, one of the other two creatures came at her from the side, catching her arm with its huge teeth and ripping a large chunk of her skin away from her upper arm, revealing the muscle beneath.

What she didn't realise was that these were the three top-level bucks of a baboon troop. The animals were treating her as a threat to their troop and were dealing with it in the only way they knew how — by attacking.

Carly screamed and stared with saucer-like eyes at the large buck in front of her, not knowing that these were the worst possible things she could do.

CHAPTER EIGHTY

Graham decided to continue walking towards where he'd seen the herd of wildebeest and zebra feeding and away from the cover of the trees, on the hope that they would be near a water source.

'Wildebeest survive,' he thought. *'Or, at least most of them do. Why can't I be like them and survive out here, too?'*

He knew there was a waterhole somewhere in the area, which was near to the river also, having been there before, but he had no idea where it was in relation to the cave area in which he'd been placed.

'Perhaps they've put Carly where I was before, or perhaps they still cannot use this area after they'd evacuated me,' he considered.

Walking became harder with every step he took, as the soles of his feet were massively blistered now and cut-sore. He was surprised at how he had found this deeply placed need to survive. It was strange, knowing how he was back at home and how lazy he was ordinarily; this new-found fortitude was a revelation to him.

As he continued to walk, he caught something move in the corner of his eye. At the same time, he heard a sharp, shrill call. As he turned to look where the movement and sound had come from, his heart abruptly beat faster.

Where he'd seen the movement was a mound, and next to the mound was an entrance to what appeared to be an animal's den. The hole looked like one in a rabbit warren and the ground around it was well worn, with many dirt pathways leading away from it.

Then he saw a creature scurry towards the hole and disappear into it very quickly out of sight. Instantly, he knew what he'd seen — a meerkat. He recognised it from a program he'd watched not that many months ago. As he surveyed the area, he realised that there were numerous holes and mounds around where he stood.

His heart was still pounding, as the movement had surprised him; he knew all too well that movement of any kind could represent all sorts of danger. This time, though, he knew he could relax a bit. Meerkats didn't represent any threat to him.

Then suddenly he heard another sound, and another movement caught his eye. Off in the distance he saw what appeared to be a vehicle moving along at speed. It was throwing up a huge amount of dust as it roared along.

The vehicle was heading his way and as it drove past the wildebeest and zebra, they scattered, which created yet more dust clouds in their wake.

His heart beat rose once more, knowing that this would mean another stint in a cage eating dog food. He began to run in the opposite direction, away from the vehicle.

As he ran, he could clearly hear the engine getting closer behind him.

Turing to see how close the vehicle was, he saw dust billowing out from the back, which made it seem as though it were on fire. The noise of the tyres on the rough ground and the sound of the suspension being put through its paces got even louder.

The Land Rover was soon almost upon him and then it came to a grinding stop. As it did so, a huge dust cloud erupted around the vehicle, almost completely engulfing it, so that he could hardly see its occupants.

As it began to settle, both the driver and his passenger jumped out of the vehicle and ran towards him. He realised instantly that the man who was the passenger had a rifle. As the two men approached him, the driver smiled and greeted him in a South African accent: 'Hey, you're safe. Thank goodness we found you in time!'

Graham's face broke into a smile. When the two reached him, he saw the man holding the gun also had brought some clothes, which he handed to Graham.

'Here, put these on,' he said. 'You must be really sore from the sun and now you can cover yourself up.'

Overcome with emotion at his rescue, Graham fell to his knees, unable to instantly respond. The men waited patiently until he could collect himself.

'Thank you so much,' he finally managed to say, then: 'How did you find me? Where are the men who kidnapped me?'

The driver was a tall man with tanned skin who was dressed in a khaki uniform and wearing a hat and sunglasses. He had a hardened look, but his face softened as he smiled back at Graham and said, 'Looking at your skin, you must be so sore. You are safe now. Your kidnappers have been arrested by the police.'

'Oh, thank God! I wasn't sure whether you were those men again, coming to catch me and put me back in that horrible animal cage,' Graham replied.

'How did you find me and how did you find out about what they were up to?'

'When we raided their camp, we found their equipment, which they were using to track you,' the driver explained

'Somewhere on you there is a tracking device, but seeing that you're naked, it must be under your skin somewhere.'

With this Graham felt to the back of his neck, where he knew there was something under his skin.

'That makes sense — I've got something under my skin back here,' Graham told the men, as he moved the lump on his neck.

'You've been treated like an animal,' the man with the gun said with disgust. 'But you are one of the lucky ones. We're not quite sure, but we do know that some of the people they captured have not survived the experience.'

'What happened to them?' Graham asked, as if he didn't already know, having nearly succumbed to the lions before being saved in the nick of time by his captors.

'We're not absolutely certain, but we know there were at least two others that didn't survive. They were killed by wild animals, we are sure of that,' the driver said, with a sad look on his face.

'Here, put these clothes on to cover your dignity and to help keep your skin from getting any more sun,' the driver said, again with comforting concern for Graham.

'We can talk more about this once we are in the Land Rover heading for the other person out here. What's your name?' he then asked.

'Graham. My name's Graham. Other person? Is that Carly?' Graham questioned impatiently, as he began to get dressed.

'And where are you from?' he asked Graham.

'I'm from England, a small town called Chelmsford. What about Carly? You mentioned another person. That must be Carly,' Graham replied, repeating his question with urgency, as if the man hadn't heard him the first time.

'I guess it could be Carly. We must move quickly to find her, too. How do you know her name?' he asked.

'She was in one of the other cages after I was recaptured by the kidnappers, who for some reason saved me from being eaten alive by the lions,' Graham said.

'I was knocked out by a stun gun and when I awoke, she was gone, so I have to assume she is out here somewhere, too. Have you found her location?' he pressed the men for an answer.

'We are going to see if she is still alive. We only have the one tracker unit and you were closest, so hurry up and get dressed and into the vehicle, mate,' the driver pushed.

'We must get to her quickly, as she is a few kilometres from here,' he continued, as Graham finished donning the clothes and climbed into the back of the vehicle.

'By the way, we're rangers. I'm Jack, and this is my colleague, Ian,' the driver offered. 'And that's Kyle in the back,' he added, as Kyle nodded and smiled at Graham to acknowledge him.

The men explained to Graham that he was in the Luangwa Valley in Zambia, which is one of Africa's prime wildlife sanctuaries, with big concentrations and varieties of game. They described the region as the 'real Africa' and told him that he was really lucky to survive, as there were plenty of predators, including lions, cheetahs, and leopards, roaming this valley.

Almost before Graham had a chance to settle into his seat, the vehicle lurched forward and they were on their way. The typical sound of the Land

Rover resonated through the vehicle, with the noise of a worn diff whining and the sound of the tyres running on the uneven African dirt.

As Graham looked forward, he could see the tracking device held by Ian. It was making an audible beeping sound and the screen had a red dot which flashed in time with the beeps.

'Is that Carly?' Graham asked anxiously.

'It must be, and she's not too far away from here, so let's hope we're not too late,' Ian said with urgency in his voice.

As they talked about what they'd found where Graham had been caged, they discussed Druker, the blue-eyed man whose real name authorities had found out was Blake Caldwell. They told him about his office and the terminals he had, which were monitoring each one of his captives when they were out in the wild.

'He and his crew also seemed to have good communications in place to make sure they monitored the movement of tourists and other visitors around the area,' Ian said.

'Although this Druker guy seemed to own a significant slice of this land, the law mandates that there is free movement of tourists across each person's property, in order for them to fully enjoy the wonders of this region,' he continued.

The rangers went on to explain to Graham that Druker had been discovered because one of the men they'd captured was an American tourist game hunter. The place he was staying had reported that he, along with his guide, had not returned from a hunting trip.

A police investigative team with a skilled tracker of their own followed the tyre tracks of the missing Land Rover and found it had been driven into the river. Sharpshooters had kept the crocodiles away while it had been pulled out of the water and identified. Then they followed the tracks of Druker's vehicle back to his home base, were they found a Winchester Model 70 rifle that had belonged to the neighbouring property owner, Dravin.

The rangers also described how Druker had been bribing the officials at the airport to turn a blind eye to what he was doing.

'You should have seen his face when we turned up with the police,' Ian said to Graham.

As they spoke about the twisted men who had kidnapped Graham and he recounted what had happened to him over the last couple of days, the Land Rover jumped and hopped across the bumpy terrain, making it difficult for its occupants to stay seated.

As they finally approached a thicker set of trees and bushes, Jack slowed the vehicle down.

'We are getting close,' he said.

CHAPTER EIGHTY-ONE

The barking sounds from the baboon troop intensified, as more male baboons joined in the attack. Carly didn't realise that despite their size, these creatures would readily attack and kill leopards in the same way and sometimes tear them apart. The three lead baboons took it in turns to jump in and tear at her skin, and now both her legs were in tatters, with blood gushing from her wounds.

The noise was almost unbearable and the pain she felt was immense, and although her veins ran with an overdose of adrenalin, the anaesthetic effect was not enough to numb the agony her attackers were inflicting.

'Get back! Go Away!' she shrieked.

But the attack was unrelenting, and the baboons came at her from all angles now. They were grabbing at her skin and ripping it apart like she was some kind of rag doll.

'Leave me alone!'

She had tried to fend off the baboons by screaming at them, then waving her tattered arms. All was in vain. Instead of frightening them away, it seemed to incite yet more anger in the animals, which took her screams as a challenge. She then realised that sitting there and being attacked was futile and attempted to get up to run away, but as she did so, one of the lead bucks jumped on her back and dug its huge canines into her neck.

She screamed out in pain as the animal's teeth bore into her neck muscle. Reacting instinctively, she reached back to grab the creature and managed to throw if off. But no sooner had she done this than another baboon was upon her and digging its teeth into her bare flesh, too.

Her screams were drowned out by the commotion made by the baboon troop, which now amounted to 50 or more of the enraged creatures. The barking they made, combined with a shrill sound made by others nearby, was so loud that the noise could probably be heard quite some distance away.

Despite how much they'd wounded her, and in spite of how much blood she had lost, Carly managed to stay on her feet, as one baboon clawed into her back, whilst sinking its teeth into the soft skin of her shoulder and the trapezius muscles. Two other baboons tore at her calves, then one sank its teeth into her Achilles tendon at the back of her foot, trying to bring her down to the ground.

Meanwhile, another attacked her knee and sank its teeth right into the knee joint. The pain from this bite alone made her scream even louder. She looked down in terror at the baboon that was biting into her knee, and as she did, it looked up with its orange-coloured eyes. As the creature looked her in the eyes, it was as if it knew where to bite for the best effect to bring her down.

This bite was so intense and painful, she involuntarily dropped to her knees, as it must have severed tendons and muscles in her knee and leg. With her mind reeling, she finally fell over on the ground with a thump, whilst several of the baboons tore at her bare back.

She was now losing blood at a huge rate from the sheer number of tears to her flesh. She knew that some of the bites were right down to the bone, as she could feel it and could even hear the sound of tooth on bone, as these vicious creatures ripped at her torso and limbs.

'Surely,' she thought, *'there must be someone out here to save me. Someone will hear the sound of these creatures and come to my rescue.'* Her mind then managed somehow to drift off to scenes of home. For an instant, she almost could objectify this experience, as horrendous as it was, and question logically how she'd ended up here, being attacked by these wild animals.

But the mental reprieve didn't last for long.

She lifted her head up from the dirt to see a baboon chewing on a piece of her skin, then another baboon came in and ripped at her face.

The pain from this injury was like she'd been burnt with a red hot poker. The animal jerked at a piece of skin it had managed to tear away from her face, and bit by bit her face was torn away.

Although pretty numb all over from the effects of an overdose of adrenalin, she could also feel another animal sitting on her back, biting into the large latissimus muscle. As it did, her arms were lifted backwards.

Carly had little life left in her, but a final, desperate urge to survive overcame her. She struggled to her hands and knees and tried to crawl away, but as she did more baboons came in from each side, biting at her elbows and at her legs to bring her back down once more. She ignored the almost unbearable pain to stand up, but as she did her legs buckled and she fell back to the ground. She tried one last time, screaming more weakly now, as the creatures came at her in unrelenting waves, like piranhas savaging a piece of meat dangled in the water.

Finally, she began to lose consciousness. Her blood loss had passed the threshold where her body simply had to give up. For a fleeting instant, her mind cast back to what Graham had said. He had told her about being rescued from lions and, even now not fully accepting how bad things were for her, she kept hoping she was going to be rescued at the last second as he had been. Then all went blank. Darkness fell over her mind and the last bit of life drained from her body.

The largest male baboon stood atop Carly's unmoving form in a strange kind of victory stance and let out a loud, triumphant bark.

CHAPTER EIGHTY-TWO

'Keep your eyes peeled. She's not moving, which might not be a good sign,' Jack said.

The bush was too thick for the Land Rover to go any further, so he pulled up and turned the engine off.

'We need to go on foot the rest of the way. You stay in the vehicle with Kyle, whilst we go and find her.'

'But I want to go with you!' Graham protested.

'No, you've been through enough and we'll be quicker without you,' Jack replied.

But before he or Ian could protest any more, Graham had jumped out of the vehicle and had joined them.

'I'll keep up, don't you worry,' he said.

The three of them walked on into the bush, as Jack and Ian accepted that it would be quicker to simply move on than to stand and argue.

It wasn't long before the tracker indicated that Carly was only metres away, and then they found her bloodied body lying on the ground, unmoving. But more terrifying than that was the scene they were witnessing, as atop her body were several baboons, with many more around her. Ian lifted his gun and fired a shot across the top of the animals, which all immediately scattered.

Graham was the first to break the silence. 'No! No, this can't be!' he protested. 'She didn't deserve this ending!'

Even though he hadn't known her, he felt that because of what he'd been through himself, and because he'd spoken to her, albeit briefly, he sensed that the two of them had some kind of bond, a deeper connection.

Baboons ran away in all directions as the party drew near. Then, as they stood above her mangled body in silence, the men heard what sounded like the bark of a dog. Jack looked around towards the sound and could still see a few baboons in the low branches only 15 or so metres away.

'She must have walked into their troop and they got aggressive,' Jack said. 'They sometimes do this to leopards and other predators that wander unknowingly into their territory, and when they feel threatened, they will attack like this.'

'It looks like we were just that little bit too late,' Ian said.

Graham felt sick as he looked at Carly's blood-soaked body and then began to cry. His tears were a combination of sadness for her and of relief for being found before he'd suffered a similar fate. He followed slowly behind as the two rangers carried her ravaged form back to the Land Rover.

Once they'd loaded Carly into the back of the Land Rover and covered her over, they began the journey back to the local town, where, once her family had been notified, arrangements would be made to ship her body back to England for burial.

The police were left to finish off at Druker's place, arresting all the men who worked there and gathering what evidence they needed for a prosecution in court.

When they arrived at the local township, Graham was first of all seen by a local doctor. After he had been given a once over, and his cuts and blisters had been cleaned and/or bandaged, he was taken to a small bed and breakfast so that he could eat and shower. Next day, after a night of exhausted sleep, he was taken to the police station in order to give evidence about his ordeal both at Druker's place and out in the wild on two harrowing occasions.

After the authorities had collected all the evidence they needed, they had arranged for Graham to return home, which was on a Kenyan Airways flight to London Heathrow. It was the first time that he'd knowingly flown. The officials had told the stewards to look after him and he was flown business class all the way. He was met at the other end by his parents, who he managed to contact and to whom he had explained all that had happened.

The news media, of course, got hold of the bizarre story right away, and Graham, as the lone survivor among the victims, was the subject of numerous interviews and their subsequent stories. He was particularly annoyed by how the ordeals he and his fellow victims had undergone were depicted in lurid fashion by the tabloid press.

It was through the news media, however, that Graham later learnt that Druker was being held on Zambia's death row in Lusaka. It was through them also that he discovered Zambia still has the death penalty, even though they've not acted upon this since 1997.

He was not sure about Druker's accomplices and what happened to them, but Graham felt happy that the man leading the whole operation, was at least serving a long sentence for the heinous crimes he'd committed and might even be put to death at some point.

Still, his satisfaction about justice being carried out did nothing to diminish the terrifying dreams he had each night about lions chasing him and digging with their razor-sharp claws into his naked back, or the residual aches and pains in his battered body that took months to completely heal.

Later, after seeking counselling for the trauma he'd undergone, Graham had to accept that some emotional scars might never fully disappear. He finally came to understand that the best he could do was to get on with his life by drawing on the compassion that had been awakened in him by poor Carly's fate.

He updated his CV and began to seriously look for employment, specifically in the healthcare industry. His new-found sincerity, and the widespread publicity he had received, helped him to land a job. As a hospital nurse assistant, he soon was recognised for his reliability and willingness to comfort patients in pain whenever he could.

Graham had learnt in the hardest of all possible ways that life only has value when you find a meaningful purpose for living it.

THE END

Printed in Great Britain
by Amazon